SPACE DOGS

by Justin Ball & Evan Croker

Alfred A. Knopf   New York

THIS IS A BORZOI BOOK PUBLISHED BY ALFRED A. KNOPF

All rights reserved. Published in the United States by Alfred A. Knopf, an imprint of Random House Children's Books, a division of Random House, Inc., New York, and simultaneously in Canada by Random House of Canada Limited, Toronto. Distributed by Random House, Inc., New York.
KNOPF, BORZOI BOOKS, and the colophon are registered trademarks of Random House, Inc.

www.randomhouse.com/kids

Educators and librarians, for a variety of teaching tools, visit us at www.randomhouse.com/teachers

Library of Congress Cataloging-in-Publication Data
Ball, Justin.
Space dogs / by Justin Ball and Evan Croker.
p. cm.
SUMMARY: Commanders Belka and Strelka, of the planet Gersbach, board their dog-shaped vehicle and head for Earth, where they encounter Lucy Buckley and her family, attempt to capture two power-seeking renegades, and hope to save their own planet from destruction.
ISBN: 0-375-83256-4 (trade) — ISBN: 0-375-93256-9 (lib. bdg.)
ISBN-13: 978-0-375-83256-7 (trade) — ISBN-13: 978-0-375-93256-4 (lib. bdg.)
[1. Science fiction. 2. Humorous stories.] I. Croker, Evan. II. Title.
PZ7.B19878Spa 2006
[Fic]—dc22   2005025966

Printed in the United States of America
April 2006
10   9   8   7   6   5   4   3   2   1
First Edition

For the Ball clan, and many thanks to Greg.—J.B.

For Yvette, who told me to cross the line.—E.C.

Prologue

In 1957 the Soviet Union launched a small silver ball into orbit around the Earth. Sputnik was the world's first artificial satellite, and it amazed everyone with its ability to travel at 18,000 miles per hour and go "beep." With this great success under their belts, the Russian scientists at Star City decided they would send up something that would fly even faster and go "woof."

It is doubtful that humans will ever know what dogs think about, which is a pity because we could probably learn quite a lot from them. Dogs appear to have a nice take on life. Eat well, get lots of sleep, chase a ball whenever possible, and, if someone's nice to you, be nice to them. They don't understand much more than that. So when a little stray dog called Laika was plucked from the streets of Moscow, she would have had no idea that she was about to become a national hero. As she was checked, tested, weighed, and measured, she wouldn't have understood anything about gravity and escape velocity. All she'd have known was that dog biscuits taste good and that it was much warmer inside than outside on the street. She also wouldn't have had a clue as to why, on one cold, dark morning, she was taken out to a tall, mysterious tower and placed inside a small metal container at the top. Nor would she have had any idea at all why the big, chunky human—who had given her all the biscuits and who now closed the hatch shutting her in—had a small, shiny tear in one eye.

The time it took for the electrical signal to reach the rocket's engine seemed like a lifetime to the Deputy Chief Mission Controller. He glanced at his superior, the Chief Mission Controller, but by the time he looked back, the rocket had cleared the launchpad tower. The engine screamed, smoke billowed, and a proud Russian voice blared from every loudspeaker on the base. A hundred heartbeats later the craft had punched through the outer limits of the atmosphere and was sailing a silent orbit around the planet Earth.

"Orbital tracking?" the Deputy Chief Mission Controller asked.

"Normal," replied one of his scientists.

"Pressurization?"

"Normal," came the answer.

"Electrical responses?"

"Normal, sir," yet another spoke up.

The Deputy Chief Mission Controller abruptly left his nicely padded, high-backed chair and strode the ten steps to where the Chief Mission Controller sat. His chair had a bit more padding, a slightly higher back, and was situated on a raised platform so that he could look out over the whole Mission Operations Room. A broad grin broke out across the Deputy Chief Mission Controller's face. "Zero ten minutes and everything is normal."

The corners of the Chief Mission Controller's mouth turned slightly upward and he nodded slowly. He was jubilant. A buzz of elation quickly sped throughout the control room. Soon everyone was shaking hands and slapping each other's back. Only one rather chunky technician with biscuit crumbs in his lab-coat pocket stood motionless. His eyes were still fixed on the spot in the morning sky where the rocket disappeared from view.

From an orbit of eleven hundred miles, the view is quite magnificent. It is a view of the Earth that is enjoyed by very few humans and even fewer dogs. So it really was a pity that Laika's craft had no windows. If it did, she could have seen the continents and brilliant blue oceans as they slowly passed below her. She could have stretched out her paw and covered half of Africa. Her tail could have flicked from California to New York in a fraction of a second. But she could see none of it: the clouds or the forests or the deserts beneath her, the rich field of stars above her, or the fiery, gold-rimmed circle that lay directly in her path.

Scientists today know very little about space wormholes, and the scientists at Star City who tracked Laika's progress knew nothing at all. The Deputy Chief Mission Controller stood before the Chief Mission Controller with absolutely no explanation as to why Laika's spacecraft had just simply disappeared from their radar screens.

"No reason at all, sir. All systems were completely normal, and then it was gone. Just gone," he said nervously.

The corners of the Chief Mission Controller's mouth dropped. He said nothing as he stared with growing intensity at his Deputy.

"I suppose the craft just exploded into a million pieces," the Deputy speculated.

Everyone in the Mission Operations Room sat at their stations in silence. Only a soft sobbing sound could be heard coming from the far corner.

Traveling through the wormhole was a bit like being sucked down the plughole of a sink, so while Laika could see nothing, she certainly felt something. She bounced about inside her craft, finding herself upside down, backward, forward, and sideways all at the same time. She didn't like this at all, so she did what dogs do in an emergency. She barked. And she kept on barking all the way down the whirling tunnel. The buffeting grew and grew until, for no logical doggy reason, it stopped. There was a weird floating silence for a moment, followed by a low whistling noise. In the darkness of the capsule a familiar feeling descended on Laika's body. It was gravity, and it was pulling the craft and its canine passenger down. The whistling continued steadily until it was abruptly replaced by a ferocious symphony of snapping, breaking, and scraping. Laika was thrown violently from side to side and top to bottom. The whacks and smacks exploded all around her until there was one very large thud. Laika's journey was over.

A startled bushwalker stumbled upon Laika's crashed capsule in much the same way you stumble upon a ten-story building. The canine astronaut and her spaceship were *huge* in comparison with the tiny inhabitants of the strange planet she'd landed on—the people of the planet Gersbach stood only as tall as Laika's paw.

At first the Gersbacians were apprehensive of Laika's enormous size, her curious language, and her habit of burying small government buildings; but they were soon won over by her playful good nature. As the years passed, the people grew extremely fond of her, and Laika ended up living a much happier life than she would have on the streets of Moscow.

In the decades that followed, Gersbach's scientists became increasingly curious about Laika's home planet on the other side of the wormhole. It was only a matter of time until they sent someone through.

one

Lucy Buckley stood at the outer rim of the solar system, approximately three and a half billion miles from the Sun and about two and a half yards from the girls' bathroom. Lucy was Pluto, the smallest, most distant, and least significant of all the planets, which was typical really. She held a small marble reluctantly in the air. Neptune, holding a tennis ball, turned around and called out to her.

"Go back further!"

"I can't! There's no room!" Lucy shouted.

Sam Chan dashed out from behind the big gum tree and looped behind Lucy. "How long are we supposed to be here?" she asked, but Sam had already run back toward the center of the solar system. "Hey, Uranus!" she called out.

"What?" the boy in front of her snapped back, feeling that he'd been insulted, but not quite sure why.

"How long are we going to have to stay here?"

"I don't know!"

"Saturn!" Lucy shouted to Brittany Ferris and her group of very bored-looking, marble-holding moons.

"Don't ask us. We don't know either. Ask Jupiter."

Lucy looked across to the giant, swirling, storming mass that was Melissa Blume. A tiny speck of a planet like Lucy knew better than to ask anything of the biggest and most terrible world in the solar system. Melissa, holding a basketball proudly, sneered at Lucy and her small marble.

Sam Chan rushed past Lucy again, and again she didn't have a chance to ask him anything before he was back circling Bradley Ditchfield, who held on to a large yellow beach ball.

"Now pay attention, Year 6!" their teacher, Ms. Felton, called out. "What Dr. Macheski is demonstrating to you is how our solar system is laid out. Bradley is the Sun, and so he is in the middle. Hold up the beach ball, Bradley. Then we have Mercury, Venus, Earth, Mars, and all the other planets, going all the way out to Lucy, who is Pluto. Hold up your marble, Lucy. That's right, isn't it, Dr. Macheski?"

"Yes, but you should be moving around the Sun," Dr. Macheski said earnestly to the class in his still-prominent Russian accent. "All the planets orbit the Sun."

"Well, I think they have the idea," said Ms. Felton.

"The boy who is Halley's Comet is right," Dr. Macheski said, indicating Sam, who orbited Ms. Felton so fast her dress blew up.

The Sun giggled.

"Does anyone have a question for Dr. Macheski?" Ms. Felton asked the class.

"Why did you come from Russia to live here?" Lucy Buckley

called from her lonely post at the edge of the solar system. She didn't know exactly where Russia was, but she knew it was at least as far away as her hometown of Tubby Flats.

"Does anyone have a *sensible* question for Dr. Macheski?" Ms. Felton continued.

It was a sensible question! Lucy felt like shouting back. She didn't, of course. She just squirmed about in her uncomfortable new school shoes as Halley's Comet flew past one more time.

"Lucy," Ms. Felton said, "wouldn't you rather ask Dr. Macheski where his rockets flew in the solar system?"

Lucy felt like shouting, "If I wanted to know about his boring rockets, I would have asked about that, but I didn't because I don't care! I want to know what he felt like when he came to live in some strange new place with strange new people because *I* know what that's like!"

But she didn't, of course.

"Who cares anyway," Bradley Ditchfield spoke up, bouncing the Sun up and down roughly. "Dad says the Americans have always had much better rockets than the Russians."

Lucy was always amazed at how rude city kids could be. It wasn't right to speak to Dr. Macheski like that, she thought, even if he was old and had very strange eyebrows. Dr. Macheski, on the other hand, didn't seem to mind at all. In fact, he instantly rose to the challenge.

"That's where you're quite wrong, my friend. At the beginning we in the Soviet Union led the world in the space race. We were the first to—"

"Have the Russians got any aliens?" Bradley Ditchfield demanded.

The class snapped silent. Even Sam Chan stopped being

3

Halley's Comet for a moment. Dr. Macheski always regretted getting this type of question, as it invariably pushed his rocketry achievements into the background.

"No one has any aliens, Bradley," Ms. Felton said.

"The Americans do," Bradley insisted. "They keep them in a top-secret hangar in the desert. Everybody knows that."

"Well, as you can see here," Dr. Macheski said, smiling warmly as he spoke to the class, "the solar system is very big. Lucy is the most distant planet from the Sun, and if she really was on Pluto and Bradley really was on the Sun, it'd take him ten years to fly to her. And remember, the solar system is just our local neighborhood. To fly to the nearest star similar to our Sun would take *thousands* of years. And you have to ask yourself, why would aliens bother?"

Dr. Macheski's answer wasn't quite as exciting as the class had hoped. But their spirits elevated when the school bell rang for lunch. Before Ms. Felton could say a word, the class had rushed off to orbit the cafeteria.

At much the same time Lucy and Sam were standing impatiently in the cafeteria line, Commander Belka Sparkleman was standing in one of Gersbach City's main public corridors. He was trying to remove a packet of Moody Chews from a vending machine. The sweets had become stuck, and it looked dangerously like he was going to lose his money units. He was just about to make a sign warning future customers when the machine, the corridor, and his whole body began to shake. The tremor was over in a few seconds, but Belka noted they were now coming very regularly.

He looked at the machine with alarm; its entire contents had emptied onto the floor. He was putting a call through to the vending company when an alert from Space Command interrupted him. He was wanted immediately. He looked with concern at the machine, but his priority was obvious. He collared a group of passing junior school students and placed them in charge of the machine and its stock. Belka noted their eagerness to help out as he headed off. At least there are *some* responsible citizens left in this town, he thought.

As Belka strode the Main Corridor to Space Command, he noticed ahead the strangely familiar gait of one of his Academy classmates—Strelka Frunkmaster. Belka had never really gotten to know Strelka during their training as Galactanauts. He hadn't seemed like Academy material. His shoulders slouched, he was unkempt in his dress, and he never appeared to share the enthusiasm that Belka and his fellow students had for their work. Belka also never really cared for the way Strelka referred to him as "Golden Boy." Strelka did, however, finish second in their class—after Belka, of course.

As they were checked through the Main Entrance, Belka thought Strelka must have improved his ways or else he wouldn't have lasted this long. When they entered the same elevator and he noticed the food stains down the front of Strelka's ill-fitting uniform, he reconsidered. They walked side by side all the way to the Chief Controller's office without once acknowledging each other. It wasn't until they stood together in the briefing room and the Chief introduced Belka to Strelka that they exchanged their first words.

"Golden Boy!" Strelka exclaimed, as if he had just noticed him.

"That's *Commander* Golden Boy!" Belka responded, annoyed.

"Commander *Belka*," the Chief said, covering for Belka's mistake. "You will be working with Commander Strelka on a very important mission."

"Important mission, sir?" Belka's ears pricked up.

"It's voluntary. I'll say that up front because it's not just very important, it's actually very dangerous too."

Belka leaned forward intently. Strelka's eyes strayed toward the exit.

"Well . . . ," the Chief said, "as you're no doubt aware, the wormhole has just reopened."

"Yes. Yes." The mere mention of his obsession filled Belka with excitement.

"And, as you're also no doubt aware, our city, in fact all of Gersbach, has been experiencing terrible land tremors."

"Part of my Living Unit's roof collapsed," Strelka announced.

"With the way you probably keep the place, I can't imagine it would make much difference," Belka muttered.

Strelka didn't react. He was rarely offended by criticism. In fact, he usually agreed with it.

"It seems the two events are not unrelated," the Chief continued, sounding troubled. "An invisible force—a Disturbance Of Gravity—appears to be flowing from the wormhole and causing this havoc. This has never occurred before. It's been happening from the moment the wormhole opened three days ago and we can't stop it."

"What are our options?" Belka asked.

"Not many. The hole opens for eleven days every year—"

"Yes. Yes, I know," interrupted Belka. He was a wormhole expert and felt almost insulted to be told the basics.

"We have no way of shutting the hole, and our geologists don't think the planet can take much more of this battering. The Disturbance Of Gravity is undermining the core of our planet. Frankly, our world is on the brink of total destruction."

There was a heavy pause. Then Belka asked, "So what can we do?"

"Well, ever since the arrival of Laika forty-nine years ago, we have been working on a special and very secret mission. A mission to travel through the wormhole to the world we know exists on the other side."

Belka's head was spinning. He was excited, intrigued, and a little bit annoyed that he had not been told of this before.

"Based on what we could learn from studying Laika, we have constructed a vehicle designed to travel through the hole and explore the surface of the alien planet." The Chief swept his hand across a sensor, and an image of a spacecraft appeared on the board before them. It was a large silver ball, just like any other in the Gersbach fleet. Belka and Strelka were not impressed.

"It is powerful enough to fly against the flow of the hole and even to withstand this new force coming from it. That is, assuming the tunnel isn't too long, and of course, we don't know exactly how long it is," the Chief confided.

Strelka glanced toward the exit again.

"So, that is the ship to get you there, and this is the vehicle that will be used on the planet itself," the Chief said, switching to the next image.

Belka and Strelka stepped back and studied it with

amazement. They had never seen a craft like it. "And you've actually constructed one of these?" Belka asked.

"We've built two of them, in fact. A prototype and an updated version," the Chief told them. "We were going to wait until the next time the hole opened before we risked a live crew, but now, of course, we can't wait. We need you to find the cause of the Disturbance Of Gravity and neutralize it."

"We volunteer for the mission!" Belka declared.

The Chief turned to Strelka, who mumbled, "Yeah, why not?"

"Which craft are we taking? The improved model?" Belka asked.

"Yes. You have no choice anyway. The prototype has been stolen."

Belka was shocked. Strelka picked some food from his teeth. The Chief flicked to the next image. It was the surly face of Colonel Bars and that of a young woman neither man recognized. Strelka's interest was suddenly raised.

"Who's she?" Strelka asked as casually as he could.

"Colonel Bars," Belka announced ominously, ignoring Strelka. "I thought he was locked up."

"He was, until three days ago. That's when he was broken out of prison," the Chief said.

"And *she* is . . . ?" Strelka repeated, raising his tone slightly.

"That is Flanger Damka—his accomplice. We thought she was just an innocent victim of Bars, but we were obviously wrong about that too." The Chief was clearly bitter.

"It could all be a misunderstanding," Strelka suggested. "Let's not judge her too soon."

"She instigated the breakout, and she was at Bars' side when they stole the prototype. No, she's in it up to her eyes."

"They're very nice eyes," Strelka said feebly in her defense.

"But where are these two now?" Belka demanded.

"They went through the wormhole."

Belka was stunned by this news and, deep down, very disappointed. *He* wanted to be the first one through the wormhole. It was always his greatest dream. He took a deep breath.

"So you want us to capture these renegades as well?"

"If at all possible. You must understand that if they manage to get hold of whatever is causing the Disturbance Of Gravity . . . well, they'd have complete power over our world."

"We'll bring Bars to justice, sir," Belka said.

"And Flanger Damka," added the Chief.

"I'm sure she's just a bit confused," Strelka said. "Perhaps she's got problems at home. She probably just needs a hug."

"When do we leave?" Belka asked.

"In two hours."

"It's too nice an afternoon to stay inside," Ms. Felton announced to the class. "Let's spend the rest of the day outside at the big oak tree! Bring your natural history books."

Lucy Buckley couldn't believe her ears. To her, living in the city was like always being stuck inside without ever being allowed out. She felt like she was on detention for something she hadn't even done, so before Ms. Felton could change her mind, Lucy grabbed her book and was the first out the door. She dashed ahead to the sprawling tree that dominated one end of the playground. Lucy scaled it like a little monkey and sat on one of the thick boughs, looking smugly down on her classmates.

"When I said at the oak tree, Lucy, I meant we'd all sit *under* it," Ms. Felton called out. "Not in it."

The whole class burst into laughter. They laughed because this new girl from the country was really dumb, but secretly most of them laughed with relief that they weren't expected to climb up there too.

"She looks just like a little monkey!" Bradley Ditchfield called out.

"A *bush* monkey!" Melissa Blume added.

And then it was on. They all started chanting, "Bush monkey! Bush monkey! Bush monkey!"

Lucy looked down on the mob and didn't move. She just clung to the branch and stayed there. She stayed there while Ms. Felton silenced the class and started them on their natural science assignment. Lucy looked down on the city kids as they wandered around the playground trying to find an insect, or flower, or anything the least little bit alive. Lucy stayed on the branch until all the class had gone home and only Ms. Felton and Sam Chan remained.

"Come down, Lucy. Everyone's gone now," Ms. Felton called up.

Lucy didn't reply.

"I'm very impressed, you know," Ms. Felton continued. "You're very . . . athletic. You'll be a star on Sports Day."

The roar of a motorbike turned Ms. Felton's head toward a young man revving a black bike at the front gate. He was staring at her and holding a second helmet.

"You can get down okay, can't you?" Ms. Felton called up.

"Of course," Lucy snapped.

"Why don't you get down now?"

"Because I don't want to get down now."

The young man revved his engine again. "Um . . . well . . ." Ms. Felton dithered.

"Oh, go on! Your boyfriend's waiting for you! I'll be all right!"

"Well, don't stay up there too long," Ms. Felton said, then nodded to Sam. "Sam's here. You'll make sure Lucy gets down okay, won't you?"

Sam nodded.

The engine revved again, and Ms. Felton scurried off.

"Talk about irresponsible, leaving me up a tree," Lucy said as she watched them ride off.

"Are you sure you can get down?" Sam said, breaking his silence at last.

"So you *can* talk," Lucy said. "I haven't heard you say anything before. I thought you were . . ."

"Aloof." Sam finished her sentence.

"Is that what you are?"

"Yes. I'm very aloof. You won't find many boys my age as aloof as me."

"Does being aloof mean you're really smart?"

"Not necessarily. You can be dumb *and* aloof, but I'm not."

"I'm dumb," Lucy said quietly.

"Hard to say."

"I can't get down."

"Come down the same way you went up."

"I can't remember how I got up," Lucy said, getting a bit panicky. "I've climbed a million trees. Getting down should be easy, but I just can't do it."

"Put your foot down. I'll guide you."

It took quite a lot of coaxing, but eventually Lucy made it back to the ground in one piece.

"Thanks a lot," Lucy said as they walked away from the tree.

"You're not dumb, you know," Sam said.

"You reckon?"

"No. You're just aloof, like me."

two

Belka and Strelka were allowed to go to their Living Units to grab some essential items and exactly two hours later were stepping into their new craft. The basic controls were familiar, but many new features were not. This was going to be a learning experience. Belka unloaded the items he had brought and placed them in his Personal Storage Unit. Strelka had brought nothing. He had spent the last two hours gathering as many images of Flanger Damka as he could from Space Command's data bank and was now putting them up around his side of the cabin. Belka looked at him with contempt.

"If we have to capture her, we need to know what she looks like, don't we?" Strelka explained. Then he added, "We'll need to share your toothbrush. I didn't have time to get mine."

Belka was about to lose his temper but was cut short by the Chief Controller's voice bursting over the intercom.

"All ready to go, boys?"

The Galactanauts climbed into their seats and strapped themselves in. "All ready for liftoff, sir!" Belka said, taking charge.

"You set, Commander Strelka?"

Strelka let out a small burp. "All set." He straightened a
photo of Flanger Damka.

"I'll initiate launch sequence. Any last-minute questions?"

"No." Belka braced himself.

"Okay—five, four, three . . ."

"Wait! Wait! I have a question," Strelka said urgently.

"What is it?"

"Is his seat bigger than mine?"

Belka rolled his eyes.

The Chief hesitated. "I don't know. It shouldn't be."

"It *looks* bigger," Strelka said.

"It doesn't matter," Belka snapped.

"We're both the same rank. Your seat shouldn't be any
bigger."

"It's not any bigger, but we'll swap if you want!"

Belka leapt up, grabbed Strelka by the collar, and threw
him into the vacated seat. He then strapped himself hurriedly
into Strelka's.

"Are you all set now?" the Chief questioned hesitantly.

"Yes!" Belka said.

"Okay! Five, four, three . . ."

"No, this isn't any bigger. We'll swap back," Strelka said,
getting up.

"Push the button!" Belka screamed.

The craft's engines exploded into life, and the g-force
pinned them to their seats. As they hurtled toward the wormhole, Belka struggled to read the meter in front of him.

"Approaching wormhole opening. Engaging power surge," he said, forcing his words out. The battering was greater than anything they had ever experienced, but Belka managed to set the booster off at exactly the right time. There was a deafening crash, and the cabin was plunged, spinning, into darkness.

Suddenly the spinning stopped and the lights came back on. Strelka looked up at the two large screens in front of him and saw a maze of swirling colors enveloping the ship. They'd made it into the wormhole. He breathed a sigh of relief.

"Mission control! Mission control!" Belka called desperately. "We've lost all vision!" He was struggling beneath a pile of Flanger Damka pictures that had come off the wall during the chaos.

Strelka hesitated, considering whether it would be more interesting to leave Belka under the pile. But Belka soon realized his ridiculous situation and slapped the photos off like they were a horde of insects.

"We're on our way," Strelka said, checking his instruments.

"We're inside?" Belka leapt up with excitement, immediately forgetting he had reason to be annoyed with Strelka.

"In fact, I think we're almost there."

They looked up at the screens and, off in the distance, saw a small pinprick of black among the whirlpool of colors. They headed directly for it. The black dot grew and grew as they approached. Then, without any particular fuss, they sailed straight through it.

Belka stared in awe at the screens and the dazzling image of the large new world that filled them. This was his dream come true, and it had all happened so quickly. Just a couple of hours ago he was in his Living Unit, and now he was floating above a sight that no Gersbacian had ever seen before. Apart from possibly Bars and Flanger Damka, he suddenly remembered—a thought that soured the moment slightly.

"It's really quite beautiful, don't you think?" Belka said, trying to share the mood with Strelka.

"In a very blue sort of a way, I suppose." Strelka pressed a button, and a location monitor rose from the console. A white pinpoint of light blinked to one side of its round screen. "I've got a location on the Disturbance Of Gravity source."

A second pinpoint of light, this one blue, flickered into life on the location monitor. "And I think Bars' craft is close by it," Strelka added.

"Locking on and preparing for entry." Belka pushed his guidance column forward. A jet fired, and the silver ball dipped into the atmosphere. Sparks, then flames, erupted around their tiny craft. It sliced straight through and, a few seconds later, emerged into a brilliant blue sky.

The powerful gravitational pull of the new world took the Galactanauts completely by surprise. Belka suddenly realized how low they were when he looked at the screens and saw the tops of enormous trees rushing toward them. Their craft smashed through thick branches, setting off a blaze of warning lights around the cabin. Belka veered to avoid a huge, wooden pole festooned with wires and spun them toward a green open space in the distance. Frantically trying to decrease speed, Belka eased the craft close to the ground. He deployed full air brakes—but knew the touchdown would be rough. The Galactanauts braced themselves and hit the surface of the planet Earth with a sickening THUD. A shower of sparks sprayed around them, and a damage report flashed across the screens.

Belka and Strelka were violently thrown about as the silver ball bounced between several large, brightly colored plastic structures. They ricocheted off the base of an enormous tree and finally came to rest in the middle of a large pit of what appeared to be sand. Belka looked at Strelka and, quite uncharacteristically, Strelka actually looked back.

"Looks like we've made it," Belka said, braving a smile. "Almost in one piece."

"I can't see any life-forms in the immediate area," replied Strelka, searching the screens.

"Right. Jettison outer shell, and let's put this explorer vehicle through its paces."

Strelka pushed a button and pulled a small lever. The silver ball slowly opened up. There, standing in the center, was something that looked exactly—in every detail—like a small, mutty dog.

three

It was commonly thought that Laika was the only alien to arrive on Gersbach from the planet Earth, but this wasn't actually the case. Laika had some stowaways onboard. In fact, Laika had some stowaways on herself. As with most dogs, Laika's fur coat was home to quite a number of tiny freeloaders known as fleas. For years the fleas were happy to stay on Laika's body and lived there unbeknownst to the Gersbacian people. After Laika passed away, however, they were left homeless and, frankly, pretty annoyed. To the average human they are nothing more than an annoying pest, easily remedied by a quick scratch and giving the dog a bath. To the tiny people of Gersbach, however, they were terrible blood-sucking rodents with the power to jump vast distances and give bites that left hideous wounds. Several Gersbacians almost lost their lives in vicious attacks by roaming packs of hungry fleas. Panic gripped the city, with people afraid to travel unaccompanied, and shops and schools were closed by the flea menace. The Guardian Service was scrambled into action, and at their head was their most valiant officer, Colonel Bars.

Bars was a sturdy, seasoned warrior who battled his enemy using both brute force and superior intellect. His first goal was to capture one of the foul creatures and run a full scientific examination to see how it ticked. He did this after bravely offering himself as a tempting meal and then engaging in vicious hand-to-hand combat. He traded the beast blow for blow and bite for bite until it lay beaten at his feet. Forty-eight hours later he emerged from his lab with a chemical formula that would stop the fleas in their tracks.

Bars' solution was sprayed from one end of the land to the other, and in no time at all the fleas were completely defeated. The few remaining survivors were rounded up and locked away. Colonel Bars, who actually held a sneaking admiration for his former foes' mindless strength and viciousness, argued with the government to be allowed to develop the captive fleas into a special fighting force. He wanted to breed an invincible army of ruthless flea soldiers. The Gersbach people, however, have always been a peaceful race, abhorring war and violence; so, while acknowledging their debt to Bars, they decided to decline his offer. Instead, they had the remaining fleas perform in a circus for all the people to enjoy.

Bars felt deeply insulted and bitter that his scheme had been rejected, but he was a determined man and, let's face it, not a particularly nice one. So he stole a few fleas and set up a secret underground lab where he bred many more. He genetically engineered each one to be more powerful and deadly than the last. Soon there was a small army of terrible beasts that owed allegiance to one man: Colonel Bars. Then he set about creating his masterpiece. Disguised by the blackness of night, a small squad of his sneaky flea offsiders crept into Gersbach's most exclusive Private Ladies' College and crept out again carrying the smartest and prettiest of all the boarders—Flanger Damka. She was the school captain, class valedictorian, and swimming champion and sang in a popular band called Underneath Peach. Unsurprisingly, all the other students disliked her intensely, so when she disappeared, her absence wasn't reported until late the next morning. As the staff rushed about in a panic trying to locate the missing girl, Bars' terrible experiment was already well under way.

Undisturbed in his lab, he toiled and sweated over his captive for hour after hour, stretching all his skills as surgeon, scientist, and embittered maniac. His scheme was so bizarre even Bars himself was uncertain if he would really succeed. But as he peeled away the last of the bandages, he knew his dream was now a reality. From the outside Flanger Damka looked exactly as she did before. She was slender and elegant, with glistening dark skin and hair that cascaded over her shoulders like a waterfall. Inside, however, it was a different story.

"I feel a bit funny," were her first words to Bars. "Who are you?" were her next.

"My name is Colonel Bars."

"Are you a nice person?" she asked, without seeming at all afraid.

"No. Are you?"

"No, not really, but I don't need to be." She looked around the roomful of ugly fleas. "Who are these guys?"

"They are my friends."

"Have you brought me here to be your friend too?"

"I want you to be my best friend," Bars told her.

For some strange reason she didn't find the thought of being this weird man's best friend revolting. Some peculiar feeling deep inside her made him and his little black, bouncing friends quite attractive.

"I am very special, you understand, so I already have a lot of friends, although none of them seem to like me very much, and I certainly don't like any of them," Flanger explained. "It really comes down to what you can do for me."

"I've already done it," Bars said in an intriguing manner. She answered this with an expectant stare. "Jump over there," he said, pointing to the far end of the lab.

"I don't jump for just anyone," she retorted.

"Do it!" he bellowed in a voice that startled her so much she leapt in the air. Flanger's fright turned to amazement when she found herself all the way down the other end of the lab. Then her amazement turned into something close to excitement as she leapt all the way back again.

"That's not bad, I suppose," she said, downplaying her delight. Then a rush of excitement seized her uncontrollably, and she found herself bounding recklessly around the room. Bars was pleased as he watched the spectacle. In front of him was the evidence that he was indeed a genius, with the ability to seize control of the entire planet. Behind him, unfortunately, was a row of Guardian Service officers who had just managed to locate his secret lab.

Bars was whisked off to spend a long time as a guest in Gersbach's most secure prison, and Flanger Damka was taken back to school. Her teachers hoped that she would soon recover from her terrible ordeal and eventually forget about the appalling Colonel Bars. She did recover, and went on to set stunning new records in track and field, although she did give up swimming for some reason. One thing was certain—she didn't forget the intriguing Colonel Bars.

ᴦ ᴏ ᴜ ᴦ

Beth Buckley stood frozen on the spot. The box she was holding nearly fell from her arms as the full horror of what she saw struck her.

Beth Buckley was the still quite youthful, but very tired-looking, mother of Lucy Buckley. The spot on which she stood frozen was the front lawn of their small, neat house in an unpopular suburb near the city's edge. The box she held was full of small, peppermint-flavored balls, and what she saw was about two feet tall and wearing a pointy red hat.

"Tom!" she called out in a loud, grumpy voice, and then immediately said it again even louder and grumpier.

Tom Buckley appeared at the front door. Tom was a solid man. He was tall and sturdy, with shoulders that seemed made to hoist up heavy objects and arms that forced things together that would much prefer to stay apart. Of course, here in the city there wasn't as much that needed to be lifted, and he couldn't really lift things with his bad back anyway. When he did lift things, he just seemed to get in trouble.

"You're not putting this here," Beth told him.

"What's wrong with it?" Tom asked sheepishly.

"It's awful. You said so yourself. I remember your exact words—'It's awful,' " she explained with the weary edge that pervaded her voice all the time nowadays.

Tom nodded. Sitting on the lawn, for all to see, was probably the world's most awful garden gnome. It could better be described as a rock. It had some sort of vague gnome shape. There was something like a hat and a bit sticking out that could be a beard.

"I suppose it's not a really *good* gnome," Tom conceded.

"It's a terrible gnome, Tom. You couldn't get a worse gnome," Beth insisted. "It's not even made out of proper gnome stuff." She gave it a little cautious kick. "What is it? It's not cement. It's just some rock your brother found. I don't even want to think about what he's used to paint it. Probably toxic waste."

"Come on, love. It was nice of him to give us a farewell gift. He made it himself," Tom tried to reason.

"He made it himself because he's cheap. He didn't want to spend any money."

"We can't just throw it away."

"Well, you didn't have to put it out here for the whole neighborhood to see. Why didn't you leave it out back?"

"Ah, that stupid-lookin' sausage dog wouldn't leave it alone. He's obsessed with it."

"He's probably trying to bury the ugly thing, and here I was thinking he was a dumb animal," Beth said, moving toward the house.

"What's that doing there?" a voice yelped.

Beth turned to see her youngest daughter, Lucy, staring at the gnome with disgust. "Your father put it there."

"If any of my friends see that!" Lucy bellowed at her father.

"I thought you said you didn't have any friends. That's why we brought you here, wasn't it? Just so you wouldn't have any friends," Tom said. Lucy was about to reply but suddenly found herself struggling under a cardboard box full of peppermint balls.

"Take that inside, then help your father do something with Mr. Gnome."

"Who put that there?!" the fourteen-year-old voice of Amy—Lucy's perpetually worried-looking sister—cried out.

"I did," Tom answered in exasperation. "But don't worry, your mother's called the police. She's having me arrested."

Amy rolled her eyes as she stomped toward the house.

"Wait," Beth commanded. Amy stopped without looking at her. "There are more boxes in the car." A mother's statement is usually also an order.

A few minutes later all the boxes were piled up in the center of the lounge room. While Amy made loud comments about how "even the slaves on Roman galleys were allowed to change out of their school uniforms before they had to row anything," Dad and Lucy headed toward that big troublemaker of a garden gnome.

*   *   *

A few miles away in the center of a small suburban park stood a terrier dog. It looked just like any other you'd see in a park. It was mainly white, with a few patches of black and tan on its sleek fur coat. It had a cute little tail, a stout, robust-looking body, deep brown eyes, two black ears that sat up like sails on the top of its head, and a brown collar around its neck. It was exactly like any other dog except for one very eerie difference. It was completely motionless. It just stood there, staring blankly ahead.

Belka looked at Strelka. Strelka looked at Belka. Strelka raised his eyebrows slightly and then turned back to the controls in front of him. They had just opened the control panel for their dog-shaped Earth explorer and were immediately impressed by its gleaming newness. A giddy "new car" smell wafted about the cabin. Its cool, streamlined design was the very latest in spacecraft ergonomic development. The buttons had calm, relaxing colors and shapes, and the guidance columns were designed for comfort and ease of use.

The two Galactanauts stared at the controls for an inordinate length of time. No amount of friendly colors or nicely padded handles could make up for the fact that they had no idea how to use them.

"You first," Strelka said abruptly.

"Yes, of course. We'll soon get the hang of it," Belka replied, doing a pretty good job of feigning confidence. He reached across and gripped the handle of his control column. He hesitated for a second, then pushed forward.

Nothing happened. He pushed again and nothing happened for a second time. He expected to see a very smug Strelka staring expectantly at him, so he waited for a moment before looking up. "Well, I don't—" Belka began, but cut himself off when he saw Strelka reading something. "What's that?"

Strelka ignored him, but Belka could see it was the vehicle's manual. Unclasping his seat belt, Belka leaned over to take a furtive glimpse but fell back in his seat when Strelka reached across him and hit a switch. With a pleasant humming noise, various lights and dials lit up around them.

"Try it now," Strelka said, without any hint of smugness.

Belka found this apparent lack of smugness particularly annoying, but he pushed forward on the control stick and, to his relief, the dog-shaped craft lurched forward. Outside, one of the craft's furry front paws had taken one small step, with the opposite rear leg following in unison. Belka pushed forward again, and the corresponding set of paws did the same. It perfectly replicated the movements they had seen Laika make on Gersbach, as well as those of a million other dogs on Earth they had never seen.

"Okay. That's good. I think I've got her measure now." Belka's two short steps had him brimming with confidence. "She handles pretty well. Have a try."

Strelka slowly reached for his guidance column.

"Don't be nervous. Just gently ease it forward," Belka said reassuringly.

Strelka pushed the stick and the paws stepped one pace.

"There, you see? You'll soon get the hang of it," Belka said. "Now let's try something a little more ambitious."

"Okay!" Strelka said with a rush of excitement that immediately had Belka on edge. Strelka jerked his controls to the left and then to the right. The furry head of the dog vehicle turned from side to side. Inside the cockpit the twin screens in front of them displayed the view seen by the dog's keen brown eyes. Strelka rapidly turned the head from side to side again, causing them to be flung about in their seats.

"Be careful, will you!" Belka reached for his seat belt.

Strelka nodded deliberately. At the same time, he moved the stick back and forth, causing the dog's head to nod up and down in time with his own.

"Just stop it!" Belka roared as they were thrown forward, then backward, several times. "Look, Commander, we have a very important mission to complete. And we can't afford to make any mistakes. You do remember that the future of our whole world depends on us, don't you?"

"Yeah. I know." Strelka sounded as if he wasn't listening.

"Let's get moving," Belka ordered. "What's the position of the Disturbance Of Gravity?"

"The D.O.G. is a distance of 2.75. Not far," Strelka said, looking at the location monitor.

Belka strapped himself into his seat, pushed his guidance column forward, and the craft broke into a smooth, steady trot. Strelka turned a dial on his panel, and the pointy black ears atop the dog-craft's head rotated to the left in unison.

"Correct course 37 degrees port," Strelka said.

The tail swung out as Belka steered them to the left, increasing speed gradually as his confidence started to grow. "Steering's pretty smooth," he reported happily.

Suddenly a grating buzz shattered the fragile calm. "Life-form approaching, possibly hostile," the computer announced.

Belka slammed the stick back, and the craft's paws grabbed the earth. The Galactanauts looked up at the screens and saw a furry object speeding directly for them.

"It's closing fast," Strelka said.

"Stay calm!"

Strelka looked at him with mild surprise. "I am," he said.

The object bounding toward them was now close enough to

be identified as a large Labrador. Of course, the Galactanauts didn't identify it as a Labrador. They didn't know what a Labrador was. To them it was an Earthling. This was to be their first Earthling encounter.

"Closing . . . ," Strelka said.

"Bring up the translator," Belka commanded.

"On," Strelka said, activating the language-translating computer.

Belka drew a deep breath as the significance of the moment hit him. Gersbacian meets Earthling. Two worlds coming together. The hands of two great civilizations stretching out across the universe. This was it. This was First Contact. A thud threw Belka and Strelka forward in their seats.

"He's stuck his nose in our butt," Strelka announced, checking his instruments.

Belka looked out the forward screens and was startled to find a complete absence of Earthling. He spun their craft around to face the alien, but the creature continued to pursue their tail. With their screens filled with a giant Labrador bottom, Belka leaned on his column, trying to outturn the probing snout. After several rotations he tugged back on the stick, slamming their rear end onto the ground. The Labrador leapt back, cocked his head to one side, unfurled his slobbering tongue, and stared at them with wide-open eyes.

Belka recovered his composure and reached for the translator microphone. This was going to be a big test for Gersbach technology. Belka stared at the creature, unsure what to say.

Strelka intervened: "I have a gun and I'm not afraid to use it."

Lights on the panel instantly flashed, and they could feel the jaw of their craft's snout opening.

"No! Cancel! Cancel that!" Belka yelled out.

The lights cut out and Belka confidently spoke up. "Good afternoon, Fellow Earth Citizen."

"Just like a native," Strelka muttered.

The lights started up again, and the mouth erupted into a loud burst of barking. A complex system of hydraulics pushed the lips and jaws up and down and back and forth to exactly mimic a real dog's yaps. The Labrador looked puzzled for a moment, then delivered an intense stream of woofs in reply. The computer went into a flurry of activity, then issued the translation.

"Smooth green donkey. Pharmaceutical bucket."

Belka glanced at Strelka. Strelka shrugged. Belka spoke again. "Why, yes, my good donkey. I have many pharmaceuticals . . . in my . . . um . . . bucket." His fumbling words were instantly turned into a series of barks and whimpers.

The Earth dog gave a heated response: "Humpty foul buttons and buttons and buttons close furnishings."

"It's like you've known each other for years," Strelka said dryly.

"Well, it must be some local slang," retorted Belka, who always had the utmost confidence in Gersbach technology.

"Welcome to the Planet of the Idiots," Strelka said, then spoke into the translator. "Because *you're* an idiot, aren't you?"

"What are you doing?" Belka yelped in a panic. "We're supposed to be undercover! You'll give us away!"

The Labrador cocked his head to one side and woofed back. "Johnson fine picket repeat smudge muffin eleven," the computer translated without hesitation.

"Face it. We've been duped," Strelka declared adamantly. "There is no way that imbecile of a creature is the dominant life-form on this planet. I never understood the fuss made about Laika back home. Stupid creature."

Belka said nothing. What could he say? He just stared at the Earthling, now sitting back and taking a close interest in its own hindquarters. A piercing alarm issued from the computer, and warning lights glowed an angry red.

"Life-form approaching," the onboard computer warned.

"Incoming moron," Strelka muttered as they turned their ship's head to a shape in the distance. They looked at the screens and this time saw a much larger alien heading toward them. This one looked familiar. It had two arms, two legs, and walked upright. It was just like *them*—only much, much larger. Strelka focused the translator on the new being. Its voice became clear.

"Where are you, boy? What're you up to?" the translation came out.

"Did you hear that?" Belka said, awestruck.

"Yes, I did," Strelka replied, without any awe.

"Its speech had a logical translation! It means that the big creature is probably the dominant life-form after all!" Belka declared.

"The one that looks exactly like us is the *smart* one?" Strelka was fond of sarcasm.

"Yes." Belka was starting to get annoyed. He was not a fan of sarcasm.

"And the creature who's sitting there licking his backside is the *not-so-smart* one?"

"There's nothing you don't know about, is there?" Belka snapped. "You've met loads of alien life-forms haven't you? You have them 'round to play charades every weekend, I daresay!"

"Contact!" Strelka yelled.

For a moment Belka thought it was a joke he didn't understand (but was bound to be at his expense) until he felt the cockpit shake violently. Outside, the large human was whacking his hand up and down on their craft's doggy head.

"Hello there, boy!" The giant man patted them with altogether too much vigor. "What's your name, then? What's your name? Eh?" He turned to the Labrador. "Got yourself a little friend here, Jasper?"

The Galactanauts listened to the translation as they bounced about in their seats. Belka was about to reply when they felt themselves being raised in the air. The man held them above his head and looked up, smiling. His rapid stream of questions didn't miss a beat as he quickly lowered them. His huge face grinned just inches from their nose, then he lifted them up as far as his arms could stretch. Then he did it again and again.

"Who's a good boy? Are you a good boy? Are you? Are you a good boy?"

Belka and Strelka clung desperately to their straps as the monstrous leering face plunged back and forth on their screens. Belka managed to grab the translator. "Yes! We are a good boy! Repeat! We are a good boy!" he yelled.

The translator snapped into action, and a short round of barks burst from their vehicle's mouth.

"Are you? Eh? What's that you say? You are? You are a good boy?" the giant human shouted enthusiastically as he spun them onto their back and dropped them to the ground. Loose items were hurled about the cabin, and the Galactanauts were flung upside down. The giant used his great hands to grab the furry belly of their craft, and he briskly rocked them from side to side, continuing his babble. "You're a good boy, aren't you? And you've got a rubby tum tummy, haven't you? A rubby tum tummy tum! Who's got a tickly tummy? You have! You've got a tickly tum tum!"

This was not quite the line of interrogation that Belka had expected from his first encounter with an intelligent life-form, nor did he expect to have his own backside pressing down against his face when it was being delivered. "Yes, we have got a tummy and it's very, very rubby!" he cried out.

The ensuing woofs only caused the giant man to hoist them back up into the air and start shaking them in front of his face. The Galactanauts fell from their seats again. Strelka stuck out his hand and whacked a switch on the translator. He got to his knees and stared into the huge eyes that filled their screens. He spoke into the translator in a slow, deliberate voice. To Belka's dismay, Strelka's words were immediately translated into the Earth being's own language.

"Listen, Earth person. You either put me down or I will kill you. It's as simple as that."

The human giant's visible signs of life paused instantly.

"You and your furry friend," Strelka added.

The human brain is very much like a computer, in that it sometimes takes a little while to process a piece of data. In the time it took the large Earthling's brain to analyze this bizarre input, he had already placed the Gersbacian All Terrain Vehicle back on the Earth's surface. By the time his brain was saying, "Quit application, save all work, shut down, go home, have a rest," Belka and Strelka were charging across the park as fast as their mechanical paws would take them.

FIVE

When the sun goes down on planet Earth, its inhabitants return to their various shelters to engage in bonding activities with the other members of their family unit.

Taking small, white, peppermint-flavored balls from one large plastic bag and putting them into several smaller plastic bags may not be the most stimulating of family activities. But if a family was always short of income, then putting small, peppermint-flavored balls into plastic bags would probably be the family activity for them. And in the case of the Buckley family, it was.

"Let's think of a way to make this fun!" Tom Buckley said cheerfully when Beth hauled in the very first batch of Novelty Mints five months ago. It was his attempt to raise their spirits, but as everyone seemed to prefer to leave their spirits exactly where they were, he hadn't bothered to say it again. For the most part, none of them said anything much as they counted, bagged, and labeled the peppermint balls. A lot of talk about their day would break their concentration and slow down the task at hand. This would mean less time to spend doing their own activities. Only Lucy would spark up occasionally.

"They're *all* white. They're *all* round. They're *all* peppermint," Lucy observed. "So why are they called *Novelty* Mints?"

Beth stopped sorting and placed two peppermint balls on the coffee table. "Some of them are *bigger* than the other ones."

"Oh . . . ," Lucy said, looking at the two balls, not completely convinced that it was *that* big a novelty. The two balls were swept off the table into the last little plastic bag by Amy, who quickly slapped a label on it and threw it into the last box.

"Okay, we're finished." She pushed the filled boxes into the next room out of sight.

"Why are you in such a rush?" Tom asked.

"Miranda's coming over."

"Oh, right," Tom said. "Who's Miranda?"

"Miranda Hunter," Amy snapped. All this talking was slowing her down.

"Have I met Miranda Hunter?" Tom asked.

"She's one of Amy's stuck-up friends, who thinks she's so fantastic because she's got the biggest boobs in their class," Lucy explained.

"Miranda's a model actually," Amy said. "She's had her picture in a catalog, *and* she's done catwalk. And Dion Van Steenwyk goes out with her."

"Yeah, because she's got really big boobs," Lucy answered back.

"Who's Dion Van Steenwyk?" Tom asked to interrupt the escalation of hostilities.

"He's a really great guy. He's really smart," Amy explained.

"He's just some guy at school who all the girls love because he's soooo good-looking," Lucy said.

"He's really successful," Amy retorted. "He's got his own business on the Net. He's even got his own credit card."

"Maybe I should ask him for a job."

Amy knew he wasn't serious, but just the thought of her father talking to Dion Van Steenwyk about possible employment made her shudder. And the thought of him talking to Miranda about anything at all made her break into a cold sweat. Amy looked at her family and started to panic. She looked at her country hick parents and her pesky little sister. She looked at her dump of a house, and she looked at the boxes and boxes of stupid little peppermint-flavored balls. Amy froze up as a hundred hysterical thoughts spun around inside her head.

Why did I invite Miranda over?

She'll think I'm a joke!

It's going to be a disaster!

I've got to phone her and call it off!

Amy was snapped back to reality by a harsh buzzing noise. It was the doorbell. It was Miranda Hunter.

"Turn down here," Strelka said, reading from the location monitor. "To port," he added.

Belka adjusted their course without comment.

Strelka looked up at him and then said, "Not far now."

Again Belka said nothing, but much more intensely this time. Strelka stared at him for a moment until Belka broke his silence.

"Officially not impressed," he said, keeping his eyes on the road ahead.

Strelka didn't reply.

"We can't afford to break our cover, Commander Strelka," Belka lectured. He waited for a response but heard none, so he looked at Strelka directly. The moment he did, Strelka turned away and looked out through the screens. "That stunt back there could have blown the whole mission."

"Life-form ahead," Strelka reported.

Standing in the darkness ahead was a small, furry quadruped. "What is it?" Belka asked as he pulled them to a halt.

Strelka studied it closely. "I don't know what it is, but it's an ugly little creature."

"What do you mean?"

"Well, look at it. What a stupid-looking face," Strelka said. "And look how long those stupid whisker things on its nose are."

Belka was surprised at Strelka's outburst. He agreed it wasn't a very attractive animal, and it did seem to sport a particularly smug expression he didn't care for. He didn't much like the way it flicked its tail about either. Nevertheless, Belka was not one to judge someone on appearances.

"Good evening, sir," Belka spoke into the translator.

The quadruped just sat and listened to the short series of woofs, then let out a very strange sound. It went something like: *Meow.*

The computer spat out its translation: "Yer mother!"

"My mother?" Belka said to Strelka. "What about my mother?"

"It's an insult," Strelka prompted.

"An insult? About my mother?" Belka asked. "It's probably some error in the translation."

"No. Look at its arrogant expression," Strelka stressed. "Let's kick its butt."

"No, Commander. We can't afford to be sidetracked." Belka spoke into the translator again. "Well, sir, it was nice meeting you, but we have to be on our way."

"Yer mother!" the creature meowed.

"Come on," Strelka urged. "Just one bite."

"Look, sir," Belka said firmly but politely to the stranger. "I don't know what personal issues you have with me, but I don't have the time to discuss them right now. I really do have to be on my way."

"Yer mother," came the reply.

"Oh, just stand aside, you lout!" Belka snapped. He could tolerate bad manners for only so long. He shoved the control column forward, and they charged at the evil little beast. The creature, however, was very nimble, and the moment they made their move, it slipped out of sight.

"Where's it gone?" Belka asked.

"Up there!" Strelka pointed to the sinister being looking down on them from a nearby wall.

"It's quick," Belka said, giving the beast its due.

"We can still get it." Strelka flicked on the nostril-mounted headlights and caught the creature in a circle of light.

Belka snapped off the lights. "Don't draw attention to us."

"You'll keep, buddy!" Strelka shouted at the beast, which was translated into a short, vicious burst of snarly woofs. The little animal on the wall just stared blankly as it watched the dog-shaped craft head off into the darkness.

Inside their All Terrain Vehicle the air between Belka and

Strelka had cleared slightly. It's remarkable how the irrational hatred of the same thing can bring people closer together.

Belka leaned over and punched a code into the computer with his free hand. An image of the prototype craft stolen by Colonel Bars and Flanger Damka appeared on the screen in front of them.

"That's the outlaws' vehicle," he warned. "Keep a careful lookout for it."

"Funny-lookin' dog, you know," Tom Buckley said as he eyed the long, barrel-shaped animal tied to the clothesline.

If someone asked you to make a dog but you didn't know much about dogs, you'd probably come up with something that looked very much like a dachshund. It has a long, basic body with a little leg in each corner. Its head sticks up somewhere near the front end, and a simple tail hangs off the rear. A dachshund looks like a first attempt at a dog, and, in the case of Nicky the sausage dog, it was.

"It's not a working dog. Not the sausage dog," Tom Buckley said to Lucy. "Your cousin Des had one on his property. Just sat around yapping all day. Stupid dogs really. Look at that one just staring at the gnome. Obsessed with it."

"You don't like Nicky very much, do you, Dad?" Lucy asked.

"It's always looking at me in a funny way," Tom said suspiciously.

Lucy was starting to think that her father was forming an obsession of his own. There was a time, not long ago, when a little dog like that would have made no impression on him. He had hundreds of sheep to worry about.

She studied her father. She thought back to the campfires

that used to make his smiling face glow against the country night sky. Now, against the city sky, she could barely make out his face at all. The sun had gone down, but it was still light. Back in the country the night would wrap Lucy up in a blanket of dazzling stars. She'd spin around, running her fingers through them, then fall to the earth and let them wash over her body. From her new home she could see only two—and they seemed old and worn out.

"Where did all the stars go, Dad?" Lucy asked.

"Oh, they're still there, doll," he explained. "You just can't see them with all the bright city lights."

Lucy looked at the sky for a little while until something flashed in the corner of her eye. In the big tree at the side of the house was a strange object made of thin metal cylinders.

"What's that in the tree, Dad?"

Tom became uncomfortable. "It's . . . well . . . it's a television antenna," he said, not looking at it.

"What's it doing in the tree? Why didn't you put it on the roof?" Lucy asked.

"I *did* put it on the roof," Tom said. "It fell down. Landed in the tree. Don't tell your mother. She doesn't need to know, not after all that business with the gnome."

"So get it down," Lucy suggested.

"How can I get up a tree with my back? Hard enough getting up a ladder to the roof," Tom said tetchily.

"Only asking."

"Hey!" Tom said. "*You* could get it."

Lucy recoiled. "No, I can't. It's too high."

"What are you talking about? I've seen you climb much higher than that."

"No . . ." Lucy shook her head.

"Go on, sweetheart. Just climb up there and knock it down to me. Where's my little monkey?"

"Don't call me that!" Lucy exploded.

"What's the matter?"

"They all call me that!"

"Who does?"

"All those stupid kids at that stupid, stupid school! I hate it here in the city! I wish we never left!"

"Well, we all just have to try and make the most of it," Tom said quietly. He walked back inside.

"I don't think I can," Lucy said.

S I X

"There's something wrong with your mirror, Amy," Miranda Hunter said as she applied yet another layer of makeup.

Amy's stomach jumped. Everything Miranda said made her nervous. This was supposed to be two friends messing around with makeup and talking about boys. It felt more like a visit from a detective who was bound to find the dead bodies she'd hidden under the bed.

"What's wrong with it?" Amy asked meekly.

"It's too small and it's not lit well enough," Miranda explained. "I can barely see what I'm doing."

"I know. It's so hopeless."

"You need a proper makeup mirror like mine," Miranda advised.

"It's not my real one," Amy said, trying to plead her case. "That's back in the country. In storage."

"Of course, you need proper makeup to go with it," Miranda

added, turning up her nose at Amy's pathetic range of cosmetics.

Amy Buckley didn't want much from life. She just wanted a successful career involving international travel and lots of new clothes. She wanted a gorgeous husband and two really good-looking and talented kids and a big house on the harbor and one in France. And she wanted to be famous, although she wasn't quite sure for what—maybe for missionary work in Africa. She also wanted to be really wealthy, but if she had all the rest, and love, that wasn't so important. She didn't really know how to get any of these things, but she knew that coming to live in the city was the first step in the right direction. Being a friend of Miranda Hunter was the second.

"Dion's coming to pick me up soon," Miranda announced.

"He's coming here?" Amy was filled with both excitement and dread. She wondered how quickly she could get a restraining order put on her father. If she called the police, could she order one instantly over the phone?

"How long have you been going out with Dion?" Amy asked.

"We're not going out," Miranda corrected her.

"You're not?"

"Everybody thinks we are, but we're only friends. We just really hit it off, you know," Miranda said casually.

"Do you want to go out with him?"

"I don't know. Maybe," Miranda said, even more casually.

"He's really gorgeous." Amy was unable to suppress a big grin.

"He's pretty cute, I suppose." If Miranda acted any more

casual, she'd be flat out on the floor. She then threw a monkey wrench in the works. "Do you have a boyfriend?"

"No," Amy admitted. *What was she thinking? How did she think she could ever be a friend of Miranda Hunter without having a really cool boyfriend?* Amy was now fighting for her life, so she did something risky. She told the truth. "I used to," she said. "Back in the country."

"Really?" Miranda said, genuinely interested for the first time all evening. Her reaction excited Amy but also filled her with fear. It was dangerous territory because Amy Buckley was, in fact, a girl with a dark secret, and this dark secret was a double-edged sword. On the one hand, everybody wants to know a girl with a dark secret, but on the other hand, if anyone actually found out what that dark secret was, everybody would *stop* wanting to know her.

"Show me his photo."

Amy nervously fetched the evidence.

"Hey, he's okay," Miranda said. "Why'd you break up?"

"It just didn't work out," Amy said vaguely.

"Did you get dumped?"

"Yeah."

"For another girl?"

Amy's throat went dry. She couldn't answer.

"Hey, that's cool. Even I got dumped once," Miranda said, letting up a bit. "What was she like? What was her name?"

Amy hesitated for a long time before finally uttering the name she had never wanted to hear again. "Winona."

In the backyard something stood out over the rumble of traffic. Lucy listened hard and found herself drawn to the sullen sausage dog. It was music. She took a step toward it and then another. It was definitely deep, throbbing music, and it seemed to be getting louder as she got closer.

Inside the head of Nicky the sausage dog, Flanger Damka and several shaggy fat fleas bounced about wildly to excruciatingly loud heavy metal. They joyously flung themselves around the stark, featureless prototype cockpit, swinging on the bundles of wires hanging from the roof. They danced along the exposed piping and happily crashed into each other.

Outside, Lucy leaned over the little dog, and if ears could squint, that's exactly what hers would be doing.

Colonel Bars was livid as he charged into the sausage dog cabin. One slaphappy flea soared across his path, and Bars instantly sent it flying back the way it came with an angry smack of his hand. This flea hit another flea, which hit another, which collided with Flanger, and in a moment the whole party had collapsed into a tangled pile. Bars ripped a wire from the console, cutting the music off dead.

"Are you trying to bring the whole Earthling world down on us?" Bars roared.

"It's just a bit of music." Flanger flexed her knees just slightly and effortlessly leapt across the cabin into one of the pilot seats. "Just a bit of fun."

"We'll have fun later. Oww!" Bars yelped. He reached down the back of his pants, pulled out one large flea, and tossed it across the cockpit. It bounced off the floor, jumped onto Flanger's head, and stared at Bars like a naughty puppy.

"We've got work to—" Bars was suddenly distracted by

something—or by nothing, actually. He looked around the room. The fleas had vanished.

"I'm going to count to three, then it's spray time," he announced ominously. "One . . ."

Bars' trousers erupted into chaos as a dozen fleas frantically evacuated and leapt onto Flanger. The super fleas weren't all that intelligent, but they knew what certain words meant.

"I thought this was going to be fun," Flanger moaned as she swiveled around on her chair. The fleas had formed a single column on top of her head that nearly reached the ceiling. The column tipped toward Bars, and the top flea stared at him until he smacked it away, causing the whole troupe to crash into the control panel.

"When we have the Disturbance Of Gravity, we will have the power to do *anything we want,*" Bars told Flanger, moving toward her slowly. "Then, I promise, you will have more fun than a barrel of monkeys." He leaned over her and spoke with increasing menace. "A whole barrel of monkeys. Okay? A great big barrel completely filled right up to the brim with as many monkeys as you can possibly jam in there," he said, violently forcing his hands into an imaginary barrel. "More fun than that. Okay?"

"Whatever." Flanger swung to face the forward screens. "Oh look!" she said with mock interest. "A little Earthling."

Bars snapped his head up to see the image of Lucy's face poking about. "Oh, terrific," he muttered and jumped into his pilot seat. "Translator on," he ordered.

"Nicky, do you have music in your head?" Lucy's voice came over the cockpit speakers.

"No!" Bars shouted into the translator. A short, sharp woof was relayed to Lucy.

"You do?" Lucy's voice was translated.

"Definitely not, you idiot!" The three barks that followed failed to convey Bars' frustrated tone.

"Is that yes or no?" Lucy asked.

"I'll give you yes or no," Bars muttered as he reached for the control column. As he grabbed it, a red circular targeting sight appeared on the screen in front of him. He pushed the column forward and the dachshund's head lowered. The target tracked over Lucy's body and down her leg.

"Well, Nicky? Do you? I definitely heard something," Lucy asked stubbornly.

When Lucy's calf was lined up in his sight, Bars pushed the red button on top of his stick. The craft's mouth snarled and lunged at her leg. "Back off, Earth thing!" Bars cried.

Lucy jumped back to avoid the bite. She looked at the dog with more resentment than fear. "Nicky, if you don't want to be nice, you don't have to be; but you don't have to be nasty either. We didn't have to take you in. We could have left you to roam the streets and get run over by a steamroller. You're a nasty, rude, ungrateful dog, and music *does* come out of your head. I heard it *and* I'm telling my father!" Lucy turned and stormed off.

Bars and Flanger Damka sat in silence until the little girl was inside the house. "What a little creep," Bars said.

"Yeah," Flanger agreed.

seven

The wail of its high-pitched engine could be heard well before the red-and-black motorized scooter rounded the corner and tore down the Buckleys' street. Its gold-helmeted rider stood proudly as the scooter conquered every obstacle this average suburban street had to throw at it. It jumped up and down the gutter. It zigzagged between the native shrubs. It flew along the Plunkets' front wall. It easily cleared the unfinished drainage ditch outside Mrs. Pappas' house, did a perfect figure eight around the recycling bins of number seventeen, then glided gracefully to a halt just outside the Buckleys' front door.

The two girls were already leaning out of Amy's window when Dion Van Steenwyk lifted his gold helmet and let his short dreadlocks fall free. As he tucked the helmet under his arm and stepped toward the house, Miranda raced to Amy's door as quickly as coolness allows (which is still pretty quick).

"Hey, I'll see you later. It was fun," Miranda said. Just before she left, she stopped and turned to Amy. "She must be really beautiful."

"Who?"

"Winona."

"Why?" Amy asked timidly.

"For your boyfriend to dump you. She'd have to be gorgeous because you're really cool," Miranda pronounced, then left.

It took a few moments for her to realize that Miranda had given her a big compliment, but when she did, Amy started to glow. This was quite possibly the greatest success she had ever had in her whole life. She was floating on air. Unfortunately, her father had just taken over the shift at Air Traffic Control.

"Quite a vehicle you've got there," Tom said to Dion, pointing to his converted scooter.

"It's great on gas," Dion said, sauntering into the house. "Very economical."

"Do you need a license?"

"I don't know." Dion shrugged. "It's just a scooter with a lawn-mower engine."

"Hiya!" Miranda arrived, beaming at Dion.

"Finished gossiping, have you?" Tom smiled.

"Oh yeah," Miranda said. "Amy was telling me all about Winona."

"Winona?" Tom asked.

Amy rushed over, but when she saw her father already talking with Miranda, she knew it was too late. It was like a surgeon saying, "There's nothing more we can do now" as he turns off the life-support equipment. Her fate was sealed.

"She must have been really beautiful," Miranda said.

"Well, I don't know if you'd call her beautiful. She was a cow."

"A cow?"

"A blue Jersey longhorn."

"What?!" Miranda exclaimed. "You mean a *real* cow?"

Amy was so horrified she felt sick. Everything in the room started to blur. The only thing that stood out was Miranda's face as it went from shock to delight.

"She was a pretty good-looking cow, though," Tom chuckled, completely oblivious to Amy's distress. "That's what Amy didn't understand. Her boyfriend raised it from a calf. He gave Winona too much attention, so Amy put it on the line. It's me or the cow. He chose the cow."

"You got dumped for a cow?" Miranda said.

"Gee, she was mad too. She even asked Bob Thurston to take it down to the slaughterhouse on his next run. You know, sort of like 'by mistake.' She offered to pay him and everything." Tom couldn't help smiling as he recalled. "You tried to have Winona whacked, didn't you, love?" he chortled, looking at his daughter. The chortling stopped when he saw the rage on Amy's face.

"What's your problem?" he asked. "Wasn't I supposed to say anything?"

Amy used all her energy to spit out just three words, and Tom felt the power of each one of them. *"It's—really— embarrassing!"*

"Oh, come on. These are your friends. Just a bit of a laugh. Right?"

Miranda pushed her grinning face into Amy's. "Oh, yeah. Don't worry. Forget about it."

"Hey, it's cool," Dion spoke up. Both girls were quickly

drawn to his smooth, firm tone. "We all have our hearts broken by livestock sometimes."

"Yeah?" Amy asked, calming.

"Sure," he said, gazing into her eyes.

Amy tried to meet his look, but felt coy and stared at his mouth instead. She noticed two small fine lines that turned upward at each corner. Dion's expression never changed very much, but these two lines made him look like he always had a sneaky little grin.

Miranda was staring too. She was staring at them staring at each other, and she didn't care for that very much at all. She grabbed Dion's arm and guided him out the front door. "Come on. We've got to go."

Amy followed them, still gazing at Dion as he mounted his scooter. Miranda jumped on behind and wrapped her arms around him. "Bye, Ames," she said as she nestled her head between Dion's shoulder blades. "And don't worry—your secret's safe with me."

Dion fired up the scooter and it whined into the night.

Amy was gripped by a cold gloom. Deep within, however, a small, glowing ember of rage began to warm her. The ember burst into flames, which became a seething volcano. The volcano erupted, shooting a thick magma of fury throughout her entire being.

Amy stormed inside to confront her father.

"HOW COULD YOU TELL HER ABOUT WINONA?" Amy shouted.

"You're too sensitive about that whole thing, you know," Tom said. "Your boyfriend wasn't a cow-kisser; he just didn't like you telling him what to do. No guy does."

"You're such an embarrassment!" Amy howled.

"Well, I'm supposed to be an embarrassment," Tom said, not looking up from his newspaper. "My father was an embarrassment to me. His father was an embarrassment to him. Grandpa Buckley, he was a really embarrassing man."

He lowered his paper to look at her but found she had gone. Amy was already lying on her bed in serious sulk mode.

This was going to ruin her life for sure.

Miranda would see to that.

Amy buried her head under the pillow. She twisted and turned, but all she could see was Miranda's smirking face, although, just occasionally, she got a flash of Dion's face also. Dion didn't smirk at her. She really wasn't quite sure what kind of look it was. It was sort of a smirk, but there was just a little bit more to it than that. Amy lay there trying to work out exactly what that certain something was, and pretty soon that's all she was thinking about. She was finally distracted by a mechanical chugging sound that seemed to be getting closer.

Lucy marched into the room and went straight up to her Dad. "Daddy, Nicky the dog has music in his head."

Tom looked up from his paper again. "You're not a teenager yet, are you?"

"No. I'm eleven."

"Then why can't I understand what you're talking about?" Tom asked.

Lucy was about to reply when she became distracted by a chugging noise coming from out front. "What's that noise, Dad?"

Tom didn't reply. He walked slowly toward the front door. As the noise grew, Beth and Amy arrived and took up position behind him. A strong light hit the door and cut through the edges into the hallway. Tom stepped out onto the porch, and his eyes were blinded by a blazing light and his ears deafened by a screaming mechanical din.

"Tom!" a voice called. The light and the noise suddenly cut out. Tom's eyes adjusted quickly, and just as quickly he realized who it was. Half hanging out of the cabin of a battered old van was his brother Gavin. Gav's hand released the extinguished spotlight on the roof as steam continued to fume from it.

Tom looked at the writing on the side of the vehicle. The fresh lettering contrasted with the van's otherwise peeling paint job. It proudly stated: GAVIN BUCKLEY'S BOUTIQUE SAUSAGES.

"How's life in the big smoke, city slicker?" Gav asked heartily.

Gav wasn't quite as tall as Tom, but he was a fair bit bigger around the belly. He was wearing his good dress clothes, which were roughly as old as his mode of transport—except for his tie, which appeared to be brand-new and about as loud as he was.

"How's city life? Good, Gav," Tom replied flatly. "What brings you here?"

"Had a bit of luck. Beth!" Gav cried out, spotting her just as she was creeping back inside. In a flash he dramatically swept her feet from under her and planted a huge wet kiss on her lips. He always did this. It was funny the first time, about fifteen years before.

"How are you?" he asked, dropping her back on her feet. Then he noticed the girls. "Girls!"

Neither Amy nor Lucy answered. They just ran as fast as they could back inside. A lot of uncles might find such a reaction insulting, but not Uncle Gav. Gav simply didn't understand insults.

"You haven't changed a bit, Beth," Gav said as they walked down the hall.

"It's only been six months," Beth replied, extracting herself from his grip.

"I expected to see you swanning around in a long gown, sipping champagne." Gav followed her into the kitchen.

"Well, I'm not."

"No, you're still a country girl. You still smell like a sheep," he said admiringly.

"Gee, thanks a lot, Gavin."

"A woman *should* smell a bit like a sheep," Gav declared. "My mother smelled *exactly* like a sheep."

"Mum didn't smell anything like a sheep, Gav," Tom spoke up.

"Well, she did to me."

"Let's not spend all night talking about sheep, Gavin," Beth suggested.

"Well, I told Tom—the boutique sausage market."

"Going all right then, is it?" Tom buried his head in the paper.

"Haven't looked back. Leaps and bounds. I told you, didn't I?"

"Yeah, you did, Gav."

"You wouldn't have lost the farm. You wouldn't have worked so hard and hurt your back. You'd still be in Tubby Flats," Gav continued, oblivious to Tom's blackening mood.

"Yep," Tom said as he flicked a page over.

"Still keeping those kangaroos at bay, Gavin?" Beth said, trying to turn the conversation. A second later Gav was just a few inches from her face.

"The boutique sausage market is in love with them, Beth. I

can't knock 'em over quick enough! Sure, sheep are a lot of fun, but where's the demand nowadays?" Gav turned back to Tom. "I definitely told you that."

"So what brings you here, Gavin?" Beth said as her husband fumed.

"I was telling Tom. Had a bit of luck. Won a contest in *Country Guns and Beef* magazine. A weekend in a fancy city hotel. All expenses! Ha! Ha!" Gav could hardly contain himself.

"Bet Judy's enjoying that," Beth said, referring to Gav's long-suffering wife.

"Oh, she's not well again."

"Poor Judy. Sick." Beth stared at him.

"Oh well, the processing plant's going full bore, so someone's got to stay and keep the blades turning." He headed toward the kitchen and spotted Amy with Nicky the dachshund. Nicky was bent over a bowl of dog food, staring at it blankly.

"Oh, come on, Nicky. Just a bit more," Amy encouraged him. "You hardly eat anything."

Inside, Colonel Bars stared at the bowl of cheap dog food on the forward screens. "I'm going to have to go in again!" he called over his shoulder.

Flanger stomped into the cockpit, followed by her entourage of fleas. She was wearing thick gloves and a face mask and held a very large spade. "We can't fit any more in! There's nowhere to put it! And it stinks!"

"Just one more run and maybe she'll get off our backs." Bars pushed forward on the guidance column and dove toward the bowl.

* * *

"That's it, sweetie. You've got to eat. You've got to stay strong. We've both got to be strong," Amy leaned in closer and spoke very softly. "When I saw you standing there in the street, all by yourself, you know who I saw? I saw me. You know what I mean? We're both alone in this big city and nobody really wants us. But you know what? We're going to make it. We'll hang out with the best people in the best places and wear the best clothes . . . and we'll meet the best guy . . . well, I will, but he'll love you too, and he'll have a girl dog for you, and we'll all hang out together on an island."

A slightly frayed-looking Flanger appeared and stood over Bars' shoulder. "There is definitely no more room back there," she hissed at Bars. He completely ignored her. Words of fury bubbled up in Flanger's mind. She was brewing an angry tirade to hurl at him but found the dreamy words issuing from the translator were cooling down the mix.

"A poet . . . a really rich poet . . . he'll give talks to other writers while I design clothes . . . in Paris."

Flanger looked up at the looming Amy. "What's she going on about?"

"I think we're having 'a moment,' " Bars said, rolling his eyes.

"Who's this guy she's talking about?"

"I don't know."

Amy's face plunged toward them, and the whole cockpit reared up. Flanger toppled backward and fell through the cabin entrance. Bars listened for a thud but heard a large squelch instead.

"Hey, who's this little fella?" Gav asked.

"His name's Nicky." Amy knelt over him protectively.

"Funny-lookin' thing. What breed of mutt is it?"

"Purebred Freeloader," Tom called from his chair.

"It's a sausage dog," Amy said, glowering at her father.

"Sausage dog?" Gav said, his interest sparked. He started to prod the animal. "How much do you'd reckon he'd weigh?"

"It's a city dog, Gav. Be all fat. Little gate-crasher. Comes in here. Sets up shop," Tom said.

"So you don't want him, then?" Gav asked.

"Yes we do!" Amy answered.

"I could give him a home if you like," Gav offered.

"You're not taking my dog!"

"A city dog wouldn't last five minutes at your place, Gav," Tom said.

Gav tried hard to suppress a smirk. "Oh, he'd last five minutes," he said, almost to himself. "Well, what about the other one, then?"

"What other one?" Tom asked, dropping the paper.

eıght

Belka stared at the gnome-shaped object on the viewing screens. "And that's definitely the Disturbance Of Gravity?" he asked.

"That's it. That's the D.O.G.," Strelka replied. The white pinpoint of light flashed triumphantly at the center of the location monitor.

Belka studied the ugly gnome looking down on them. Their All Terrain Vehicle was just two feet from it. The back-porch light cast a weak glow over the gnome's crudely painted face.

"You know, it almost looks evil," Belka said, which reminded him of their other problem. "Where are Bars and Damka?"

"Not far." Strelka pointed to the blue light blinking on the location monitor. "Probably just behind that door."

Belka turned the ATV's head to observe the house. "Our priority is to destroy the D.O.G., then we'll tackle Bars."

The door was suddenly flung open. Standing there were two large humans and two smaller ones. "I think we're sprung," Strelka said.

"Stay calm!" Belka barked.

"I am."

"What are they saying?" Belka slapped on the translator.

"Jeez! Another one!" Tom said. "What are we? A halfway house for sponging little city dogs? Well, I'm not feeding this one too. It can hit the road!"

"Tell you what. I'll take it off your hands," Gav offered.

"You're welcome to it."

"And what are you going to use a little dog like that for?" Beth called out from the kitchen.

"Oh, come in handy. Dog like that," Gav said as he moved toward Belka and Strelka's craft. "Good ratters."

Lucy became worried. She didn't know who this new dog was, but she definitely knew who her Uncle Gavin was. She could read him like a book, and that book was called *Don't Trust This Man Under Any Circumstances*.

"You can't just take it," Beth said. "It probably belongs to someone."

"Yes, that's right!" Lucy rushed to the little dog. "It's Sam Chan's dog!"

"It's *whose* dog?" Tom asked, both confused and annoyed.

"My friend, Sam Chan," Lucy blurted out, trying to make her mind outpace her mouth. "He asked me to look after him tonight. His name's . . . F-F-F-Flumpy."

Tom stared at her. "Flumpy?" He didn't quite know what to think, but he was becoming too tired to really care. "All right.

Just keep Flumpy out of my way." He headed back inside. Lucy looked up at Uncle Gav and smiled. Glowering at her, Gav followed Tom.

"And keep Flumpy outside. The house is a Flumpy-Free Zone," Tom stated firmly. "That goes for this one too." Tom hooked his boot behind the sausage dog and nudged him into the yard.

Amy followed. She put a comforting arm around Nicky and gave Lucy a dirty look. "You just cause trouble all the time," she hissed at her little sister.

"Don't upset Flumpy," Lucy said, putting her hand on the little dog's head.

"You're so full of it."

Lucy ignored her sister's hostility and looked at the two dogs facing each other just two feet apart. "Hey, I think they like each other."

"If they resist arrest, we'll have to kill them," Belka said. "We can't afford to fool around."

"We'll tear this animal's throat out the moment the humans are gone."

Bars moved the targeting sights over the image of the new dog. "Then we'll have ourselves some D.O.G." Bars' eyes widened as he looked at the gnome. "The power is so close now, I can smell it."

"Well, I'm never going to get this smell of cheap meat out of my hair," Flanger whined. "And it's under my nails!"

Bars was about to get very annoyed with Flanger when his attention was diverted.

"Attention, Colonel Bars." Belka spoke calmly, but with all the authority that his position as an Official Representative of the Gersbach Government afforded him. "We are officers of Gersbach Space Command." He pushed his jaw forward proudly, and the message was immediately turned into a series of particularly high-pitched and whiney dog yaps.

"That's the other craft!" Bars exclaimed as the translation came through.

"What other craft?"

"They made *two* of these vehicles. This is only the prototype. That's the newer version."

Flanger's expression turned to horror. "You mean this isn't the latest one?" she wailed. "I don't believe it! This is last season's model!"

Belka started to speak again, but so did the other Gersbacians. The two craft slowly closed in on each other, their howls and woofs twice as loud and growing louder.

Belka: Colonel Bars, it is pointless to resist arrest. You are clearly in breach of every ordinance in the Gersbach Code of Good Citizenly Conduct. Oh yes, you can	Bars: If you think I'm going to let a pair of jumped-up, furbrained Boy Scouts come between me and the power that is justly mine, then you'd better go and see your shrink. If you	Strelka: Ms. Damka? We want you to understand that we in *no* way hold you responsible for any of this. We realize that at your age you come under a lot of pressure. Especially an	Flanger: Will you people just back off! I don't know why you're getting mad at us. You've got it good! You're sitting there in the lap of luxury while we have to suffer cooped up in

make threats, but if you continue to resist, we will have no alternative other than to use whatever force is necessary to place you in our custody. Both of you. Brutal force against both of you. Including you, Ms. Damka. This action may cause you personal injury or could even result in your demise!

try to touch me, I'm going to remove your craft's tail and place it as far up both your bottoms as it will go. Then after I've squashed you, I will go back and take the whole of planet Gersbach apart piece by piece. Then the good people of Gersbach may understand the meaning of gratitude.

attractive woman like yourself. You meet a guy, you fall in love, and next thing you know you're on another planet inside a giant dog. It could happen to anyone. But it's all right. No one is mad at you. When this is over, we'll get together over a meal and have a real good heart-to-heart. Just the two of us.

this piece of junk. It's hot. It's stuffy. I'm literally covered in this disgusting foul gravy stuff that I'm going to smell of for the rest of my life. I haven't had a proper bath since I've been here, and I can't get a decent shampoo anyway. "Result in my demise," you say, Commander Belka? Too late, mister. Come and look at my nails!

The feuding All Terrain Vehicles were just a dog's breath away from each other when an external party interrupted their debate. This party was wearing pajama pants and a very frayed white T-shirt.

"Shut those bloody mongrels up or I'll tell Gav he can have 'em!" Tom roared at his daughters from the back porch. "And he can take you two as well!"

Both cockpits plunged into silence. Amy gathered up Nicky

in her arms. Lucy grabbed Belka and Strelka's ATV and held it close to her chest. The two sisters stared each other down. Amy's look was one of fury. Lucy did feel a little responsible for the trouble, so all she could manage was a look of disdain.

"Well, tie them up! Away from each other. Crikey!" Tom turned and went back inside.

"Tie that thing up way over there!" Amy pointed to the far end of the yard as she hurled a leash at Lucy. "Keep it away from Nicky."

The two girls quickly fixed restraints to the animals, gave them a comforting hug and a word of reassurance, and then stomped into the house without looking at each other. The house shook as two bedroom doors slammed in unison.

Hours later Lucy was awoken by the screech of Uncle Gav's van rattling off down the road. She looked out from her bedroom window over the quiet backyard. She saw no sheep, no tractors, no water tank, and no distant hilltop lined with scribbly-gum trees. Instead, she saw a clothesline, a toolshed, and a piece of alien material radiating an energy stream that was steadily destroying the core of a planet one hundred thousand light-years away.

She also saw a pair of ruthless outlaws determined to take control of the alien material in order to wreak havoc on that planet, and two elite Galactanauts whose mission was to destroy the alien material and arrest the two outlaws before any more harm came to their planet or anyone else's. Of course, to Lucy this all just looked like a clothesline, a toolshed, a garden gnome, and two scruffy little dogs. And even the gnome didn't look much like a gnome.

Why the dogs were glaring at each other Lucy couldn't figure out, but as she crawled under the covers, she realized she was just too tired to care.

Inside the two dog-shaped spacecraft in the backyard, however, everyone was wide-awake and on high alert. Bars stared at Belka and Strelka's ATV intently. He was almost shaking with rage.

"Those morons are not going to get their hands on the D.O.G.," he declared.

"Well, let's face it, they probably are," Flanger said. "Now, if we had taken the *new* ship and not the *old* ship . . . ," she began, but didn't finish—partly because she had made her point and partly because there was activity from their pursuers.

Belka's hand carefully pushed the control column until the leash had slowly moved into the center of his screen. "Engage the laser," he ordered.

Strelka turned a dial, and a gun sight appeared over the leash. Outside, a smooth silver barrel slid out the left nostril of the ATV's little black nose. Belka's thumb hovered over the red trigger button as he lined up the leash. He made a slight correction to the left and then pushed down.

Colonel Bars nearly leapt from his seat when he saw the bright flash of the laser. "They've got a laser!"

"Really?" Flanger said with false surprise.

"They're using it to break their restraint!"

"Well, let's do that too." Flanger searched around the

control panel. "Now, let's see. Laser? Laser? Where's the laser?"

Bars shook his head furiously and grabbed his control column. He had a desperate plan of action in mind.

Belka and Strelka sat watching the leather leash cool down so that they could measure their progress.

"It's made almost no impression," Belka sighed. "Made it very hot, that's all. The laser can't be at full power. Have we got any other weapons?"

Strelka checked the arms inventory on the computer. "There's a missile launcher with one missile. Right nostril."

"*One* missile?" Belka questioned.

"They're very expensive."

"Will it destroy the leash?"

"Yes . . . ," Strelka said, checking its specifications.

"Prepare to fire!" Belka ordered.

"And us, and the yard, and the house . . ."

"Okay. Okay. Try the laser again," Belka said, then noticed a flurry of activity over at Bars' ship. He swung the ATV's head around and saw the little sausage dog had elevated slightly. Strelka zoomed onto the dachshund's legs to ascertain why. A rocket nozzle was protruding from each of its furry paws.

"We've got to hurry!" Belka yelled as he turned back to the leash and gave it another laser blast.

"Put your straps on!" Bars yelled at Flanger as he wildly flicked switches.

Flanger's cocky attitude deserted her as she buckled up and grabbed the sides of her seat. The fleas jumped up and grabbed Flanger's sides. Bars pulled back on the control stick and hit a button so special it was hidden under a shiny cover. Outside, the jet-paws started to shake, and a second later intense flames shot out of the sausage dog. It rose slowly into the air as Bars struggled to keep the craft level. Hovering only a few inches off the ground, Bars determinedly eased the craft toward the gnome-shaped D.O.G. Just half a dachshund's head away from their goal, they came to the end of their tether. Bars increased the power, but the restraining chain was too strong for a small alien spaceship. It stretched and stretched but did not break. The strain on Bars' face was as great as that on the chain. Everything he wanted was right there, just out of reach. He prepared to put the throttle into overdrive.

Belka and Strelka watched the smoke and fumes clear from around their own restraint. Strelka raised his eyebrows slightly. "Nope. Pretty much the same," he observed.

"What's our flight system status?" Belka asked.

Strelka consulted the computer. "Not good. Three rocket legs damaged beyond repair back at your crummy Earth landing."

Belka let the comment slide. "One of us will have to go outside and use explosives on the leash," he said, staring Strelka directly in the eye.

Strelka looked back as if he didn't completely understand the statement. "One of us?" he said.

Belka threw off his harness. "Obviously, I meant *me*," he huffed as he grabbed a stack of explosives from the weapons store. "Obviously, I didn't think for a minute that you'd be interested in doing something that required you to take any sort of risk you didn't absolutely have to."

Strelka just continued giving a blank look as Belka climbed into the elevator. "But if it's not too much trouble, would you mind opening the top outer hatch for me so I can go and save everyone's backsides?" Belka asked as he closed the door behind him.

"Right away," Strelka said obediently as he flicked a switch on his panel.

Between the two ears of their dog-craft, a tiny hatch flung open and a metal elevator cabinet rose up. Inside the elevator Galactanaut Belka pushed a button, and the seal on the doors broke with a hissing gasp. A heavy invisible force struck Belka immediately, forcing him to his knees. As he crawled out, he realized that the force was the Earth's gravity. Its pull was many times stronger than it was on his home planet, and he wasn't like an Earth insect, with a body strong enough to cope with it. Belka was basically a monkey, and a very small monkey at that. He was, however, a very determined monkey, and he managed to drag himself to the edge of the ATV's head. He looked down at where the leash clipped on to the collar, which was, literally, several stories below. Gripping handfuls of the huge hairs around him, he swiveled his body around and dangled his legs over the furry cliff. The gravity and the weight of the explosives in his backpack proved too much, however, and he suddenly found himself battling not to be pulled over the edge. He won the tussle by slipping the pack off and letting it fall to the ground far below. Without the explosives Belka had no reason to continue, so he used his remaining strength to haul himself back to the elevator and toss his crumpled body into it.

From the helm of the ATV, Strelka watched Bars and Flanger

as their dog-craft hovered just out of reach of the ugly, gnome-shaped D.O.G. The elevator hissed open behind him. A disheveled and exhausted Belka staggered forward and fell into his seat. There was an awkward silence.

"So . . . um . . . how did you do?" Strelka asked.

"The gravity is too strong," Belka muttered.

"Oh, right. Yeah, it would be," Strelka nodded.

"I dropped the explosives outside."

"Uh-huh."

There was another awkward silence, broken by a bright flash and roaring noise from the dachshund ship.

One of Bars' hands was jammed forward on the throttle while he used the other to try and keep the craft stable. A high-pitched grinding sound filled the cabin as the engines strained. The cockpit rattled and shook. Bars and Flanger felt the jarring right down to the roots of their teeth. The chain that held them from their gnome prize strained but would not yield. In fact, as the engine struggled to maintain power, the chain seemed to be slowly pulling them back.

"Come on, you stubborn beast!" Bars roared over the screaming din of rockets, then felt the controls go wobbly in his hands. The ship slowly started to rise and drift toward the house. Bars tried desperately to wrestle it back to the ground, but the craft soared as high as its tether would allow. When he realized he had totally lost *all* control, Bars just sat and stared at the front viewing screens. As the ship turned upside down, the night sky slowly appeared. The sky was replaced by the tiled roof, which in turn was pushed aside by the gutters. The gutters became the side of the house, which gave way to the top of the window frame, and then the upside-down and very perplexed face of Tom Buckley. The craft hovered there for a few seconds before all noise, shaking, and power from the engines ceased.

Tom stood for a moment, his mind quite blank. He then chanced a tentative look over the window ledge. The dachshund was on its back, completely motionless on the ground below. He stepped back and tried to think, but nothing came to mind. Tom checked the dachshund again. Still there. Still upside down. He looked over to his sleeping wife and considered waking her, but a vision of the phone network of great-aunts eagerly discussing how "Tom just isn't coping in the city" stopped him. He had to take some action, however—there was the well-being of his family to consider. So he shut the window, closed the curtains, and went to bed. As an added precaution he switched off the light.

nine

The Buckleys woke up early. It's what country folks do. Even Amy woke up early, but she lay there under the covers determinedly *not* getting up. It's what city folks do.

"Get out of bed!" her father's voice boomed through her bedroom door.

"Why? It's Saturday!" she yelled back.

There was a long pause, and Amy could almost hear her father's brain ticking as he carefully considered the many reasons why she should get out of bed: the advantages to her health, the social benefits, the respect she should pay to the long tradition of her ancestors who rose early each morning to work hard and forge this country into the great nation it is today.

" 'CAUSE I TOLD YOU TO!" he shouted, and stomped off down the hall.

* * *

Tom entered the kitchen and eased open the curtain. There was Nicky. Not floating. No aerobatics at all. Just standing there at the end of his chain, staring at that darn gnome. Tom sat down. Then he got up and had another look, then sat down again before checking one more time. And that's what Tom spent most of the day doing, apart from putting peppermint-flavored balls into little plastic bags.

"Why do you keep staring at Nicky, Dad?" Lucy asked.

"I'm not staring," Tom said, snapping back the curtain.

"Is Nicky freaking you out?"

"Course not. Just a stupid sausage dog," Tom retorted.

"Nicky's really freaking you out, isn't he?"

"When's that Flumpy going back home?" Tom asked, changing the subject.

"Later on."

"Well, just keep them out of my hair. Take them for a walk around the park. Otherwise I *will* freak out."

"I don't get it," Belka said. "Walk where? Where does she want us to walk to?"

"Dunno," Strelka said. "But she seems pretty excited about it."

"Walk!" Lucy ordered the two dogs, trying to stir up some enthusiasm.

"We need to maintain our cover and please the Earthling," Belka advised.

Strelka moved the ATV's head about. "Yes. Yes. Walk. Walk," he muttered dully.

"That's more like it!" Lucy said happily, and led the dogs out the gate and down the road.

* * *

"Where are we going?" Flanger's bedraggled body slumped into the seat next to Bars.

"We're going for 'a walk' apparently," Bars said as he drove them along at a steady trot. He kept one eye on the Space Command ship jogging along next to them, and while it was obviously not a race, he couldn't help but keep his craft a nose in front.

"Could we walk a bit more quietly? I'm exhausted. I can't sleep properly in a bunk. And why haven't we got that D.O.G. thing yet?"

"When we get a chance, we'll make a break for it," Bars replied, his patience clearly tested. "Until then we have to play along with the human."

"Let's just blast off—" Flanger began.

"No! Not yet! We can't—"

Bars was cut off as the leash jerked the dachshund to a halt. He looked up at the screens. They'd reached the place all real Earth dogs most crave to be. Stretching before them was a vast, open expanse of grass. They'd reached the park.

"You mean that's it?" Flanger said. "It's just . . . well, it's just a park."

Lucy unclipped the leashes from the dogs' collars and stood back expectantly. "Well, go on," she said.

The two dogs stood motionless.

"Go on!" Lucy urged. "Walk! Run! Scamper!"

"There's nothing on scampering," Strelka said as he clicked through the computer menus.

"Just jump up and down a bit," Belka improvised. "And wag the tail. Humans love that."

Lucy looked disapprovingly at the little dog. "That's really lousy scampering," she said, then turned to the dachshund. "Still, it's better than *no* scampering at all!"

The dachshund instantly started to bounce about like Flumpy, but even more half-heartedly.

"That's the worst scampering I ever saw. Where did you guys learn to be dogs?" Lucy chastised them. She reached into her pocket and pulled out a tennis ball. She bounced it up and down on the ground with a gush of enthusiasm. "Look! Look! Look what I've got!"

"What do we do now? What is that thing?" Belka asked.

"It's a nitrogen-inflated, powdered-titanium, rubber-core ball, covered with fabric," the computer explained.

"Riiiight . . . ," Belka pondered, turning to Strelka.

"Beats me." Strelka shrugged.

"She's thrown it!" Belka shouted.

They watched the screens as the tennis ball flew through the air. It landed in the middle of the park and bounced to a stop. Strelka zoomed in. They studied the magnified image of the ball cautiously.

"Chase it!" Lucy shouted in exasperation.

Belka pushed forward on the guidance column and cantered toward the small green sphere. Bars set Nicky off after them.

"What are you doing?" Flanger whined as they bounced along. "Why don't we just go back and grab the D.O.G.? Isn't that why we came to this stupid planet?"

"We've got to wait for the right moment!" Bars snapped

back, keeping the tennis ball in his sights. He opened the throttle and surged past Belka and Strelka.

Belka was about two feet away from the tennis ball when he jumped on the brakes. Their ATV lurched to a halt inches from the dachshund, which seemed to be grinning at them as it clenched the ball victoriously between its teeth. Belka stared balefully back at Nicky. Strelka looked across at him.

"You want that ball, don't you?" he said.

"I'm considering my next move."

"He beat us to it, so now you *really* want that ball," Strelka teased.

"Look—" Belka was interrupted by Lucy calling from the edge of the park.

"Bring it back here!" she screamed.

"What kind of dogs are you?" Lucy frowned. "Haven't you ever fetched a ball before?"

There was an awkward silence.

"Well? Drop it!" she instructed Nicky, who released the ball at Lucy's feet. She picked it up and hurled it back to the center of the park.

"What's she doing?" Bars asked. "We brought it back to her and now she just throws it away again. Well, I'm not chasing after it. She can go and get it herself."

"Don't worry," Flanger said, looking at the screen. "Those idiots from Space Command will get it."

"Like heck they will!" Bars cried as he spun the ATV around and sped off after his rival.

"Shouldn't we be watching Bars?" Strelka asked as he clung to his seat.

"I'm just trying to humor the Earthling!" Belka shouted as he pushed Flumpy into overdrive. "Engage head-up tracking display!"

"Um . . . okay." Strelka flicked a switch. A complex grid of lines and numerals appeared on the forward screens, plotting the tennis ball's movement through the air. Belka pulled open Flumpy's snout and made a desperate leap at the green sphere. He missed by only half an inch, allowing the ball to hit the ground and bounce back up into the air. It didn't hit the ground a second time. Bars was too quick. He grabbed the ball and raced back to Lucy with Belka in almost reckless pursuit.

"If you slow down and try not to kill us both, I promise I'll buy you a ball of your very own," Strelka said as he was tossed about in his seat.

"It's not about the ball!" Belka snapped, slamming on the brakes. "It's about maintaining our cover so we can success-fully complete our mission!"

Strelka turned from Belka's withering gaze.

"Look! She's throwing it again!" Belka shouted, unable to suppress his excitement. It took him only a couple of seconds to have Flumpy's paws pounding the ground at full gallop. This time Belka's aim was dead on target. With Strelka making precision adjustments according to the trajectory display, Belka sprang the ATV into the air at precisely the right moment to intercept the ball. Bars was furious. Flumpy came up trumps the next time as well. But a sneaky sideswipe—causing Flumpy to break stride and lose momentum—meant that Bars won the following round.

Belka always believed in playing by the rules—but he'd

never seen the rule book on ball chasing. As both craft leapt for the next ball, he decided grabbing the dachshund's tail was quite permissible.

"You guys are really good at this," Lucy said as Belka disengaged the primary mouth hydraulic, dropping the ball at her feet. "But can you get this one?"

She tossed the ball as far and as high as she could. A lot of Earth dogs would have considered her throw to be "a hard one." But a lot of dogs don't have an onboard tracking system that can predict within 99.9999 percent accuracy that the ball will glance off the edge of the park bench @ an angle of 42.1 degrees, pass directly over the doggie-do bin @ a height of 1.35 yards (@ a speed of 17.32 miles per hour), and land 15 inches 4.37 degrees south-southwest of the slippery dip.

"You're *really* good at this!" Lucy exclaimed as she took delivery of the ball. "But you'll never get this one so quickly!"

But they did. And they got the next one, and the one after that . . . with logarithmically improving speed and accuracy. Belka and Strelka fetched the ball three more times, then Bars won the next couple. The score was exactly even when Lucy picked up the ball again.

"We should get back, so this will have to be the last one."

"So I suppose we just *have to* win this one, don't we? Even if it kills us," Strelka muttered, loud enough to pierce Belka's throbbing aura of excitement.

"Have you ever wondered why I came in first in our year at the Academy and you came in second?" Belka asked.

"Because my priorities were girls, football, really big cakes, *then* lectures, but I'm sure you have a different theory."

"It's because I believe in winning," Belka insisted. "I believe in winning every part of a venture—no matter how insignificant it may seem. If you stay vigilant and win all the little battles, the final victory will always be yours. If—"

"Bars and Damka have gone," Strelka announced calmly, checking the location monitor.

"What?!" Belka yelped. "Where?"

"Back toward the Earthling dwelling."

"Hold tight!" Belka spun Flumpy around.

"I said one more time!" Lucy shouted as the two dogs dashed down the road.

ten

The dachshund turned into the Buckleys' driveway and charged toward the side gate.

"Brace yourself—I'm not slowing down!" Bars shouted. He lowered the craft's head, and as Flanger tightened her straps, they hit the gate at full ram speed. It doesn't matter if it's a real dog or an intergalactic spacecraft—against a determined dachshund a flimsy wire gate doesn't stand a chance. Bars smashed through, leaving a tangle of wire in his wake, and steered directly for the gnome. About a foot short of it, he pulled to an abrupt stop.

Bars looked at the badly painted face of the gnome staring at them from their screens. It became the face of every citizen of Gersbach. Every one of them at his mercy. Every one of them on their knees! He lined up the gnome's bulbous red nose in his sights. A piece that size would be perfect to take back to Gersbach—portable, yet totally devastating. He opened the dachshund's mouth and pushed forward on the control stick. The gnome's nose, however, didn't get any closer.

"What's the matter now?" Flanger said, quite fed up.

"I don't know. We're stuck!"

"Don't let go!" Belka ordered, but Strelka didn't reply because it was such a stupid thing to say in the current circumstances. Strelka *didn't* let go of Flumpy's mouth control. Flumpy's mouth *didn't* let go of the dachshund's tail. If Strelka *did* let go, Bars would grab a piece of the D.O.G., fly back to Gersbach, and, well, it wouldn't be pleasant.

Belka threw the ATV into full reverse and, being the slightly more powerful, newer ship, it slowly started to drag Bars' ship back from the gnome.

"We're going the wrong way," Flanger said flatly.

"I know we're going the wrong way!" Bars yelled, still struggling to stop their reverse. "They're pulling us back!"

"When are you going to do something about them? They're really becoming annoying."

"Right now!" Bars slammed the control column to the right.

The dachshund spun around, tearing its tail free from Flumpy's mouth, and launched a fierce face-on assault. Belka reared Flumpy onto his hind legs and threw the front paws into action, blocking each of the dachshund's attacking blows. Strelka snapped the ATV's mouth back and forth, not actually making much contact but producing a lot of impressive snarling noises.

"You drive!" Belka shouted over the din of battle.

Strelka didn't have a chance to be surprised by Belka

leaping from his seat. He worked the boxing paws while Belka dashed to the Weapons Store and grabbed as much explosive as he could carry, then ran back and seized the controls again.

Belka presented Bars with an onslaught of paws, claws, teeth, and snout that left the dachshund cowering against the clothesline. Then he thrust the control column back to Strelka.

"Let me out as close as you can to the D.O.G.!" Belka ordered as he ran down to Throat Level.

Strelka grabbed the controls and swung the craft toward the gnome. Flumpy leapt six bounds and lowered his head to the gnome's shoddily painted boots. Strelka pressed a button, and with a gentle whine of hydraulics Flumpy's lower jaw opened. Belka appeared up at the throat entrance with a backpack bulging with explosives—clearly feeling the burden of gravity.

He looked at the patchy lawn stretching across the Buckley backyard. This was the surface of the most distant alien planet a Gersbacian Galactanaut had ever witnessed. Bars may have beaten him through the wormhole, but Belka would be the man to *take the first step on an alien civilized world*. He pressed a button just inside Flumpy's mouth, and the long pink tongue snapped into a flight of stairs that reached to the ground. Apprehensive yet excited, he carefully stepped down the first two steps; then he slipped on the artificial saliva that had been used to make the tongue more realistic. He made a painful, tumbling transit down the slobbery ramp and was catapulted onto the Earth's surface.

And so the first part of an alien to touch the Earth was Belka's bottom.

Belka nonetheless climbed to his feet. If he'd had a Gersbach flag, he'd have proudly planted it. Suitable words for the occasion stirred in his mind.

"That's one small step for a Gersbacian, one giant leap for—"

"Hurry up, Golden Boy," Strelka said curtly over the loudspeaker.

As Belka dug away some dirt from under the gnome and wedged in the bundle of explosives, Bars saw his chance and charged at Flumpy's unguarded rear end. The impact sent the ATV flying straight into the D.O.G., causing the enormous statue to wobble dangerously above the tiny Belka. At the same time, the Earth's powerful gravity was beginning to take its toll on the brave Galactanaut. He set the explosives' timer to one minute and staggered back to Flumpy's slobbery tongue. Before he could climb up, however, another powerful blow from Nicky sent his escape route flying out of reach.

Strelka attempted to confront his attacker, but Bars expertly locked the dachshund's jaws around the terrier's throat. Belka looked up in alarm as the two mighty ships struggled above him, but he had no choice other than to stagger as far from the impending gnome explosion as he could.

The Chief Controller at Gersbach Space Command stopped writing his report. He signed his name and then looked about the office. Something was different. Lately, signing his name had been a very difficult task with the escalating tremors afflicting the planet. Only that morning he had been endorsing a promotion in front of a grateful Space Command Lieutenant when his pen flew across the room and put a large black dot on the poor man's nose.

But it was easy to sign his name now, for the quakes had stopped.

Belka and Strelka had succeeded! And so soon! Could it be that easy?

He ran to the window and gazed up at the wormhole burning brightly in the Gersbach sky.

When the garden gnome exploded in the Buckleys' backyard, it was far more powerful than Belka had expected. Despite his exhaustion and the incessant pull of gravity, Belka managed to prop his bruised and battered body into a sitting position. He was alarmed to see Flumpy fall onto his back, flung effortlessly aside by the explosion. But he was more alarmed when the ATV's head hit the ground with a thud, and a muffled BOOM reverberated across the yard. Flumpy shook, and what looked like a puff of talcum powder shot out from the ATV's crown. It took Belka a moment to realize what had happened. The backpack of explosives he'd dropped the night before! Flumpy's head had landed directly on it and set it off! He had a vision of Strelka vaporized in the cockpit. He then had a second and distinctly genuine vision of a certain dachshund bearing down upon him.

Flanger had never seen Colonel Bars quite so enraged. "You're really mad now, aren't you?" she said, a little nervous.

Bars was too angry to reply. He was too angry to do anything other than keep the figure of Belka firmly in his sights. No one denied him a prize as fabulous as the D.O.G. without paying for it.

"You should stomp him really hard," Flanger encouraged him. "It'll do you good. Just let it all out."

Belka couldn't move. His body just wouldn't do it. He looked up at the enormous dachshund looming above him and felt the strange sense of calm a completely hopeless situation can produce. He was going to die, but he found solace in the knowledge that he had saved Gersbach from certain doom.

The dachshund of his destruction towered murderously above; then out of nowhere another figure loomed over Nicky.

"What are you up to?" Lucy asked, attaching the leash to Nicky's collar. "And did that gnome just explode?"

She knelt before Nicky, took the dachshund's head gently in her hands, and looked him in the eyes. "Did you do it?" she asked.

Bars threw his hands up in fury. "Me blow it up?! Why would I blow it up?!" he ranted at the innocent face filling the screens. "And why are you asking me anyway? I'm an Earth dog!" He turned to Flanger, almost choking with frustration. "Why do they do that? Why do these humans talk to dogs like they can understand what they're saying?" He turned back to the screens and shouted, "I'm a dumb animal, you moron!"

"Well, between you and me, I didn't like that gnome anyway," Lucy confided. "And what are you doing, you lazy little thing?" Lucy turned her attention to the upside-down Flumpy. She crawled over and started tickling the underside of the most sophisticated and expensive piece of technology within one hundred thousand square light-years.

"Are you sunbathing?" she said playfully, rolling him from side to side.

Inside, Strelka tried to recover his senses as he dangled upside down in his seat. He remembered the gnome exploding and Flumpy being blown over, but it seemed only a few seconds later another hellishly loud detonation had occurred directly above him. He must have blanked out for a while. His head felt like he'd spent a week in a subwoofer bin at a heavy metal concert. Everything sounded like it was underwater, with an annoying high-pitched squeal across the top. He pulled himself together and worked the controls, but the ATV's mechanical paws flailed in the air without effect.

"Did you blow up the gnome too?" Lucy's watery, giggling voice came through the translator. "Did you? Did you?"

Bars still had one thing on his mind—a small Galactanaut who lay floundering in his path. He slammed the control column forward. His eyes bulged red with vengeance. Two more steps and Belka would be history—but Bars suddenly found he could not take even *one* more step. The leash clipped to his craft's neck was once again spoiling his plans.

Bars did not completely lose his temper as Flanger expected. Instead, he calmly turned to her and gave her an instruction. "Go down to the Aft Navigator's Observation Section."

"The where?"

"The A.N.O.S.!" he shouted, now losing his temper. "It's at the rear! Under the tail!"

"Okay. Okay," Flanger muttered as she sulked off.

Bars immediately spun the craft around so that the dachshund's rear end was facing Belka. Now, even *with* the restraining leash, the sausage dog's rear legs were easily within stomping range.

Belka's arms and legs felt like jelly, but he still managed to throw one in front of the other as he made a desperate crawl toward his own vehicle. As the long shadow of Bars' craft engulfed him, he looked back over his shoulder. He saw the dachshund's tail rise into the air dramatically, revealing a small porthole at its base. The steel cover on the window opened like an iris on a camera, and a female's head looked out. He had only seen this woman in official photos, but he knew immediately who it was.

"So what do you want me to do *now*?" Flanger huffed into the intercom.

"Stick your head out of the A.N.O.S. and guide me onto that Galactanaut," Bars snapped back.

Flanger felt strangely uncomfortable sticking her head out of the small porthole, but she started to issue directions. "A bit to the left," she said. "Now a bit to the right. More to the right."

Bars thrust the control column from side to side and back and forth. Down below, Belka called on every reserve he had to hurl himself out of the way as a deadly rain of paws crashed around him.

"You keep missing him," Flanger said, annoyed.

"Well, tell me which way to go!"

"I am," Flanger insisted. "But you may as well not bother now."

"Why?"

"Because the other ship has already picked him up."

"What?!"

Despite hindrance from the playful young human, Strelka had managed to right the ATV and make a dash for Belka. He scooped his partner into the dark, slobbery safety of Flumpy's mouth. Belka was in a daze. It was a while before he completely realized where he was and that his partner's quick action had saved his life. Despite his slack attitude, Strelka had come through.

"Good boy, Strelka! Good boy!"

"What have you got in your mouth?" Lucy asked as she moved in for a closer look. "You're not eating something nasty, are you, Flumpy?"

eleven

"You'd better get back up here, Commander," Strelka said into the intercom as Lucy started to peer closer at Flumpy's mouth.

"Come on. Show me. What have you got in your mouth?" Lucy's voice came over the speakers.

"Really. You should come back up," Strelka advised, but Belka was too exhausted to move.

Lucy put her hand on Flumpy's snout. Strelka reacted by jerking back from her hold and throwing in a nasty growl for good measure. Lucy jumped back with fright; but her fright immediately turned into annoyance because she was getting pretty sick of little dogs with bad tempers.

"I was only trying to stop you from choking on something, you ungrateful little dog!" she shouted. Then she saw that something had dropped out of Flumpy's mouth during the tussle. She swiped it off the ground and waved it in front of the dog's face.

"What if you had choked on this? What if it had gotten stuck in your throat?" She waved it about again to stress her point, then realized with shock what it was. In her palm was a little man. A bruised, battered, exhausted little man.

"Who are you?" Lucy asked. "Are you all right?"

Belka raised his hand slightly and managed a weak, delirious smile. Lucy was amazed. She thought she'd seen every toy on the market, but this was incredible.

"You're so realistic. Where does your battery go?" she asked, turning Belka upside down. Belka's eyes widened in horror, but before Lucy had a chance to check for any secret compartments, she became aware of a frantic whimpering. She looked down at Nicky. The little dachshund was sitting up in the classic begging position with its tongue hanging out.

"And just what do you want?" Lucy asked. "Do you want to play with the little man?"

Bars pumped the pant lever quickly and nodded Nicky's head back and forth. "Yes. Yes. I want to play with the little man," Bars said anxiously. "Let me play with the little man."

"Well, I don't know if I should. I'm still not sure if I like you. I haven't forgotten you tried to bite me before." Lucy turned to Flumpy, who was now also begging. "I know I'm not going to let *you* play with him. I thought you were nice, but you're just a horrible grumpy ungrateful little dog."

Strelka didn't really listen to Lucy's dressing-down. He had heard it all before. He'd been hearing it all his life, so, as he usually did, he just took matters into his own hands or, in this case, mouth. In one quick and simple action Flumpy sprang up and gobbled Belka out of Lucy's open hand. Lucy, understandably, was horrified.

"You ate him! You bad dog! You bad, *bad* dog!" she cried with rage.

"Oh, you stupid kid, we're not a dog, isn't that obvious?" Strelka snapped over Flumpy's loudspeaker.

Lucy froze. She'd never heard a dog speak before.

"Excuse me, young Earth female!" another voice boomed behind her.

Lucy spun on the spot. "Who—who said that?" She looked around the yard to see who was playing tricks on her. "Where are these voices coming from?"

"I will explain everything," Bars said through Nicky's loud-speaker.

Lucy regarded the dachshund warily. *They don't make toys this good,* she thought. She was on the verge of believing these dogs were actually talking to her . . . but that just couldn't be right.

"Is there a little man inside you too?" she asked Nicky.

"Yes!" Bars quickly insisted. "But I'm a very *good* little man. That other animal contains a pair of ruthless criminals!"

"That is patently untrue!" Belka's authoritative voice boomed from Flumpy. Lucy stepped back warily.

"We are from the planet Gersbach," Belka continued. "We are Officers of Space Command. We have come here to arrest that man—Colonel Bars—and his accomplice. *He* is the crimi-nal. Don't believe a word he utters."

"But look what they did to your beautiful statue!" Bars shouted back. "Is that the action of men of justice?"

"Well . . ." Lucy wavered. She turned to Flumpy. "Have you got a warrant or something you can show me?" she said, remem-bering a TV show she had seen recently. "Or a tiny little badge?"

A beeping sound started in Flumpy's cabin.

"You'd better check this out, Belka," Strelka said, looking at the location monitor.

"What is it?"

"You know how you just destroyed that statue made of D.O.G.?"

"Yes," Belka answered proudly.

"There's another piece of D.O.G. out there."

"Where?!"

"About one hundred miles west of here."

"Is it just a little bit?" Belka asked hopefully.

"No," Strelka answered. "It's a really, really big bit."

Flanger's attention was drawn to the dachshund's location monitor. "Bars—look!"

Bars leaned over and his eyes widened. A bright dot of light was blinking rapidly on the screen. "The D.O.G. mother lode!" he exclaimed. "Look at the size of it!"

"What's going on?" Lucy asked.

"Young woman," Belka announced over Flumpy's loudspeaker. "We must depart. Our mission requires us elsewhere."

"No, young lady!" Bars shouted. "Keep them locked up! I have an important mission they will do anything to ruin! You must release *me*!"

"Just be quiet, would you? Both of you," Lucy said, annoyed. "I should go and get my dad, but I don't want to get anyone into trouble, especially me."

"No one will be in trouble if you let me go right away," Bars lied. "But keep *them* locked up. They are extremely dangerous! Trust me—I'm your friend!"

"Shush! Both of you just stay there until I work out what to do!"

But Belka and Strelka were not about to wait around as their home planet came under a new and even bigger threat. Belka seized the controls and made a sudden break for freedom. Before Flumpy had cleared even four paw lengths, however, Lucy scooped him up in her arms.

Tom slammed open his bedroom window. "Lucy! When are you taking that silly-lookin' Flumpy back to Sam's house?"

"Right now, Daddy," Lucy said, secretly grateful for the idea. "I'm sure Sam misses him."

"Righto," said Tom, retreating to his newspaper.

* * *

Sam immediately noticed the scorch marks on Flumpy's leash, and on top of his head. He held on to the leash tightly, as Lucy had ordered.

"I don't know if Mum and Dad will like me having a dog here," he said seriously.

"Your parents are always at work anyway," Lucy snapped. "I need you to help me keep these bad men away from Colonel Bars and his mission."

"What mission? You didn't say anything about a mission!" Sam exclaimed.

"His only mission is to gain power and subjugate an innocent people!" Belka announced over the loudspeaker. "He is here on *your* planet to take control of a powerful force that will give him utter control over *our* planet!"

Sam stopped in his tracks. "Flumpy talks!" he marveled. "He talks and we can understand him!"

"All you need to understand is that they're bad-tempered, disobedient, and they make gnomes blow up," Lucy declared.

They walked up to Sam's bedroom.

"Don't let him get on the bed," Sam said cautiously.

"What?"

"You shouldn't let dogs on beds. They have things living on them that can cause diseases."

"He's got things living *in* him," Lucy said. "Didn't you hear a word I just said?"

"About Flumpy blowing up your gnome? Are you serious?"

"Yes!"

"It's just that some people even let dogs lick their face, and that's really unhygienic. I've got an uncle—"

"Attention, young Earth male," Belka's voice interrupted, full of authority.

Sam became intensely curious. "That really does come from your dog, doesn't it?" He looked closely at Flumpy's face. "How does he do that?"

"I told you. It's full of little men."

"Yeah, sure," Sam replied, looking for a switch or an antenna.

"What she says is accurate, sir. We are Officers of Gersbach Space Command," Belka said.

"That is so cool. Did you build it? You're a genius," Sam said, genuinely impressed.

"Listen, you stupid kid, we really are Space Officers, and we're really here on a very important mission!" Strelka's voice roared.

Sam's face began to drop. He didn't like this animal's tone, and he was even beginning to wonder if perhaps . . . but it just couldn't be.

"Think about it. This Earth girl is just as stupid as the rest of your primitive race," Strelka said.

"Oh, thanks," Lucy said.

"Shush, Strelka! You're not helping," Belka's voice could be heard saying.

"I'm under stress." Strelka went on in a more reasonable tone, "But think about it—how could she possibly construct a craft like this?"

Sam looked at the creature's eyes. There did seem something unusual about them. He stepped closer, looking deeper until he was looking right into the pupils. He intensified his stare so much he nearly strained his eyes. But then he saw it—a little man sitting in what appeared to be a room full of equipment. The figure waved and Sam leapt back in fright.

"Convinced yet?" Lucy asked.

"Well . . . not completely," Sam said dubiously.

Suddenly a thin red beam of light shot out of the dog's nose and struck the schoolbag hanging on Sam's cupboard door. A black dot scorched the material, and a small wisp of smoke drifted up to the ceiling.

"So what do you want us to do?" Sam asked, clearly unnerved.

"Let us off this leash."

"No!" Lucy yelped.

"We should probably do what it says," Sam suggested.

"No! We can't trust them," Lucy pleaded.

"Why do I have to keep it here?"

"Because I've got to watch the other one—Nicky," Lucy said angrily. "They've got to be kept apart, otherwise they start fighting and blowing up your—"

"That statue had to be destroyed," Belka stated. "It was emitting a force that was dangerously affecting our planet. And you must understand there is another one! Another source of danger to our planet that we must get to *immediately* and destroy! We know where it is—you must let us go there. Let us go, and I promise you'll never see us again."

"Shush! Just shush!" Lucy cried and headed to the door. "I'm going." She pointed a stern finger at Flumpy. "And you *stay!*"

"That went well," said Strelka after a pause.

But Belka wasn't listening. He was studying the location monitor and the relentless white light pulsing upon it. "This new source of D.O.G.," Belka said. "It's getting even bigger!"

Gavin Buckley stood in his top paddock and marveled at the large, stark white rock that nosed up through the dirt. He checked the chain, stretched tight between the rock and his tractor.

"Again!" Gav bellowed to his wife.

Judy Buckley was a very small woman, and she looked even smaller sitting at the wheel of the huge tractor. She stamped down her rubber boot, and the tractor surged forward. The giant rock clung to the earth like a child to its mother, then rose another yard out of the ground before stopping again.

The tractor's wheels began to spin in the dirt, and the chain threatened to break. It was obvious the rock would budge no more.

"Okay! Knock it off!" Gav ordered. Judy cut the engine.

"You're a mysterious fella, aren't you?" Gav said to the rock. He ran his hand over it. The surface was perfectly smooth, apart from where he'd knocked a bit off six months before. He'd turned it into a gnome for his brother's family in the city. Good-looking gnome, too.

Today he'd decided to pull the rest of the rock out—to find out just how big it really was. And it just kept coming and coming.

Maybe you're not a rock at all, he suddenly thought. *You look more like a bone!* His mind began ticking with possibilities. *There wouldn't be too many big bones like you, would there?*

He turned to his wife. "Jude! Fetch the shovels! We've got digging to do!"

He spun back to admire his big bone. His mind was already going at a hundred miles an hour.

twelve

As Amy approached the school gate, her brain was entirely occupied with one thing: small, white, peppermint-flavored balls. This is what she did when she didn't want to think about anything. It was like putting her brain into "standby" mode. If she did start thinking about anything, it would only be about the terrible events of last Friday evening when her stupid father blabbed about Winona. And that didn't bear any more thinking about.

She inserted herself into the crush of students bustling down the path toward the buildings. The other students seemed much taller today. She couldn't see over them. They knocked her from side to side as they rushed past and crowded her from behind. A hundred simultaneous conversations melded into one bleating din. The flowing mass finally reached the end of the brick veneer valley and burst into the main courtyard, where students milled around in small groups. As Amy approached her group of friends, the rumble of the crowd faded to a low murmur, then dissolved into a weird, breezy quiet. A strange moaning sound gradually rose up from the edges of her perception. Amy froze with recognition.

"Moo."

A sick feeling bubbled at the bottom of her stomach.

"Moooo."

But it wasn't just one moo. There were several moos, and they were coming from all around. Amy's head felt light, and sweat trickled down the back of her neck. She spun around, but there wasn't a single cow in sight.

Amy ran. She ran through the tight knots of school children that were now turning to confront her.

"Moo!" they bleated.

She veered to avoid one particularly ferocious group, only to run straight into another pack of laughing, mooing girls. The back of Amy's school uniform was soaked with sweat as she charged through the baying mob and headed for the teachers' parking lot. The frenzied herd stampeded after her, all trying to hurl the most vicious moo. Amy jumped three stairs in a bound and dashed past the science master's station wagon, out onto the empty, half-returfed soccer oval.

Above the laughs, cheers, and moos of the students watching her frenzied escape, a familiar, high-pitched howl erupted. Then an even more familiar scooter appeared behind the mob and started to slice its way through. The crowd parted as Dion Van Steenwyk leaned on the handlebars and powered after the frightened, running figure that was now halfway across the oval.

"Amy! Stop running!" Dion called to her.

Amy glanced over her shoulder but kept going. Dion took bold action, jamming his scooter's handlebars on an angle and leaping from the moving vehicle's platform. The chunky soles of his boots took the impact as he hit the ground behind Amy. In one smooth movement he bounded forward and threw both arms around her. They tumbled to the ground. As they rolled along, the barrier of Dion's strong arms sheltered Amy from the harsh earth. When they came to rest, the panting, disheveled girl looked up, and through blurry eyes she saw a gold helmet rising into the sky above her. She saw a cascade of dreadlocks and a mouth with little upturned creases in the corners.

"Moo," Dion said softly.

A warm, slightly dizzy sensation rushed through Amy's body as she found herself rising up and standing beside Dion. His arm was still around her as she heard the roar of his approaching scooter. The riderless bike had carved a graceful arc around the oval and now passed remarkably close to the point where Dion had jumped off. He casually stepped onto its platform, sweeping the still-dazed Amy with him. As the pair drove across the oval and out of the car park, an angel could have looked down from heaven and seen a girl nestling in the warm safety of her first love. Unfortunately, Mrs. Glover looked down from the history staff-room window, and all she could see was a couple of truants.

*   *   *

"Lucy," Ms. Felton said. "I thought you'd like to be the first one to try out the school's brand-new gym set."

Lucy didn't move. She just looked around the gathering of children, teachers, and the mothers on cafeteria duty that day.

"Come on, Lucy," Ms. Felton insisted. "Show everyone what a good climber you are. I was very impressed by you the other day."

Lucy walked slowly to the apparatus and looked up at its cold, mean grid of metal bars.

"Go on, Lucy. I've told all the other teachers how athletic you are." Ms. Felton was beginning to get agitated.

Lucy jumped up and grabbed the center bar. Then her hands froze. She just hung there, unable to coax herself into doing any climbing or swinging. It was almost like she was *scared* to do it.

"We're all waiting, Lucy," Ms. Felton called out.

Lucy did nothing. The cafeteria mothers left. They had to get the lunches ready and they were running behind.

"So that's all you're going to do, is it, Lucy?" Ms. Felton said, quite annoyed. "I hope you show more enthusiasm on Sports Day."

Lucy made one last supreme effort. She lifted one of her hands and fell straight down onto the ground.

"Oh, everyone just get on there and have a go!" Ms. Felton shouted as the other teachers headed back to the staff room.

The children shuffled over to the gym set and climbed on. Lucy sat on the ground and watched them crawling across the framework above her.

"And have fun!" Ms. Felton demanded.

thirteen

Belka slammed the control stick forward, and the ATV surged across Sam Chan's room. It leapt onto the bed and plunged through the gap in the curtains, screeching to a halt when its nose was barely an inch from the bars on the window. Belka pounded a button on the console, and a flurry of high-pitched barks erupted. Strelka noted the escalating desperation on Belka's face and placed his hand over Belka's.

"There's nothing there," Strelka said.

"I thought I heard something." Belka felt self-conscious. "A vehicle, or another dog animal."

"Maybe you should stop doing that. No one's going to just come and let us out."

"We've got to get out of this place! Our mission is failing," Belka said dramatically.

"We can't really do anything until the human comes back. This room is too secure."

"Why do they put solid bars on their domicile's windows? Why do they want to keep people in?"

"I think it's more to keep people out."

"What kind of planet is this?" Belka decried.

"Who knows?" Strelka looked on in disdain as Belka started hitting the "Warning Bark" button again.

"Something went past! I saw it!" Belka shouted.

Strelka leaned forward and switched off the power to the console. The barking ceased. Belka stared angrily at him until he flicked the switch back on, restoring the power.

The icy silence was shattered by the bedroom door being unlocked and Sam Chan dropping his schoolbag. Belka spun the vehicle around, dove off the bed, and landed at Sam's feet.

"Were you on my bed?" Sam asked suspiciously.

"I think we've already established that we are *not* a real dog animal and thus completely free of the disease-ridden parasites that usually accompany such a beast," Belka answered.

"I still don't want you on the bed," Sam replied firmly.

"Look here, young Earthling," Belka spoke with authority. "You must release us immediately. There is more at stake than you can possibly understand."

"So you've said," Sam replied as he switched on his computer and connected to the Internet.

"As you sit there playing with your toys, an entire civilization is on the brink of annihilation," Belka pleaded, looking to Strelka for support.

"True story." Strelka was a little lost for words.

"Lucy said she had to think about it." Sam didn't even look at them as he typed on his keyboard.

"There isn't time!"

"Mmm-mmm-mmm," Sam deliberately hummed as he concentrated on his computer screen. He typed the word "origami" into a search engine.

Belka looked at Strelka in frustration. Strelka spoke into the translator. "What's that you're looking up?"

"I have to make something using origami. It's homework," Sam answered as he called up the first site on the list.

"What's origami?"

"You get a piece of paper like this and fold it into a shape like a cat or a bird. But I don't want to do a cat or a bird. Everybody'll do cats and birds," Sam moaned as he scrolled through the second site.

Before Sam even finished speaking, Strelka had scanned the dimensions of the sheet of paper into the onboard computer and was running a series of calculations. It took only a few moments for a list of instructions to pop up.

"You want something different?" Strelka asked.

"Well, yeah," Sam said cautiously.

"Fold your paper diagonally across the middle, then turn each corner back to the center."

"Why?"

"Just try it."

Sam made the folds and then more as Strelka read them out. His curiosity grew as the paper started to take shape.

"What's it going to be?" Sam asked as he made some intricate creases.

Interested, Belka looked across at Strelka's monitor but was not pleased by what he saw. The three-dimensional model spinning in the display was a highly accurate representation of the outlaw Flanger Damka in an alluring pose.

"Hold on!" Belka spluttered into the translator. "That's not right."

"Why?" Sam asked.

"Try this instead," Belka said as he hurriedly ran another program.

Belka muted the translator and hissed at Strelka, "This has got to stop. She's a criminal."

Strelka rolled his eyes and sat back.

Belka called out to Sam as the new instructions flashed up. "Start by folding it in half."

They were a bit tricky, but Sam followed Belka's directions precisely, and after about twenty minutes he was holding a small, horn-shaped object. It had a mouthpiece and some keys along its length.

"What is it?" Sam asked, unable to disguise his fascination.

"It's a musical instrument," Belka answered.

"I can't play any musical instruments," Sam said, a little disappointed.

"Just blow and push the first button up and down."

Sam carefully placed the end in his mouth and blew gently. A perfect musical note sounded from the other end. He was amazed and blew harder. The little horn was more robust than he thought, and soon, with Belka calling out which key to press next, Sam was playing a simple little melody. "I'll admit that's pretty impressive, although the tune stinks," Sam said.

"It's the Gersbach national anthem," Belka said indignantly.

"Can I play something else?"

"Of course."

Belka led Sam through many different combinations of keys

and taught him many new tunes. It really was the most amazing folded-up piece of paper that Sam had ever seen. None of the other kids in class, with their pathetic giraffes or sailboats, were going to come within a mile of this.

"So now that you know that we're only here to help, perhaps we could discuss our departure?" Belka suggested.

"If by that you mean will I let you go, you know I can't," Sam said, still fiddling with the paper horn. "What other things can we make?"

"You're pushing the friendship a bit, but if you can get a really big square of paper . . ."

"What? What can we make?" Sam said urgently.

"Well, if you think that horn is good . . . ," Belka teased.

Sam dashed from his room and left the door ajar. Belka didn't hesitate. He ran the ATV through the gap and, while their jailer was scrabbling through the hallway cupboard for king-sized pieces of stationery, made a break for freedom.

Amy opened her eyes. *That's a nice color,* she thought, looking up at the ceiling. She rolled onto her side, keeping the duvet tucked right under her chin. *They're nice cardboard boxes too,* she thought. In fact, as her eyelids started to close again, everything seemed pretty nice in her world. Suddenly Amy's eyes snapped wide open.

Where was her world?
Where was she?
What time was it?

She sat up on a comfy couch. "Dion," she said, surprised.

"You feeling better now?" Dion asked as he turned from his computer.

The bike, the sprint across the oval, the mob of students, the mooing noises . . . the images came rushing back to her. She leapt to her feet in a fluster and grabbed her schoolbag, causing a tower of cardboard boxes to teeter forward. Dion sprang forward and shoved them back.

"Sorry!" Amy yelped.

Dion reached for the phone on his desk and pushed the intercom button. "Mrs. Van Steenwyk, could you come in here for a moment?" he said before turning to Amy. "You should sit down. You were out nearly all day."

"Sorry. I haven't been sleeping lately," Amy replied as she sat back down. She looked around the room. Everywhere there were boxes and T-shirts in various stages of packaging. Dion sat bathed in the light of two large computer monitors. At his feet a couple of computers whirred.

"Is this your business office?" Amy asked.

"Yes. Office. Bedroom. This is the hub."

Amy's eyes darted about. In the corner, behind a wall of boxes, was what looked like a bed piled with clothes and other bits and pieces of teenage boyhood. The door opened, and a woman stepped in holding a clipboard.

"Mrs. Van Steenwyk," Dion said, looking up. "This is my friend, Amy Buckley."

"Good afternoon," Mrs. Van Steenwyk said in a rather subdued manner.

"Hi," Amy replied.

"Could you bring some tea, please?" Dion instructed politely, then turned to Amy. "Tea all right?"

"Yes. Fine," Amy said, then added hastily, "but not peppermint!"

"Right away," Mrs. Van Steenwyk replied.

When Mrs. Van Steenwyk left, Amy leaned toward Dion and whispered incredulously, "Is Mrs. Van Steenwyk your mum?"

"Yes. Except between the hours of 3:30 and 7:30 P.M. Then she's Mrs. Van Steenwyk."

"She does whatever you tell her to?"

"At an hourly rate. Casual. No holiday pay, retirement benefits, or dental."

"That's so cool . . ." Amy smiled as she leaned back, taking in the air of corporate power that teetered all about her. "I should try the same thing with my folks."

"I could show you how."

"Really?" Amy said, and then was overcome with her usual self-doubt. "Oh no. I couldn't do it. I'm not good enough."

"Yes you are," Dion said warmly. "You're smart, interesting, good-looking."

"Do you think I'm good-looking?"

"Sure. And presentation is crucial in business."

"Right . . . ," she replied uncertainly.

"So if you wanted to do a bit of work for me . . . hands-on experience is the best teacher."

"Yeah!" Amy enthused.

"I can't pay you anything, of course . . ."

"That's okay! You're doing me the favor. I should be paying you!"

Dion didn't reply. He was considering something. Amy took the break to chance a question.

"Hey . . . ," she asked coyly. "Why did you do what you did today?"

"There was a damsel in distress. What else is a knight in

faded denim armor supposed to do?" He put his hands behind his head and stretched his long legs out in front of him. "Besides which I think you're—" he added tantalizingly before the intercom buzzed.

I'm what? I'm what?! Amy silently screamed as Dion answered it.

"Excuse me, Mr. Van Steenwyk. There's a call on line one. A Miss Hunter."

An angry chill ran up Amy's spine.

"Put her on," Dion said.

"Hey! Dion!" The unmistakable voice of Miranda burst from the phone.

"Hello, troublemaker," Dion said good-naturedly.

"Oh well, you know me. I'm no good," Miranda laughed.

"You certainly upset a certain Ms. Buckley."

"The girl got dumped for cattle. What can I do?" Miranda said. "Hey! You busy? Maybe I should come over?"

"I think you should. You can sort things out with Amy."

"What?!" Miranda yelped. "Is she there?!"

"Yep."

A strange gasping sound came from the phone's speaker. Amy, and even Dion, were surprised to look up and see the figure of Miranda Hunter—her cell phone still held to her head—appear at the window and then drop out of view. A second later she bounced back up into view and dropped out again. She did this a few more times in rapid succession, each time desperately trying to crane a look inside.

"Miranda," Dion called into the phone. "Are you outside?"

"I was just passing," Miranda said in a fluster.

"Maybe you should come inside."

Amy just had time to fold her arms and adjust her frown when Miranda burst through the door. The heat of a fuming Amy seared her immediately.

"I didn't tell anyone," Miranda snapped.

"Yes you did! You *must* have!" Amy snapped right back.

"I told *one* person. Big deal! I didn't tell her to tell everyone else. It's not my fault your stupid boyfriend ran off with *Winona,*" Miranda taunted, putting a particularly goofy emphasis on the name of *that* cow.

Amy clenched her fists. If this was the country, Miranda would be flat on her back nursing a bloody nose, but this was the city, and Amy knew she couldn't do that sort of thing here.

"What are you doing here, anyway?" Miranda demanded.

"Dion's going to teach me about business."

"I thought you were going to teach *me* about business," Miranda said to Dion, but in the respectful tone due the most gorgeous boy in this part of the world.

"I am," he declared. "I'll teach you both."

Amy and Miranda eyed each other. "Okay," the two girls said sullenly.

"All right! Let's get started," Dion said, tossing boxes in their direction. "Rule one. You always have to start on the ground floor."

The girls held the boxes of T-shirts gingerly, trying to cover their lack of understanding.

"I need those packaged and addressed," he prompted.

Amy flew into the task. This was perfect. She'd been doing this for the last six months, only this time it was with T-shirts instead of peppermint balls. Miranda wasn't used to such manual labor, but she had a determination that drove her on. After an hour of fervent folding, cutting, and sticking, the two apprentice tycoons had finished every order. Amy's hands were sore and covered in glue, but it was worth it. She had beaten Miranda by at least a box-and-a-quarter. She was definitely Dion's star pupil.

"You guys are great!" Dion announced.

"It was fun. I learned heaps," Amy said, rubbing her neck.

Dion reached out and grasped Amy's arm. He spun her around and began to gently massage her shoulders. A blissful tingle surged through her entire body.

"You're a great teacher!" Miranda said, trying to distract Dion with a beaming smile.

The door suddenly flung open and Mrs. Van Steenwyk marched in. This time her voice was severe and full of authority. "Come on. Your dinner's ready."

Dion sat up in his chair quite flustered. "What time is it?" he asked sheepishly.

"It's 7:35. Have you done your homework?"

"Um . . . I . . . ," Dion muttered.

"I got another call about you leaving school early. What's that all about?"

"We'd better go," Amy said, grabbing her bag.

"Yes, bye, girls," Mrs. Van Steenwyk dismissed them. "And after you've done the dishes, Dion, I want you to clear out my linen closet. It's full of your T-shirts."

fourteen

"Yer mother."

The hair on the back of Strelka's neck bristled.

"Yer mother," the creature said again.

"Just ignore it," Belka advised.

The Galactanauts looked at the animal blocking the front gate of Sam Chan's house. They'd encountered one of these beasts before. This one was predominantly ginger in color and had a shorter coat of fur, but it was every bit as rude.

"Stand aside, please," Belka said, which shot out of the ATV's mouth as three short barks and a snarl.

"Yer mother," the animal replied, stubbornly maintaining its position.

"Just give me two minutes alone with it," Strelka seethed.

"Attention, whiskered creature, we are on a very important mission," Belka said in his most official-sounding voice. This was translated as a long growl and a short whimper. "I am giving you one warning. If you do not vacate your current situation immediately, we will have no alternative other than to bite you. I repeat, leave now or you will be bitten."

"Yer mother," the feline replied with a flick of its tail.

"Let's go!" Strelka yelled. He opened the throttle and started the jaws gnashing furiously. He soon became aware, however, that the ill-mannered, whiskered animal wasn't getting any nearer—despite the fact that it appeared to be sitting in the exact same spot. It took him only a moment to work out why—a pair of eleven-year-old Earthling hands belonging to their friend Sam Chan was holding them aloft.

"I'm very disappointed." Sam tucked them under his arm and walked back into the house. "I thought we had established a level of trust."

"What can we do to convince you that we are on a very important mission to save our home planet from total destruction?" Belka said with an edge of desperation.

"Well, you could start by not hassling my cat the first chance you get," Sam said as he locked his bedroom door behind them.

"That little piece of sewer refuse had it coming!" Strelka blurted out. "Those things are bad! They should be totaled! The lot of them!"

"It was all a misunderstanding," Belka said, trying to cover for Strelka's outburst. "We had no idea that the animal was an associate of yours. In fact, we mistakenly thought that it posed *a threat* to you and your premises. That's right, isn't it, Commander Strelka?"

"Well, yes, I suppose. Our error," Strelka replied half-heartedly. "It's an easy mistake to make. It does look like a nasty, low-life thug that would happily slit your throat for—"

"Your well-being was our major concern," Belka said, cutting Strelka off. "We fully understand that we have to negotiate our departure through the appropriate diplomatic channels."

Sam sat and looked at the little dog, not knowing quite what to do. He'd been told nothing about this sort of thing at school. He knew not to talk to strangers and to look both ways when crossing the road but nothing about aliens inside small terrier dogs. School never teaches you anything you really need to know.

"Look, it's not like I don't believe you," Sam explained. "It's just that I promised Lucy that I wouldn't let you go."

"We understand your obligations. You're obviously a man of honor just like ourselves."

"Listen, it's too late now, but first thing in the morning I'll find Lucy and see what I can do," Sam said.

"That's very kind of you," Belka said. "We'll all rest now and sort it out in the morning. Good night."

"Good night," Sam said, climbing into bed.

Sam fell asleep straightaway but was woken by a noise half an hour later. He switched on his bed lamp and saw a familiar fake terrier standing by the bedroom door, holding Sam's door key in its mouth.

"Bring that to me," Sam demanded.

Flumpy trotted over and grudgingly dropped the key in his hand. Sam got out of bed irritably and scooped them up. "It's the attic for you, I'm afraid."

"It's definitely the mother lode," Bars said, checking the location monitor. He itched to escape the humans' clutches and check out the new, bigger source of D.O.G. that blinked tantalizingly on the screen. "Just look at it!"

Flanger didn't react. She had become distracted by a teenage Earthling's telephone conversation.

Amy was still on the phone after a solid hour and a half. Her folks were going to hit the roof when they saw the bill. Calling the country cost a fortune, even at this late hour, but this was an emergency. It was about Dion. She didn't have any friends in the city, so she just *had* to speak to Fiona—despite the fact Fiona was a country hick who wasted the first twenty minutes going on about the drought and her new horse.

"And he's so cool," Amy enthused.

"Wow!" came the voice from the phone.

"And he's so smart."

"Wow!"

"And he's really tall."

"Wow!"

"And he's just so completely gorgeous!"

"WOW!"

The word "wow" created problems for the dachshund's translator, so it spat out a Gersbacian word that means "the gritty dust that gathers down the side of lounge chairs." Flanger, however, didn't have any trouble following the conversation. She knew exactly what it was about because it was the same all over the galaxy. It was about a girl in love for the first time. And this was something that Flanger knew all about. Although she hadn't actually experienced it herself, she was a renowned expert on all matters youthful and female. She doled out advice on the topic every month in her column "Everybody Just Listen to Me."

"The new source of D.O.G.! I said it's the mother lode!" Bars repeated.

"Yes," Flanger said, nodding.

"You are interested in this, aren't you? You are vaguely interested in having the power to completely rule all of Gersbach?"

"Mmmm . . . ," Flanger replied. Of course she wanted to rule all of everything of whatever, sure, but she also wanted to hear more about this guy, this Dion.

"Of course, we have to get out of this room first," Bars said, clearly frustrated. "I'll try the door thing again."

He pulled back on the guidance column and Nicky stood up, then jumped off the end of Amy's bed. Bars trotted them over to her closed bedroom door and maneuvered one of the forward paws up and down in a scratching motion against it. He pulled up a whimper from the Sound FX plug-in—"pathetic: level 10."

"I can't let you out," Amy said, interrupting her rapturous diatribe about Dion. "Dad'll spew. I told you."

"I'm not supposed to be able to understand you," Bars said grumpily. "Why do they talk to their pets like they can understand? I never had conversations with any animals on Gersbach. I just ate them without any idle small talk." Nicky leapt back onto the bed and lay at Amy's feet.

"But the real problem is that so-into-herself Miranda," Amy continued on the phone, getting worked up as she explained her nemesis. "He doesn't even like her, but she won't leave him alone. She's just throwing herself at him like a real tart, and now of course she wants him to teach *her* about business too. So he's going to, because he's just too nice to say no, and now she's going to be hanging around all the time like such a blatant loser."

"There's competition," Flanger announced. "There always is for the good ones."

"Could you forget about the stupid Earthling's love life and try and think of a way we can get out of here?" Colonel Bars demanded.

"Sure!" Flanger jumped up and, in two mighty bounds, grabbed the translator unit out of the equipment rack and leapt into the exit hatch. She was gone before Bars could say a thing.

"Oh God! Have we been talking for that long?" Amy said as she glanced at her clock radio. "They're going to kill me! I'm gonna have to go. Bye."

Amy hung up the phone and lay back on her bed. It was quite a cold night, but all she could feel was warmth cascading over her. She could still feel Dion's hands on her shoulders. She could see his face rising into the sky over her and his mouth with those little creases in the corners. She could smell him—that giddy combination of sweat, *Sport* spray-on deodorant, and lawn-mower fuel. She felt like an explorer who'd been wandering in the jungle and had just stumbled across a fabulous long-lost city. All the crappy things in her life began to make sense. It was like everything was for a reason, and everything suddenly fit together.

Being in love for the first time is like that. It's a magical experience. You feel things you haven't felt before. You do things you thought you couldn't ever do, and you believe in things that you didn't think were possible. Which was very handy for the renegade crew of a stolen, dog-shaped, prototype spacecraft.

Amy idly rolled onto her side. Her eyes followed the moonlight filtering through her window onto the bedside table and the little person standing on it.

Amy looked at the figure curiously. She stared straight into its eyes, and it appeared to stare right back. *That's strange,* she thought, but the way she was feeling today, it was just another strange thing, so she wasn't alarmed. She actually felt quite detached from the whole situation. She watched her own hand slowly move toward the small young woman. When it was just an inch away, a little voice sprung out.

"Hello!" Flanger said cheerily.

All of Amy's senses kicked back in at once. It was like she'd been zapped by an electric fence. She snapped her hand away and threw herself against the wall.

"You're Amy, right?" Flanger asked with a smile.

Amy nodded. Her mouth wasn't quite working properly.

"I'm Flanger. Flanger Damka."

Amy huddled in the corner of her bed, still unable to speak.

"Just calm down. I'm not going to hurt you. I'm your friend. I'm on your side."

Amy's brain went into overdrive, seeking a logical explanation for this little person but not finding one in the immediate vicinity. Amy plunged deeper into her library of memories and experiences, sifting fruitlessly, until she was right back in early childhood with all its fairies and goblins and witches.

"Are you a fairy?" she asked tentatively.

"Yes," Flanger answered. "But a good fairy. In fact, a fantastic fairy."

This really can't be true, Amy thought, but there it was right in front of her. It's difficult *not* to believe something when it's *right there*. Then a realization struck her.

"I've gone mad," she said, almost with relief.

"What?" asked Flanger.

"Well, it's obvious, isn't it? If I've started to see fairies, then I must be crazy. I guess it's not so surprising when you think about it. I have been under enormous strain."

"Oh, you're not mad," Flanger reassured her.

"Well, you're bound to say that, aren't you? If I wasn't mad, you wouldn't exist."

"Um . . ." Flanger tried to come up with an argument.

"No. I'm crazy all right. I thought I was in love but I'm not. I'm just plain mad. It's moving to the city that's done it. And Miranda, and all those stupid peppermint balls. I clearly haven't coped. I've snapped." Amy flopped on her bed. "It's not so bad, actually, insanity. It doesn't hurt or anything. It's kind of relaxing. I'll probably wake up in a moment and I'll be wearing a straitjacket and have my parents and all sorts of doctors leaning over me, but until then I may as well try and enjoy it."

Flanger started to feel a bit uncomfortable. Sure, she wanted to rule all of Gersbach, but she didn't want to ruin a girl's first experience of true love in the process. "Look, you're really not crazy, but you *are* in love."

"Nice try," Amy said with resignation. "No, I'm sure Dion doesn't even exist. I've probably just made him up. So, do you do anything else?"

"What do you mean?"

"Well, apart from letting me know how completely out of my mind I am, do you do anything else? Do I, like, get three wishes or anything?"

"No," Flanger said, embarrassed.

"Not much of a fairy, then."

"I can help you win Dion away from this Miranda person."

"Even though he doesn't exist?"

"He does exist!"

"Do you know him? Have you met him?"

"Well, no, but he does. You know he does. You saw him today."

"Yes, but I'm crazy."

Flanger was getting exasperated—and also beginning to feel Earth's gravity. Her flea-like qualities made her able to withstand its force longer than her fellow aliens, but she would succumb soon. She made a hasty promise. "Look, tomorrow we'll go over to Dion's house, and I'll make sure you win his heart."

"Sure. Why not? What have I got to lose? What time will I meet you there? When the Sun is in the seventh moon of Jupiter?" Amy asked.

"You'll have to take me."

"How? Sitting on my shoulder?"

"Bring the dog with you. That's where I live. Inside the one you call Nicky."

"That makes sense. I mean, it doesn't make sense but it does, me being crazy and everything." Amy started to slide down under the covers. She was beginning to feel tired. "Well, all right. You can come with me, but I'm not letting you off the leash."

"Can't we forgo the whole leash thing?" Flanger pleaded.

"Dad'd kill me. When it comes to you dogs, he's as crazy as I am . . . nearly."

"Please," Flanger gasped, remembering she had to go back and face Bars. Earth's gravity was making it really hard to breathe now.

"No!" Amy insisted. "You're a figment of *my* imagination, and we'll do things *my way*."

"Okay. Okay," Flanger muttered as she bounced back toward Nicky with relief.

"Now, I just want to sleep," Amy said as she closed her eyes and settled under her duvet. "And hopefully, I'll still be as mad as a cut snake in the morning."

Fifteen

Gav Buckley wore an extremely tight T-shirt featuring a crude line drawing of a bone with the words GAV'S BIG BONE (AND GOURMET SAUSAGES) printed underneath. The actual Big Bone—being steadily unearthed from his top paddock—was much more impressive, and the scene around it was like a circus, but without any elephants.

There were tourists everywhere: some digging, some posing for photos, and yet more pouring tomato sauce over their complimentary gourmet sausages. Gav's wife, Judy, held a pile of shovels almost as tall as she was. Mounds of fresh earth grew alongside the bone as its stark whiteness blazed in the morning sunshine.

"Look, Mr. Buckley!" an excited voice called out from a group of school children. They were all holding shovels and wearing T-shirts bearing the logo: I DIG GAV'S BIG BONE. "We've dug up lots of dirt!"

"You've done a mighty job, champ. All of you," Gav said cheerily.

"Can we dig some more?" the boy asked.

"Sure you can. Just get your teacher to bring over her little plastic card again and you can go for another hour," Gav told them with a wide smile.

The buildings of Gersbach Space Command rattled under a fresh onslaught of tremors. As the Chief Controller stepped into his office, the corridor behind him collapsed, and he narrowly avoided being crushed by debris.

"That was definitely bigger than the last one," he muttered as he consulted the Seismology Center report on his computer. His brow furrowed as he realized a yet greater source of D.O.G. was assaulting them from the world beyond the wormhole.

* * *

Amy wandered into the kitchen and sat at the breakfast table. Tom was there, as was Lucy, and everyone looked tired.

"You're going to be late," Tom warned.

"I may not go to school today," Amy said in an offhand manner.

"What's the matter? You sick?"

"Yes."

"Your school rang up. They said you've been skipping classes. Is that something to do with it?"

"Yes. But it's not physical. It's up here," Amy said, pointing to her head.

"Right . . . ," Tom said.

"I've gone mad," Amy informed them.

"And when did this suddenly happen?"

"I crossed over into complete insanity last night, but it's been coming on for a while."

"You seem okay to me."

"Well, I spent the night talking to a fairy, so yes, I'm pretty certain," Amy said.

"A fairy?" Tom asked.

"Yes. A little fairy about this tall." She measured an inch with her fingers.

Tom thought this was more a matter for Beth, but she'd already left on her peppermint run. It also struck a nerve with Lucy. She stood abruptly and headed for the door.

"I'm late. I'd better go," Lucy said, and raced out.

"So . . . um . . . can this fairy fly?" Tom asked.

"Her name's Flanger, and no, she doesn't fly," Amy said, getting quite grumpy. "She sort of bounces about. She lives in Nicky."

Tom instantly recalled the other night's flying dachshund, but he didn't want to go there. There wasn't any point in both of them being crazy.

"Do you want to see a doctor?"

"No. I like being mad. It's nice," Amy replied. "But I can't go back to that school. I'll have to go to a special school where we just play games and make things out of toilet-paper rolls."

Tom smelled a rat. "Yeah, well, I didn't like school much either, but I still went," he said, reverting to his usual straightforward self. "If you're still crazy when you get home, we'll have you locked up then. Go!"

Amy jumped up and stormed into her room. She put on her school uniform, grabbed her bag, and clipped the leash to

Nicky's neck. She then stomped out the front door without another word, dragging Nicky behind her.

But she didn't go to school.

Colonel Bars kept his craft at a steady pace alongside the relentless Amy. They walked for several miles at the same quick speed until they arrived outside a human dwelling that looked very much like every other human dwelling they had seen. To Amy, however, it was the most splendid house on the whole planet. It was the home of Dion Van Steenwyk.

She sat on the front fence of the house opposite and just stared. Bars immediately began to look for an opportunity to slip out of the leash and pursue the D.O.G. that continued its tantalizing blink on the location monitor.

"Well, that's his house," Amy spoke up.

Bars was caught off guard. Flanger was still flaked out on her bunk. He put a call through, summoning her to the flight deck.

"Are you there? Or aren't I crazy anymore?" Amy asked.

Bars hit the call button again but knew he couldn't wait. He switched on the translator and spoke. "I'm still here," he said in the most feminine and friendly voice a murderous villain could muster.

"You sound really different when you're in Nicky."

"I suppose I do."

"So what's your big plan to make Dion want to go out with me instead of Miranda?"

"Okay, step one is to take the leash off me," Bars instructed.

"Well then, we'll have to go straight to step two, won't we?" Amy said. "What am I going to do about Miranda?"

Bars was annoyed but realized he had to keep playing along. He tried to put himself in the mind of a fourteen-year-old. What would he have done at that age?

"You need to sneak up behind her as quietly as you can," he explained. "Then you put one hand over her mouth, and at the same time you push your knife into the spot just under her rib cage, then draw it up through—"

"Do what?" Amy said, taken aback.

"Or a pair of scissors or any sharp object will do."

"I'm not doing that. What kind of a weirdo fairy are you?"

Flanger grabbed the translator microphone away from Bars. "Of course we won't do that. I was joking," she said hurriedly.

"Well, it'd work," Bars remarked, but too quietly for Amy to hear.

"Just give me a moment to think about it, Amy," Flanger said.

"You sound different now," Amy observed.

"I'm still half-asleep. How long have we got?"

"Hours. He won't be here until after school."

"Get her to take off the leash!" Bars urged. Flanger waved him down.

"Okay, Amy, good. That gives me plenty of time to come up with a magic spell."

"It'd better be a pretty strong spell," Amy said despondently, and settled down for the long wait.

sixteen

Lucy Buckley found it intriguing, but a little frightening. Sam Chan thought it was the best thing he'd ever seen, and hoped Dr. Macheski would show him how to build one. Ms. Felton was unsure about it—particularly as a large number of eleven-year-old children were standing just a few feet away.

"This is a *rocket,* Dr. Macheski," she said with a frown.

"Of course it's a rocket," the eccentric old Russian replied. "As promised, today we're having a launch demonstration."

"But I thought it'd be some kind of *toy* rocket made of cardboard, like a firecracker or something."

"A firecracker!" Dr. Macheski snorted. "In my day we used to launch rockets *eight stories tall!*"

"Oh, please let him launch it!" Sam shouted.

"Yes, please, miss!" Bradley Ditchfield added.

"It's just that this is a six-foot-tall, metal, lethal-looking, well, missile!" Ms. Felton said, tapping the base of it with her foot.

"Ah, don't do that," said Dr. Macheski. "That's a tank of liquid oxygen."

"Please, miss!" Lucy's class choroused.

"Trust me, Ms. Felton," said Dr. Macheski, guiding her to a safe distance from the launch site. "I am a professional! Now stand well back, children, it's time for the countdown!" He picked up a remote control. "Ten, nine, eight, seven . . ."

"Six, five, four . . . ," the class joined in.

"Three, two . . . one!"

Dr. Macheski flipped a large red switch and Macheski One shot into the sky atop a ball of fire. It sliced angrily through the air, leaving a trail of flame and thick black smoke.

"Oh my God! FIRE!" Ms. Felton yelled. Sparks from the launch had set a large pile of leaves ablaze, and flaming cinders were drifting on a breeze toward the school. "BRING THAT THING DOWN NOW!"

"But this is the automatic part of the flight . . . ," Dr. Macheski began.

"You mean you don't have control of it?"

"I should, soon."

"You mean *you're not sure*?"

Dr. Macheski looked awkward for a moment. "They never let me test it at the Rocketry Club. They kept arguing that liquid hydrogen oxidized with liquid oxygen contravenes all safety regulations."

"Does it?"

"Well, it's incredibly explosive, and somewhat unstable, but how else can you get sufficient thrust?"

The rocket hurtled ever higher before there was a series of loud, metallic scraping sounds. Guidance fins broke from its body, spinning like flung daggers through the air before demolishing the greenhouse where Year 5 had been growing their hydroponic tomatoes.

Ms. Felton shrieked as she saw the building shatter and shards of glass shower the grounds. "Control that thing RIGHT NOW, Macheski!"

Dr. Macheski seized the remote control. He pulled a small lever downward. The rocket performed a wobbly turn and roared back toward the class.

"Do not be frightened, children," Dr. Macheski said.

Lucy's class began to run in every direction.

"Do not be scared!" he ordered. "It will run out of fuel and land safely, just watch!"

The rocket powered onward, picking up speed, the trail of fire growing longer behind it.

"Any minute now," said Dr. Macheski. "Any moment now it'll run out of fuel."

The rocket accelerated further.

"What happens if it doesn't run out of fuel?" Sam asked.

"Oh, well, the fuel will explode on impact. We had a lot of that in the old days. They were always blowing up."

Ms. Felton let out a little yelp before scooping Sam and Lucy under each arm and bundling them toward the school. Macheski One streaked earthward.

A retro-rocket fired from the missile's far side and swung it clear of the library by the barest margin. Another burst of flame shot from its belly, and the rocket leveled, just four feet above the ground. It was directly behind Ms. Felton, Sam, and Lucy— accelerating swiftly as it hungrily consumed its remaining fuel.

A growling rumble made Ms. Felton look back. Her face

drained of color as she saw the black, flaming cylinder thundering behind her, *following them into the school corridor*!

The rocket shot past classroom doors, bright red cinders dropping from its tail. Year 1's art display was set alight as dense smoke billowed through the school.

"LET US DOWN, MS. FELTON!" Lucy yelled, but her teacher was in a blind panic. Lucy wrenched herself free and tumbled to the floor. Unbalanced, Ms. Felton and Sam came crashing down with her. Lucy sprang to her feet and turned to face the howling roar coming up behind her. She could clearly make out the rivets on the rocket's nose.

She had to act.

But couldn't.

"Jump, Lucy!" she heard Sam call distantly. "Jump out of the way! Lucy! JUMP OUT OF THE WAY!"

The next thing she knew, Sam had dragged her and Ms. Felton into the girls' bathroom. He slammed the heavy door and sprang back. The rocket's shadow raced past the frosted glass, and an intense flash of blue flame scorched the door.

Sam took a mop from Mr. Jenkins, the janitor, who was cowering in the last cubicle, and used it to lever open the hot and blistered door. Lucy stepped into the corridor and saw the rocket set fire to the school's trophy cabinet before making a loud sort of farting sound. In a final burst of energy it smashed through the front doors and dropped into the pond. In a sea of bubbles and steam it settled on the bottom, finally spent and silent.

The last thing Lucy saw at school that day was Ms. Felton giving Dr. Macheski the most severe talking to. The Russian nodded and fumbled as he scooped his rocket from the water. He put it in the back of his car, a battered Datsun 180B.

"Maybe next time I'll use my smaller rocket?" Lucy heard Dr. Macheski ask.

* * *

The citizens of the planet Gersbach regarded the wormhole with dread. Usually its appearance in the sky signaled festivals and wild marriage proposals, but now it was a passageway for some deadly, escalating force that was literally rocking the planet's foundations. As Gersbacians went to work and caught the hoverbus to school, the ground split and twisted beneath them. Frequently when they arrived, there was no work or school to go to. Everyone had horror stories of tremors, quakes, missing garages, and cliff faces crashing into the sea. It was hard to ignore the constant rumbling deep below Gersbach's surface, as though the Gersbacians were walking on a sleeping giant suffering massive digestive troubles.

The government told the citizens to just sit it out. The wormhole was due to close in a few days, and the trouble would surely go with it. A little pamphlet and fridge magnet sent to every Gersbacian home said there was nothing to be alarmed about. But even a child could tell an event of catastrophic proportions was bearing down upon them.

seventeen

It's said that soldiers in the field spend only one percent of the time actually fighting the enemy. The other ninety-nine percent of the time is spent fighting the boredom, and inside the ATV Strelka was right in the thick of it. He emerged slowly from Flumpy's bathroom facility after his fourth shower for the day, dripping on the cabin floor.

"Impressive design in there," he said, drumming up conversation. "Compact and efficient."

"Yes, we're lucky to have one," Belka noted. "The prototype craft only features a basic latrine."

"How can Flanger stand *that*?" Strelka asked with genuine concern.

"When you meet Ms. Damka, you could win her over to our way of thinking with the lure of a hot shower."

"Yeah, you think?" Strelka asked earnestly.

"I'm kidding, Strelka."

"Oh."

Belka consulted the location monitor and noticed Bars' ship was now stationary, parked some distance from the Buckley residence. He presumed one of the Buckley girls was responsible.

Strelka flopped into his seat with a sigh and swung his feet up on the console. Belka knew that this was his thinking position. Belka had no new ideas for escape either, so he looked up wistfully one more time at the small window that cast a pale light into their attic prison.

"That's the way out. That window," Belka sighed.

"I *know*. You keep saying that."

"But how do we get up there?"

Lucy didn't know much about King Tutankhamen, but they actually had quite a lot in common. By the time he was Lucy's age, Tutankhamen was king of Egypt, and three thousand years ago Egypt was the most powerful country in the world. By age eleven he had to make important decisions all the time, affecting the lives of thousands and thousands of people. Lucy Buckley only had to make *one* decision, but it could affect everybody on the planet—maybe even two planets.

She had to decide which alien was telling her the truth. Colonel Bars claimed Belka and Strelka were criminals. Belka and Strelka said Colonel Bars was a criminal who wanted to take over their home planet.

Lucy just didn't know who to believe.

There was no way she could make such an important decision without speaking to Colonel Bars again—but that would prove difficult. Nicky the sausage dog was usually holed up with her sister, and Amy was loath to let anyone near him.

Lucy flopped onto the couch. She resented the fact that a girl her age had to decide the fate of the universe anyway. King Tut had all sorts of adults advising him—not to mention Ra, the sun god. All Lucy had were a couple of dogs that weren't even real dogs. But she did have one loyal friend to advise her. He wasn't quite as spectacular as Ra, but he lived around the corner. As she dialed Sam's number, she thought if she ever did meet King Tut, she would hold his head under a faucet and tell him how easy he had it.

"I just don't know who to believe," Lucy whispered into the phone.

"I reckon Belka and Strelka are okay. I think they're telling the truth," Sam Chan's voice said at the other end.

"You've still got them locked up, haven't you?" Lucy asked urgently.

"Yeah, they're locked in the attic. What about Colonel Bars?"

"Nicky's always with Amy. She doesn't let him out of her sight."

"Does she know who's *inside* Nicky?"

"I don't think so," Lucy said. "Although she *has* been acting weird."

"Belka and Strelka say Bars is a criminal," Sam warned. "If Bars is really dangerous, you should tell your dad."

Lucy was considering this when she heard a thumping sound coming down the hallway. "Gotta go!" she cried out and hung up, just as an alien being lurched into the room. This alien wasn't an inch tall and driving a dog, however. This one was the size of a fully grown human.

Lucy gasped as she looked at the intruder towering above

her. She saw it was wearing a tall helmet made of a transparent plastic material. A thick, flexible tube ran from the helmet to a large metal cylinder strapped to the alien's back.

Lucy switched her gaze to the big hand stretching out to her. She cowered from the white padded gauntlet that resembled a cricketer's batting glove. She studied it closer. It *was* a cricketer's batting glove. Lucy looked up at the alien's face. It was her father.

"Come on, Commander!" Tom ordered, grabbing her hand.

He hurried her out to the backyard and sprang onto the tattered old hammock. Clutching Lucy to his chest, Tom lay down as far as the vacuum cleaner on his back would allow.

"Prepare for liftoff, Commander!" Tom shouted. "Five, four, three, two, one—BLAST OFF!"

Lucy clung tightly to her father's arms folded firmly across her. He rocked her from side to side, making loud rocket-engine noises. When she started to relax from the initial shock, Lucy realized that her father was just playing one of his games. They weren't actually going to take off (although with the week she'd been having, she couldn't be completely sure).

"Go with throttle up!" Tom commanded.

"Roger!" Lucy replied. She nestled into her father's chest and looked up at the blue sky. Her father hadn't been in this sort of mood for ages. She was beginning to feel safe. Safe from the kids at school. Safe from the dogs and the confusing aliens inside them. She was wondering if she could tell her father about them when a mysterious astral body darkened the sky. It was her mother.

Beth didn't say anything. She just removed the blender jug from Tom's head and took it back to the kitchen. A short while later, when the Buckley astronauts were rapidly approaching the Andromeda galaxy, Beth reappeared. She removed Tom's Chest Respiration Unit and put it back with the other frying pans.

"Equipment failure!" Tom cried out. "Prepare for emergency landing!"

Lucy clutched her father's forearm even tighter as the hammock plunged through the stormy atmosphere of an uncharted planet. It shook from side to side until Tom hurled them onto the ground, which, of course, meant that they had landed. The two astronauts climbed quickly to their feet and surveyed their surroundings.

"What a strange, cold, hostile place!" Tom observed.

"It sure is," Lucy agreed as she looked across their backyard. It looked more alien and hostile than ever.

"What do you think that is, Commander?" Tom asked.

"The back door?"

"Yes—that portal to an alien dwelling. We have to approach it with extreme caution."

Lucy slipped her hand into her father's big, chunky glove as they stepped toward it. A Strange Being suddenly appeared, framed dramatically by the doorway.

"Alien life-form!" Tom declared.

Beth stared at him.

"It's an interesting-looking creature," Tom said as he studied her face. "Weird but strangely attractive."

"You know we have a mountain of peppermints that need packaging," Beth said without humor.

"It speaks!" Tom said. "Can you understand its language, Commander Lucy?"

"The sooner you two start packaging, the sooner you can go back to your games," Beth said.

"No, I can't understand it," Lucy grinned.

"We come in peace," Tom said slowly and clearly to Beth.

"Just get in there. Both of you!"

"We mean you no harm," Tom continued.

"I'LL DO IT ALL BY MYSELF THEN!" Beth screamed. "Like everything else around here!"

"Jeez, love," Tom said, dropping his spaceman persona. "We're just having some fun."

"I'd like to have fun too, but I don't have *time*! I have to keep things going. I have to keep the money coming in!" Beth raged.

"Oh, fair go!" Tom retorted. "I'm trying to get work. It's not easy with a bad back."

Lucy shrank back as the two creatures clashed.

"Well, can't you do *anything*? You can't even put a gnome in the right place." She marched over to the small, scorched pit where the gnome once stood. "I mean, what have you done with it now? It's gone! It's completely gone!"

Tom looked at his feet. Lucy nearly said something but decided to keep quiet.

"Is it going to suddenly pop out of the next box I deliver?" Beth continued.

"Give me a break, Beth," Tom said.

"I'm just so sick of being the one who has to keep this family together." Beth's eyes filled with tears. "It's so easy for you because you don't care!"

"I care!" Tom shouted.

"No you don't. You don't know anything about your children. Lucy's very unhappy."

"I'm not! I'm *really* happy!" Lucy lied, producing the biggest forced smile she could.

"No you're not. You're miserable," Beth snapped.

"Okay." Lucy's face dropped.

"And where's Amy?" Beth continued.

"She's . . . um . . ."

"She wasn't at school again today. I got a call. You don't even know where your daughter is. Is she with this Dion boy? We don't know anything about him. Who knows what they're up to?"

"Oh, she's a sensible girl," Tom assured her.

"She's been acting like a fruitcake lately," Beth insisted.

"Well, she's at the fruitcake age."

"I want changes, Tom," Beth said. "I know we've got our share of problems, but I can't cope by myself. I want big changes!"

Beth turned and stomped into the house, leaving the two astronauts stranded on the planet's surface.

"Abort mission, Commander," Tom said to Lucy. "Return to base."

eighteen

As Amy sat waiting during the long afternoon, she felt her madness steadily taking a tighter grip. Everything around her became slightly hazy. She became light-headed and her mouth was parched.

Sure signs of craziness.

Of course, the fact that she hadn't drunk or eaten anything all day could have had something to do with it too, but she was also talking with a dog, and *that* could have no other explanation. They had spoken about many things. There was a lot of chat about leashes and why they were very bad for dogs, but eventually the conversation turned more to Amy and, of course, Dion. Flanger the fairy had all sorts of advice. She told Amy all she knew about guys, and she did actually appear to know a lot. She talked about what guys look for in girls and how they like to be treated. She told her about relationships and compromise and mutual respect and partnership goal-setting and self-confidence and body image and trust and conflict resolution and quite a lot about establishing the boundaries of one's own personal space.

"Yes, but you *can* wave your magic wand and make Dion *like* me, can't you?" Amy asked impatiently.

"Yes," Flanger said, deflated.

Amy was snapped out of a doze by a motorized scooter whose two-stroke howl seemed unusually proud this afternoon, almost noble. As Dion swung into his driveway, Amy's heart began to race, and that weird, giddy sensation enveloped her. She hauled Nicky over to Dion's house. Amy was there before Dion even had a chance to step off his cast-metal mount. As he took off his helmet and those sexy dreadlocks tumbled free, Amy's heart somehow tumbled with them. Momentarily transfixed by his beautiful face, she suddenly began to question her own madness.

Dion is just too fabulous.

I'm not clever enough to have made him up.

Then she remembered. Fairy, talking dog, strange euphoric feeling, prior history of abnormally high stress. No, she was crazy all right. Textbook case.

I hope Dion doesn't realize that I've gone mad, Amy thought. *He probably won't. Guys don't notice things like that. They notice if you suddenly get fat, but complete insanity they're usually a bit slow to pick up on.*

A terrible voice interrupted her pondering.

"You weren't at school today," Miranda Hunter said with a kind of dainty sneer. "We thought maybe you had left for good. We thought you might have moooooooved." Miranda sniggered at her own joke.

Amy was so besotted with Dion she hadn't even noticed Miranda had ridden in with him. Miranda stepped off the scooter, ready for battle.

Damn, Amy cursed. Miranda was bound to see that Amy was crazy and tell Dion. But then again, she had probably made up Dion anyway. He was probably only Amy's hallucination, so it didn't really matter what Dion thought, did it? But why would she have made up someone as awful as Miranda Hunter? It didn't make sense, but that's what being mad is really all about, Amy concluded, her head starting to spin a little. *Insanity is so confusing.*

"So, lesson two in being successful in business," Dion announced with a gorgeous grin as they walked into his National Head Office (or bedroom if you prefer), "is concerned with distribution of product to the marketplace."

He pointed to a pile of boxes, T-shirts, envelopes, and labels. It was even larger than the pile they'd tackled the day before.

"Um . . . didn't we learn all about this yesterday?" Amy questioned.

"What have I said about the importance of taking one step at a time? What have I said about the ladder to success and the lowest rung?" Dion said with good-natured firmness.

"Yes, but we're really, really good at that now, so perhaps today we could learn about the computer or something," Amy ventured.

"You know, things are going pretty well at the moment," Dion said, ignoring Amy's suggestion. "I think it's about time I looked at taking on a full-time staff member. A sidekick.

Someone to be my right-hand man . . . or woman." Dion cast his deep blue eyes from Amy to Miranda and back again. The two girls exchanged glances, then nearly knocked each other over as they scrambled for the pile of boxes.

Colonel Bars sat at the console, fiddling with the location monitor. He had done this many times already, but it helped distract him from the stupid spectacle that was happening behind him. Flanger and the fleas were taking part in what appeared to be a weird pagan ritual. The fleas leapt about in a manic frenzy, contorting their little black bodies into all kinds of strange positions. They jumped onto Flanger, then onto each other, then onto a large computer screen on the wall. Over and over again. The image on the screen showed the human body in close anatomical detail. The complex system of reflexes was highlighted, with particular attention to points around the elbows, hands, ankles, and knees. All this frantic dancing about was, of course, a means of communication. Flanger was issuing instructions in a way that only she and her little flea cohorts would understand.

"Are you nearly finished?" Bars asked grumpily. He knew it was a means to an end, so he put up with the whole stupid rigmarole, but it seemed so undignified for a military officer of his standing to have it taking place on his bridge. He wished he could resolve the Amy situation with one of his usual methods: a rifle, a knife, or a spear gun. *Whatever happened to spear guns?* Bars fondly reminisced.

Flanger completed one last twisting and tumbling maneuver. The fleas, full of purpose, bounced into the exit hatch and were gone. Flanger leapt to the console to watch her charges do her bidding.

"He's actually pretty cute," Flanger said, observing Dion on the screens. "For an Earthling."

"Why'd you bring your dorky dog with you?" Miranda asked as she stepped over Nicky to add some finished orders to the pile. "I didn't think you'd want the competition," she added with a smirk.

Amy didn't answer. She just kept folding and sticking because, inexplicably, Miranda was going much faster this afternoon. She was ahead by at least a dozen orders. Amy'd never win Dion's heart at this rate. *When was this stupid fairy going to help her like she promised?* Amy gave Nicky a frustrated glance.

Help, however, was on the way—in the form of a squad of tiny insects. The fleas had lined up on the curtain rail and were preparing to take action. As Miranda passed below, they stepped off, paratrooper style, and landed without any discernible impact on her shoulder. They immediately scurried off in separate directions, heading toward their predesignated targets on Miranda's body.

Miranda didn't know why her scissors suddenly cut right through a sheet of preaddressed labels. It was very strange. Her hand just didn't do what she wanted it to do. It was a momentary loss of concentration, she supposed. She was going too fast.

"It's cool. I'll just print out another set," Dion said with his usual generosity of spirit.

"I'm really sorry," Miranda said, humbly taking the new labels.

Her scissors made short work of those too.

"It's okay. I can do another set," Dion said, this time not quite as graciously. "Just be a little more careful this time. They're not cheap."

This time Miranda's hands tore them in two. They all watched aghast as she then threw the remnants wildly into the air.

"I don't know what's happening! I didn't mean to do that!" Miranda cried out. She was so red-faced she was almost sweating.

Amy looked across at Nicky. The little sausage dog's tail started to wag slowly and deliberately. A smile erupted on Amy's face that she quickly converted into a look of concern.

"Maybe you're working too hard," Amy suggested. "You've probably strained yourself. Some people just can't cope with the rigors of the business world."

Dion's astonishment turned to horror. Not only had he lost nearly five dollars' worth of stationery, but he didn't have any worker's compensation coverage. If Miranda sued him . . . well, he didn't even want to think about it.

Miranda took a few deep breaths and felt she was beginning to regain her composure. Unbeknownst to her, however, the flea infiltrators were hovering over another set of her sensitive nerve endings and were about to launch phase two. With an acupuncturist's precision, each flea plunged its proboscis—the sharp, needle-like protrusion on its face—exactly into the right place on Miranda's skin. The bites were completely painless, but their effect on Miranda's reflexes was devastating.

Miranda's first kick knocked over some boxes of T-shirts. Her second kick dented Dion's filing cabinet, and the third left a bruise on his shin. The next flurry of kicks sent packaged orders flying to every part of the room. Amy jumped up on the bed to avoid being hit and watched as Dion grabbed Miranda from behind and wrestled her into a chair. Miranda frantically grabbed her own leg and tried to hold it still. Flanger's raiding party leapt clear of her hands and headed to the next ambush position. Having seemingly calmed her wayward leg, Miranda threw herself back into the chair and clung to the sides, terrified of what her body would do next. And she wasn't the only one. Dion rose warily from behind her chair and reached for the phone, making sure he kept a safe distance.

"I think you may need some help," Dion said tentatively.

"Yeah. You're sick," Amy said. "Or maybe you're possessed by the devil. Can you spin your head all the way around?"

"Maybe I should call a doctor," Dion said.

"Call an exorcist," Amy suggested.

"I'M NOT SICK!" Miranda shouted. "I'm . . . all right . . . now," she said, trying to calm down. "I just need a glass of water."

Dion put a call through on the intercom, and a moment later Mrs. Van Steenwyk came in with a jug of water and several glasses. Instantly the entire jug was poured over Mrs. Van Steenwyk's head, and Miranda was attempting to lead her around the room in a cross between a waltz and the lambada. As Mrs. Van Steenwyk slung the profusely apologetic girl over her shoulder and carried her out of the room, a group of little black fleas jumped off and headed back to base.

"You just can't get good help nowadays," Amy said to Dion with a naughty grin.

"I'm sure she'll be all right." Dion was clearly spooked by the whole episode.

"I'll help you clean up."

Dion looked at her. He was impressed by her resilience in the face of such drama. Amy looked right back. She was impressed by *everything* about him. Then, as that familiar lovely feeling took hold of her, she remembered.

I'm insane.

I'm completely out of my mind.

This is my hallucination, so I can do whatever I want.

And she knew what she wanted to do.

The last of the fleas scrambled into the dachshund cockpit, filled with the jubilation of a successfully completed mission—not that they really understood what the mission had been all about. They might have been superintelligent as far as fleas go, but they were still pretty dumb. All they really understood was that they had to bite a certain human in a certain place at a certain time. When they leapt over to the forward screens and saw an image of two humans kissing, it didn't mean very much to them, except that Flanger seemed very pleased about it—and that made them happy. Colonel Bars, however, seemed bored; but they didn't care much about him anymore. Bars looked at the elated Flanger.

"You know, I tried to engineer this part of your personality *out* when I created you," he said.

"You didn't create me!" she snapped at him. "I made me! Not you! I'm my own person!"

Bars didn't want to argue. He had a much more important matter to consider. "So, will the Earthling girl release us *now*?" he asked with restraint.

Flanger looked at the embracing humans and at the expression of bliss on Amy's face. "Oh yes," Flanger said with a grin. "It won't be long now. . . ."

nineteen

As Friday dawned, Amy was sound asleep in her bed, completely at peace with the world. Even when she slumbered, the smile refused to budge from her face. Warm, romantic dreams had swept her through the past few nights—wonderful, blissful images of roses glistening in the early morning dew; long, silken dresses from Paris; and Dion running toward her across fertile fields of wildflowers.

For Lucy, however, it was different. She was already wide awake as the gray dawn light snuck past her venetian blinds and cut an unhappy streak across the bedroom wall.

Today the dawn light foretold hell. For today was Friday. Today was School Sports Day.

Back at Tubby Flats, Lucy used to love Sports Day. Only Kathy Wyler ever seriously threatened her in the 100-yard dash, and nobody ever came near her long-jump record. Such activities came easily to her, and it was fun too. Easy as falling off a log . . . or leaping up a tree. At least, it used to be.

It was a long, reluctant walk to school that morning, and it was a relief to discover Sam by the gate. Some eager student athletes were already milling around the oval, warming up and stretching. Milling around Sam's legs, however, was a familiar terrier.

"Why did you bring Flumpy?" Lucy asked incredulously. "As if they allow dogs at a city school!"

"Well, I felt sorry for them cooped up all week," Sam explained. "I really think we should let them go. Come on—they're not bad. They've got a world to save. What do you say?" He proffered her a smile in an attempt to clinch the deal.

Lucy didn't respond. She was looking straight at Sam and registered that his mouth was moving, but she hadn't heard a word he'd said. Her mind was far too busy imagining the teasing she was about to get from Melissa Blume and Bradley Ditchfield when they saw her cheap sports clothes. And the bucketing she would receive when she failed to clear an inch in the long jump. Already that annoying feeling was creeping into her limbs like a virulent dose of flu—the feeling that made her petrified to move for fear of failure. She headed off to the dilapidated stand where her sporting house—Menzies House—was to be seated for the day.

Sam followed his unresponsive friend. "Oh well, guys," he said quietly to Flumpy, "at least you're allowed an excursion today."

Melissa Blume spotted them first. "MS. FELTON!" she bellowed. "Bush monkey—I mean Lucy Buckley—has brought a dog!"

146

Ms. Felton bustled over. For some reason she always wore a tracksuit on Sports Day, even though she was usually *less* active than on a regular school day.

"Lucy! You can't bring your dog to school," Ms. Felton scolded. "Maybe in the country you can, but not here. There are rules."

"He's *my* dog, Ms. Felton," Sam said quickly. "The vet says he needs special tablets, and I have to look after him. My parents are away."

"I see," said Ms. Felton, softening a little. She scanned the area quickly for her teaching colleagues. "Well, just keep him tied up, then. Out of sight. Under the stands."

As Sam tied Flumpy up, Lucy took a seat on the wooden bench, just avoiding a wad of fresh chewing gum no doubt left for her.

"Do all the Buckley girls have dumb animals for boyfriends?" Melissa Blume sneered.

Sam sat down next to Lucy. "Flumpy's not dumb," he said.

"Not the dog, stupid, *you*!" Melissa Blume roared with laughter. Her many cronies joined in.

It's going to be a long, long day, Lucy thought.

By midday it couldn't be put off any longer. Lucy had ducked and weaved her long-jump turn a couple of times by (1) not being in the stand when her group was called, and (2) feigning a limp when the Sports Master came around to catch the stragglers. Eventually Ms. Felton caught her by the water fountains and marched her over to the long-jump line. Sam, quite coincidentally, was right in front of her and, before long, found himself standing uncertainly on the starting line.

"This'll be good!" Bradley Ditchfield yelled from the stands.

Sam hurtled forward. There was no precision in his awkward run. It appeared he was just going to continue his sprint across the sand pit when he tripped and fell flat on his face. Even Mr. Purcell, Year 4's humorless teacher, who was reluctantly recording the students' long-jump efforts, had to stifle a laugh.

"Have another go," he suggested.

Sam did. He misjudged his leap this time around and managed to land painfully on his knees. Mr. Purcell disqualified him.

"Next," he said, gazing at his clipboard. "Lisa," he read incorrectly.

Lucy walked unsteadily to the line. The maroon path of battered synthetic material seemed to stretch a vast distance to the sea of choppy sand. Mr. Purcell suddenly recognized her.

"Aren't you the little monkey up the tree? The bush girl?" he asked. "This should be easy for you. Score some points for Menzies House—they desperately need them."

His comments were intended to be good-natured. It was in fact the most pleasantly intentioned and good-natured thing Mr. Purcell had said to any student since 1979. But the words "bush" and "monkey" pulverized the last crumbling walls defending Lucy's confidence.

Her feet turned to heavy blocks on the starting line.

"When you're ready," Mr. Purcell said patiently.

"C'mon, Bush Monkey!" a distant Melissa Blume howled.

"Yeah, show us how it's done, Monkey Girl!" Bradley Ditchfield added. A chorus of similar comments began to drift across the field.

"Can't I just skip it?" Lucy asked feebly.

"No, we don't do the hop, skip, and jump event," Mr. Purcell replied, misunderstanding her.

"I mean I don't want to do this *at all*," Lucy said.

"Well, you have to," Mr. Purcell said, losing his friendliness under the hot sun.

"Why?"

"Don't you dare talk back to a teacher like that!" Mr. Purcell snapped. "You jump right now, young lady, or there'll be some serious consequences!"

Such an outburst, of course, drew the attention of the entire school. Melissa Blume and Bradley Ditchfield led an ever louder chant of "Bush Monkey, jump! BUSH MONKEY, JUMP!"

The rival houses of Chifley, Hughes, and Holt were amazed that the Menzies would pick on one of their own team. They certainly couldn't afford to. They were so far down in points that even the Holt House looked set to beat them.

"What's going on here?" Ms. Felton demanded, storming into the long-jump area.

"Lisa won't jump," Mr. Purcell explained.

"You jump right now, Miss Buckley, or you can explain yourself to the Headmaster!" Ms. Felton ordered.

Lucy ran forward blindly. Tears obscured her vision, so she could barely make out the track. She tripped off the edge and fell heavily into the sandpit. A great chunk of it ended up in her mouth.

Menzies House erupted into malicious laughter.

"I reckon even your *dog* can do better than you!" Bradley sniggered. He'd located Flumpy under the stands, untied the leash, and pushed the ATV onto the track. Year 5's 400-yard race just avoided tripping over him.

* * *

"The gate's open!" Strelka yelled gleefully in the cockpit. He spun the ATV toward the open school gate and set Flumpy running. The pavement rushed beneath their paws, and freedom—the wide-open rickety gate with the beckoning road beyond—was only yards away. Belka, however, kept casting glances back to Lucy. She remained prone in the long-jump pit, her face buried in the sand, abuse from Menzies House showering down upon her.

A casual observer would have thought her dead, lying still and broken as she was. The image of this lonely Earth child, however, drifting farther and farther behind them on the rearview screens, played upon Belka's mind.

Strelka was surprised when Belka took the controls and raced the ATV back to Lucy. Belka poked Flumpy's wet nose into Lucy's ear and spoke quietly over the loudspeaker to her.

"Get to your feet and stand strong, Lucy," he urged. "Don't give those kids the satisfaction of seeing you beaten. Get up and face them!"

Lucy turned to Flumpy in surprise, stood slowly, and wiped away her tears. She walked back to the stands and took a seat next to the bruised Sam.

Melissa Blume hurled rude comments at her but was silenced when Lucy shot her a baleful glance. Like most bullies, Melissa Blume knew only how to dish it out, never to take it, and she wilted quickly under Lucy's steely gaze.

Pretty soon the comments stopped and Lucy and Sam sat out the afternoon in peace. They even got a free hot dog at lunchtime from a kindly parent volunteer.

* * *

The Sports Master blew his whistle one last time, and Sports Day was over for another year. Hughes House came in first, followed closely by Chifley. Holt had its best run in years by coming third, and Menzies came a resounding last. Holt and Menzies had been neck and neck for a while, until Sam stumbled across the hurdles and managed to trip up Menzies' one good competitor in the lane next to him.

"Even your dog's weird," Melissa Blume said as she brushed past Lucy on her way out of school. "Bradley let him off and he runs over to you! I would've run out the gate if I'd had the chance!"

She shrugged and walked off.

Lucy looked at the terrier trotting at the end of Sam's leash. Flumpy patiently kept pace beside Sam as he hobbled forward.

"You could have escaped, couldn't you?" Lucy asked.

"Yes," Belka replied over the loudspeaker.

"But you didn't."

"No."

"Why not?"

"Well," Belka said with a sigh, "you needed a friend."

twenty

The pale light of Saturday morning edged through Sam Chan's attic window and found Flumpy lying dejected on the floor.

There's nothing as stark as the four walls of a prison after you've had the opportunity to escape. Since Belka had chosen to rescue Lucy rather than continue their mission the previous day, Strelka had said nothing. He just stared at Belka and took a lot of showers.

He stepped from the bathroom facility, dripped across to the console, and resumed his staring with renewed vigor. He put his feet up on the control panel with a heavy sigh.

To avoid him Belka looked up at the attic window one more time.

An unusual shadow passed across it, then a lorikeet fluttered into view, its vivid, multicolored plumage quite a stunning contrast to their ugly prison. It settled by the window and pecked at some berries.

Belka and Strelka looked at the bird in amazement. They'd never seen a winged, flying creature before—Gersbach just didn't have them.

"What a remarkable animal," Belka said, reaching for the ship's camera unit.

"Yeah, if only it could do something useful like—OWW!" Strelka shrieked.

Water had dripped from his feet into the translator unit and given him a mild electric shock. The translator made a fizzing sound and switched itself on.

"*Fool!*" Belka scolded. "The stupidity of you! As if we haven't enough problems, and now you're deliberately damaging our one means of communication!"

"Oh yeah?" Strelka bit back. "Who crashed on Earth in the first place? Huh? Who dropped a bunch of explosives that almost took off my head? Who put some whiney little Earth girl ahead of our entire planet? Huh? HUH?"

"Oh yes?" Belka fumed, rising to his feet and jabbing a finger at his colleague. "Who's the badly dressed, swaggering, so-laid-back-I'm-lying-down reprobate who managed to fall *backward* onto a pack of explosives, threaten the cat of the one human who could release us, and has a RIDICULOUS crush on a juvenile delinquent who is the accomplice of the man hell-bent on destroying Gersbach?"

"Gee, I dunno. Me?" Strelka countered.

Belka became aware that Flumpy's jaws were moving and their argument was being translated into a series of curious squawking sounds.

The lorikeet had stopped eating and was looking at them intently.

"I mean, if you could stop pontificating for just one minute," Strelka continued, "and get us help, then maybe—"

The lorikeet instantly tried to open the window, pecking at the glass with its beak.

"Say that again!" Belka ordered.

His tone flummoxed Strelka. "I said get us *help*! HELP US!" he shouted.

And then Strelka noticed it. The lorikeet had heard the order and was determined to enter the attic, head-butting the window frame in an attempt to get inside.

Strelka looked at the bird with dawning realization and yanked the translator microphone toward him.

"Flying creature," he said to the lorikeet. "Fly around in a little circle."

The command translated into a series of squawks. The lorikeet promptly flew in a little circle and then recommenced pecking at the window. Belka's eyes widened in excitement.

"The translator—it's tuned itself to the animals! Insect creature!" he ordered, looking at a passing cockroach. "Jump up and down!" The cockroach did so and continued on its way. Belka turned to Strelka and, remarkably, had nothing to say. His mind was far too busy calculating possibilities for escape.

Sam Chan walked out into his backyard, dragging a basket of laundry behind him. He was startled when a sulphur-crested cockatoo soared into the yard and screeched at the attic window above. Flumpy's face looked back at it, his damp nose pressed against the glass. Five more cockatoos arrived, and the group appeared to engage in a conversation of strange squawks. It looked like Flumpy was ordering the creatures about!

Sam ducked as more and more cockies swooped into the yard. Everywhere he looked, the blue sky was blotted out by hundreds of white wings accompanied by an extraordinary din of high-pitched screeching. Sam took cover in the far end of the backyard as the attic window suddenly burst from its frame and tumbled to the ground. He ran inside, bounded up the stairs, and flung open the attic door.

What he saw made him ill. A seething army of cockroaches—shiny, black, brown, and scuttling—had formed themselves into an eight-foot-high ramp from the floor to the attic window. Flumpy had marched up the throbbing, made-to-order escape route (even though each crunchy step made Belka feel a little queasy) and then head-butted the window clean out of its frame. Sam was incredibly impressed. But also sick to his stomach at the thought that his house had so many cockroaches for the aliens to call upon.

What Sam Chan saw next he would never forget.

Flumpy, perched on the windowsill, issued a complex series of barks and squawks. The cockatoos, hovering anxiously outside, squawked in reply. They arranged themselves noisily into square flying formations, then layered themselves into a solid, flapping platform. Flumpy stepped carefully from the window ledge onto the backs of the nearest cockies. They squawked angrily under his weight but beat their wings all the harder to keep their passenger aloft. Flumpy directed them, ordering the birds into a more efficient formation. Then the dense squadron of cockatoos rose as one and disappeared over the treetops. Sam gathered his jaw from the ground and ran to get his bike.

* * *

When you're in love, everything seems better. Everything looks better, feels better, and tastes better. Even the air smells cleaner and fresher. This was certainly the case for Amy Buckley, and it wasn't all in her mind. Things *were* actually a lot better for her. She could now walk into the school playground and not hear a single moo. The other kids talked to her and listened intently to what she had to say. Miranda didn't speak to Amy, of course. She just skulked around in the corner of the courtyard with her few remaining friends saying "It won't last!" very loudly. School was now a breeze for Amy. She knew all the answers in class, and if she didn't, it didn't bother her because she had the only answer that really mattered: Dion Van Steenwyk. This had been the best week of her life. She didn't know if she was crazy, or if Flanger the fairy existed or not, and she didn't care.

Dion was a happy man too. He'd just had an order from the local soccer club for two hundred long-sleeve T-shirts embossed with their logo in full color—front and back. Not only that, but his new line was selling well among his schoolmates, and his scooter was running like a dream. He was starting to like Amy Buckley too. She was a great help in the office, as well as a really good kisser.

"We're almost out of time!" Colonel Bars announced as he stood at the door of Flanger's tiny cabin. He'd been running some wormhole calculations on the ship's computer and was alarmed at the result. "We've only got a few Earth hours left! We have to go right away or we won't get back to Gersbach before the wormhole closes!"

"I guess . . . ," Flanger said without much enthusiasm.

"Go in there and get that Earth girl to let us off the leash. Now!"

Flanger leapt over Bars' head so quickly he didn't have the chance to turn around before she spoke again.

"I suppose we shouldn't wait any longer." She strode into the cockpit with her flea posse in tow.

"Have you been stalling?" Bars asked with sudden realization.

"What do you mean?" Flanger reached for the translator microphone.

"You're more interested in the love life of some stupid human child than you are about ruling all of Gersbach, aren't you?"

"No . . . ," Flanger replied innocently. "Being a ruthless despot is important too."

"Why do I waste my time with women?" Bars cursed, stomping back and forth across the flight deck.

"I just wanted to see how things turned out, that's all."

"Well, let's just stay here forever, because I wouldn't want to break her little heart," Bars said sarcastically.

Flanger ignored his comment and spoke sweetly into the microphone, "Amy?"

Amy was sitting with her diary in the backyard, analyzing her last conversation with Dion. But she gave the wonderful Flanger her fullest attention. "Yes, Flanger?"

"How's Dion?"

"He's great," Amy said with her usual glow.

"Good. So now I've solved all your problems, I think it's about time you did me a little favor."

"You're not leaving, are you?" Amy asked with a touch of panic.

157

"Let me off the leash."

"I can't. Dad won't let me."

"I'm not going anywhere. Don't worry. I just need to walk around a bit."

"You won't run away?"

"I promise I won't run away."

"Well . . . okay."

Amy hesitated for a second, then snapped the chain off the little dog's collar.

The dachshund immediately took off in a burst of smoke and flame, almost burning a hole in Amy's jeans. Lucy ran out of the house just in time to see the dachshund's hind legs dent the neighbors' satellite dish as it flew west as fast as it could.

"Wow! Nicky can fly!" Lucy exclaimed. "Where's Colonel Bars going?"

"You mean Flanger, stupid," Amy hissed, angry at the dachshund for flying away.

Then she hesitated.

When you suddenly realize something you thought was your big secret is not a secret at all, you get a little warm flush and your bones feel a bit rubbery. When you realize it's your stupid little sister who knows all about your big secret, the warm flush turns to a sickly burning sensation and your legs wobble about uncontrollably.

"What do *you* know about all this?" Amy demanded.

"About Colonel Bars inside the dachshund?" Lucy answered.

"Flanger lives inside Nicky!"

"Well, there was a little man in there last time I looked!" Lucy had endured quite enough of her sister's short temper.

Amy looked confused as the dachshund rose steadily over the rooftops. "It's not just Nicky," Lucy explained. "It's Flumpy too. Belka and Strelka are in Flumpy, and Colonel Bars lives in Nicky. They're all from the planet Gersbach."

"No!" Amy insisted. "Flanger is in Nicky and she's a . . ." Amy was about to say *fairy* but decided against it. "There are *aliens* living inside the dogs?"

"Yes. Tiny men."

"Do you mean I was telling a MAN about my PERSONAL AF-FAIRS?!" she shrieked. "Why didn't you tell me there was a man in there? This is SO embarrassing, and it's ALL YOUR FAULT!"

But Lucy wasn't listening. She had learned to switch off her sister's voice when it reached a certain number of decibels. The vapor trail of the dachshund had taken all of her attention. As it slowly disappeared in the sky, so too did the cloud of confusion that had been surrounding Lucy for days. Belka and Strelka had to be right. Bars couldn't be trusted. He was on the run, and that's what criminals do. Also, he seemed to have been feeding Amy a bunch of lies. Bars was not very nice at all. Lucy made up her mind to help Belka and Strelka. She just hoped that they weren't too mad at her.

Sam pedaled his bike speedily, puffing deep breaths, his hands sweating and slipping on the handlebars. He could not keep his eyes off the amazing flying circus flapping and squawking ahead. Over a hundred sulphur-crested cockatoos flew in a solid platform with Flumpy balanced on top, his head thrust proudly forward, commanding the extraordinary exam-ple of cocky cooperation screeching beneath his paws.

"Look!" Belka shouted. "Bars and Flanger Damka!"

Strelka looked at the familiar Buckley home coming up on their left. The dachshund had just launched from the backyard before turning and denting the neighbors' satellite dish.

"Tell the birds to follow the dachshund!" Belka commanded. Strelka relayed the order through the translator, but the flying platform only seemed to lose altitude in response.

"THE BIRDS ARE TIRING!" Sam shouted to the street. As the street was empty, nobody heard him, but it did relieve the tension. He was suddenly overtaken by a motorized scooter with a gold-helmeted rider. Sam followed it into the Buckley backyard, to see Amy and Lucy gazing up at the receding form of Nicky.

Dion propped his scooter against the shed and placed his helmet carefully on the ground. He swaggered over to Amy, and a smile burst across her face. She began to speak but was cut off as a screeching crackle of cockatoos exploded into view. The birds, exhausted from carrying Flumpy, dropped as one into the Buckley backyard and suddenly dispersed, flapping off to perch in the surrounding trees. Dislodged, the ATV collided with Dion, who cushioned its fall. Flumpy immediately checked the dachshund's progress, then ran to the shed. Dion sat up amidst a pile of cockatoo feathers, automatically smoothing down his hair. Though disoriented, he reacted immediately to the familiar sound of his scooter's engine. Flumpy had pulled the starter ripcord with his mouth.

Dion's face dropped in silent horror as he saw the terrier pilot the scooter down the driveway, execute a wobbly left turn, and accelerate down the street. He made a curious strangled sound and sprinted two blocks in pursuit, but the dog-driven scooter shrank to a point in the distance. Dion doubled over as a painful stitch bit into his side.

He was almost run over by Sam's speeding bicycle and swiveled just in time to avoid losing the end of his nose on Lucy's. A moment later Amy ran up to join him.

"That . . . dog . . . ," Dion wheezed, rearing to his full height and looking angrily up and down the street. "It took my scooter!"

"Well, Flumpy's an unusual breed . . . ," Amy began, desperate to conceal stories of aliens in dogs, at least until she fully understood what was going on herself.

"Taxi!" yelled Dion, leaping in front of a battered cab that was speeding down the street. The taxi screeched to an unceremonious halt in a cloud of blue smoke. Amy heard loud, unusual techno music thundering within.

Not far away, in his large backyard, Dr. Macheski twitched his eyebrows with excitement. A little wary of his all-too-powerful rocket, Macheski One, which still sat in disgrace in his car after the school demonstration, today he was testing a new *mini*-rocket engine upon his rotary clothesline.

The rotary clothesline was the perfect contraption for rocket testing, Macheski thought, and he wished they'd had a large version of it in the USSR back in the 1950s. He checked the wire harness on the foot-long rocket and stood back a respectful distance. He pressed the red button on the remote control and enjoyed the spectacle of the small rocket gaining speed, whisking the clothesline around and around. The rocket was so powerful that it flew from its harness and landed in the open trunk of his Datsun 180B in the driveway.

His backyard, it must be noted, had three concrete launch pads, each littered with the remnants of a hundred mini-rocket launches, the scorched earth bearing testament to a man reliving long-past Soviet space race glories. From above, the layout of his backyard looked like a miniature Cape Canaveral, and indeed, Flanger gave it a passing glance as the dachshund flew overhead. Dr. Macheski heard the sound of its engines and quickly looked up from his rocket test.

He grabbed his nearby telescope. His wild eyebrows rose in stunned curiosity as he saw smoke and fire streaming from all four paws of a *flying dachshund*—the legs angling occasionally to steer the creature through the air.

Dr. Macheski ran to the driveway and slammed the trunk shut. Revving up his Datsun 180B, he headed after the flying dog in eager pursuit.

At full throttle Nicky the dachshund was cruising at an altitude of fifteen yards and at a steady thirty miles an hour. And this modest cruise was burning up fuel at an alarming rate.

"What's our ETA at the D.O.G.?" snapped Bars, flicking off a flea that was actually taking a nap against his ear.

"It'll take three hours to get there," replied Flanger, looking up from the computer. "In this fast, modern ship you got us."

"Well, at least we're airborne," Bars said with an icy smile.

Belka and Strelka had settled Flumpy into the best position for driving the curious Earth vehicle—reared up on his hind legs with his front paws draped over the scooter handles. The ATV's head looked around one side of the steering column.

"What speed are we doing?" Belka asked.

"Thirty miles an hour," replied Strelka. "Which appears to be as fast as this thing will go."

He dialed up ATV Weapons Command on his screen and rotated the laser from its left nostril position to storage. His fingers sped across to "ATV Utilities," found the item labeled "MagHook," and rotated it into place. When he pressed down on the red button atop the guidance column, a magnetized grappling hook shot from the ATV's nose, securing itself to the rear bumper bar of the state transit bus in front of them. The Galactanauts were flung back in their seats as the scooter's speed increased rapidly. Belka and Strelka found themselves gaining on the dachshund above them, then overtaking it and streaking ahead.

"Good work," Belka said, turning to the location monitor. The D.O.G. position inched closer as the dachshund location pointer fell away behind them. "Looks like we're finally ahead of the game."

twenty-one

Lucy and Sam rode past a traffic jam and weaved through an excursion of Boy Scouts, just managing to keep Flumpy's small scooter in sight. Suddenly they saw it racing after a bus. They gave chase as fast as they could, before hitting the brakes at a frustrating red light.

As the flying dachshund zoomed out of sight, Dr. Macheski came to a halt in traffic gridlock, thumping his steering wheel in frustration. A taxi breezed by in the transit lane to his left, emitting the loudest young-people's music he'd ever heard. The bent sign by the roadside read: TRANSIT LANE. BUSES, TAXIS ONLY. It certainly didn't say "Buses, taxis, those on verge of major scientific discovery only."

Macheski thought that's what it *should* read, so he pulled into the transit lane and shot forward. Only those who dare to break the rules make the great discoveries, he figured.

The bus towing Flumpy screeched to a halt behind a breakdown, and Strelka quickly demagnetized the grappling hook, retracting it into the left nostril.

The scooter continued its fifty-mile-an-hour momentum down the road and just cleared the giant bus. Looking at the rear display, Strelka saw Lucy and Sam cycling behind them.

"Our little jailers are after us again," he muttered.

"Least of our trouble," Belka said. "Visual confirmation! Bars and Flanger Damka above and behind us . . ." He inspected the instruments. "And turning port .75!"

The dachshund was heading west across suburban rooftops.

"At this rate they'll get to the D.O.G. first," Belka said. "We can't match their pace stuck here on the ground!" He smacked the console in frustration. "I'm sick of being the underdog!"

Strelka noticed a group of seagulls pecking at crumbs by a bus shelter. "Well, let's bring Nicky down to us," he suggested. He flipped on the translator and spoke in a voice that resembled an airport announcement rather than a fervent battle order. "Attention all flying creatures. Please attack the flying dog animal. Use all appropriate strength to bring it to the ground. Group your attacks. Thank you."

A squadron of nearby lorikeets responded immediately. They didn't really know why they were responding—it was an instinctual thing; they just suddenly felt the urge to split into rows and crash into the flying dachshund, one wave after another. Meanwhile, a murder of crows primed their beaks for a series of spectacular runs at the dog's flying belly.

* * *

"GREAT LICKS OF LAIKA!" Bars yelled. A crazed, squawking mob of birds was pushing the dachshund deliberately and forcibly toward the ground. Bars set Nicky's rocket paws at full power, but when an enormous contingent of pigeons and seagulls joined in the melee, he accepted the inevitable. Flanger grimaced, holding her hair in place as the dachshund struck the ground. While Bars picked himself off the deck and straightened his uniform in barely contained anger, Flanger switched the windshield wipers to full strength, dislodging a nasty deposit of pigeon excrement from the forward screens.

Then Bars spotted a gap in the fence surrounding a construction site. "That way! That's where we're going!" he shouted and switched the prototype craft to "Foot Mode."

Flumpy bounced over the gutter, and Belka almost lost the ATV paws' grip on the scooter handles. He corrected course and followed the dachshund into the construction zone past a fleet of parked, official-looking cars. A flustered man in a suit and safety helmet tried to grab the dachshund but missed. Belka aimed the scooter straight at the man, forcing him to leap out of their path. A moment later the man jumped the other way to avoid serious injury from two kids on bikes.

"You can't go in there!" he yelled. "Invited guests only!"

But the party of intruders had disappeared into the gaping mouth of the new M12 Motorway Tunnel.

Flanger looked up at the gleaming newness of the subterranean roadway as fluorescent light strips whizzed past overhead.

"Wow," she said sarcastically. "Finally something that looks post-ice-age on planet Earth."

"Just shut up and keep tracking the D.O.G.," Bars snapped. A flea bounced into his lap and snuggled up to him. Bars slapped it toward Flanger. "And keep your pets on YOUR SIDE of the cockpit!"

Belka and Strelka were finally gaining on the dachshund. The sausage dog's squat legs were running as fast as possible, but the scooter was almost on top of it, the motor shaking and smoking in protest at the speed demanded.

"Stand by to deploy MagHook," Belka ordered. Strelka's finger hovered over the red button.

"Stand by for takeoff," Bars commanded, and Flanger punched some buttons. A red warning signal flashed on the console.

"Purge problem," she said.

"Purge problem!" Bars roared. "Why?"

Flanger read the ship's diagnostic report. "Fuel-line blockage, rear left. Due to impact damage. Fuel is quite low by the way."

"I'm going back there! Keep this thing at full speed." Bars glanced at Belka and Strelka's ATV in the rear display. "And keep *them* at bay," he added.

Flanger grabbed the controls. "How?" she sneered. "Shall I tell them to 'sit'?"

"Just use your pretty little head," Bars snapped and left the cockpit.

Flumpy pulled in behind the pounding rear quarters of the dachshund, and soon the scooter's front wheel was just inches from the dachshund's tail. Strelka's hand hovered over the

MagHook release, the red target crosshairs on the forward screen illuminated over the dachshund's glossy black rear end.

"Fire!" Belka shouted eagerly.

The MagHook shot forward . . . but fell short of its target, dangling and scraping across the road. Belka looked at Strelka in confusion. The dachshund moved out of reach, its little legs pounding the asphalt, and if anything seemed to accelerate away from them.

"We're slowing down!" Belka realized.

"The scooter's fuel supply," Strelka said. "It must be running out . . ."

Giant rubber wheels rolled into view on either side of Flumpy. It was Lucy and Sam on their bicycles.

Bars made his way into the foul-smelling cargo hold of his ship. The dachshund's long, cylindrical body was like a dark, cavernous warehouse, and he had to grip the cold walkway railing securely as the vehicle's rather nauseating running motion tossed him up and down. The cargo doors below were covered in dog food, shoveled there by Flanger after Amy's numerous feeding sessions. The stench of rotting low-grade meat, gravy, and a nasty jelly-like substance was quite overpowering, and Bars moved quickly aft to investigate the fuel-line problem in the left rear leg.

"But we want to help you!" Sam pleaded, cycling beside Flumpy's scooter.

"Oh yes?" Flumpy appeared to say, though it was really Belka over the loudspeaker. "By locking us up again? Oh yes, you're a big help!" Belka was a highly trained Gersbacian Space

Officer and could maintain his indignation under the most arduous of conditions.

"We're sorry!" Lucy puffed, straining hard to ride beside them and talk at the same time. She looked at Sam. "Well, *I'm* sorry. It was *my* fault. I should've trusted you. On Sports Day you really helped me, and now I really want to help you."

"We could actually use some help," came Strelka's voice of reason. "We're not making a lot of progress by ourselves."

"Very well," Belka said. The scooter's engine burnt the last of its fuel and cut out. Flumpy and the scooter rolled a few more feet down the road and, unceremoniously, fell over.

Dr. Macheski glimpsed the dogs vanishing into the motorway construction site and pulled over to investigate. In front of him the music-blaring taxi had skidded to a halt, and a vocal, dread-locked boy was trying to scale a fence to get in. He wasn't succeeding. A pleasant-looking teenage girl was trying to placate the youth, but she wasn't succeeding either. With an angry yell and shake of his fist, the boy leapt back into the taxi and almost left without his companion. Dr. Macheski studied his road map to see where the new motorway tunnel emerged.

twenty-two

Colonel Bars thundered back into the dachshund cabin, a nasty smell of dog food, hydraulic fluid, and fuel wafting from him. A spray of oil decorated his uniform like a sash. "Prepare for take-off," he said to Flanger. "Pump the fuel lines first!"

"Ready?" Belka asked over the loudspeaker.

"Yes," said Lucy and Sam.

It was a curious sight. The steering column of Dion's scooter had been removed and used as a connecting strut from Lucy's bike, to the scooter, to Sam's bike—forming a rigid, six-wheeled machine. Lucy sat atop her bicycle, leaning down to the right, with the scooter's ripcord starter in her hand. Sam sat facing backward on the scooter platform, one hand gripping his bike for stability, the other holding the scooter's accelerator. His legs held Flumpy snugly over the scooter's engine while a tube dangled from between Flumpy's rear legs into the fuel tank.

"We're feeding the scooter's engine rocket fuel," Belka told Lucy and Sam. "It'll give us more kick. Start her up, Lucy!"

Lucy pulled the cord and the engine roared into life. Within ten seconds the unwieldy six-wheeler was racing at a startling sixty miles an hour.

As the dachshund ran, streams of rocket fuel trailed from its feet. In their rear display Flanger and Bars noticed a strange, multiwheeled contraption gaining on them with alarming speed.

"Close fuel dump," Bars ordered. "Take off!"

Nicky's galloping paws roared to life with fire and steam, and the sausage dog was airborne once more. The pool of leaked rocket fuel ignited beneath it, and two rivers of fire snaked back through the tunnel.

Lucy saw it first—a distant burst of flame and then what appeared to be train tracks of fire shooting toward them. She screamed. Sam and Flumpy looked back at the commotion. Lucy tried to steer the scooter/bike out of the way, but the slight veer to the left wasn't nearly enough. The twin trails of fire scorched across the ground, and a haze of heat rose to the roof. Lucy smelled the burning fuel, then felt a thick wall of heat bearing down upon her.

* * *

Beth Buckley, boxes of peppermint balls under each arm, nudged open the front door with her foot. She let herself in, placed the boxes on the couch, and managed to stop herself yelling again about open doors and security in the city.

"Hello, love," said Tom, paper in hand.

"Where are the girls?"

"Out back, I guess."

Beth looked out into the yard. "No they're not."

The State Premier stood before a wall of cameras, reporters, government officials, and representatives of the construction company. They all stood before a thin wall of sandstone in the middle of the M12 Motorway Tunnel as a powerful earth-boring machine idled nearby. The Premier took the scissors from the Minister for Transport and approached the purple ribbon that had been draped across the stone barrier.

"Thank you, Anton," he said. "And so it's with great pleasure I cut this ribbon, to allow the two halves of the M12 Motorway Tunnel to connect." There was polite applause and the flashing of photography as he cut the ribbon and then used a hammer to tap the wall. The wafer-thin rock tumbled clear, revealing the rest of the tunnel gleaming on the other side.

Suddenly a loud warning screeched from a walkie-talkie: "FIRE IN SECTIONS F AND G! OH NO! AND H!"

The group looked down the tunnel nervously and saw a distant ball of flame. The next moment they were all drenched by a powerful—and icy—sprinkler system.

Lucy had never relished the touch of beautiful cold water quite that way before. A moment earlier a monster of fire was about to consume them, then just as suddenly it was destroyed, evaporating in a dense fog of steam as their strange bike machine powered forward. Through the rain she could just make out Nicky flying ahead, but they were catching up to him. She looked at Sam, who had very bravely placed his body over Flumpy to protect him from the elements.

"Ah, right, well done, Sam," Strelka said over the loud-speaker. "Now if you could just aim us upward."

The dachshund had reached maximum airborne speed. Lucy, Sam, and Flumpy rolled up underneath it.

"Slow down, Sam," Belka said. Sam eased off the accelerator and aimed Flumpy at the belly of the dachshund above. "Prepare MagHook, Strelka," Belka added.

The earth-boring machine plowed effortlessly through the rock remnants and formed a nice large hole. Though very wet, the Premier and Minister for Transport were determined to complete the tunnel-opening ceremony. They prepared to step through.

"Fire!" Belka commanded. The MagHook shot from Flumpy's nose and hit home between Nicky's front paws. Strelka hit the recoil function, and the MagHook cable winched Flumpy from Sam's arms toward the dachshund. The sausage dog, suddenly burdened with extra weight, sank toward the ground. Flumpy wheeled crazily through the air beneath the straining Nicky. Lucy and Sam's machine just kept pace underneath.

The Premier was about to be the first to officially step through the hole in the rock wall when he was flung aside by an airborne dachshund holding a terrier. A couple of kids riding very fast bicycles swooped after them.

"Keep up, Sam!" urged Lucy.

"I'm trying to!" Sam was revving the scooter's engine as fast as he could. "I think rocket fuel's really bad for this motor . . ."

And just then the scooter's engine rattled loudly, blew a cloud of smoke, and disintegrated—fanning a blanket of debris across the motorway.

"The ATVs are designed to lock together nose to tail," Belka explained, gripping his chair as their craft dangled precariously beneath the dachshund. "With automatic lock-on when in proximity."

"Oh, good. Then you can just stroll aboard and give them a damn good talking to," Strelka said.

SPLAT! Something brown hit their forward screens. SPLAT SPLAT! More blobs of the ugly stuff rained down on them.

"What's that?" Belka asked, more annoyed than alarmed.

Flanger had opened the cargo doors of the dachshund and was shoveling the unwanted dog food onto Flumpy. Great dollops of disgusting brown meat and slime splattered down, often ending up on Flumpy's face and obscuring the cockpit's vision.

Belka fired the laser at their assailant, but Flanger easily leapt out of the way. She only sniggered and shoveled dog food at them faster. Soon Flumpy's face looked like a deliciously layered hot fudge sundae—just a lot smellier.

Bars was tiring of his enemies' attempts to thwart him. He saw an exhaust shaft in the tunnel ceiling ahead and hit upon a risky way out of the predicament. He savagely braked to a halt beneath the opening. Flumpy was thrown back and forth beneath the dachshund, but the sturdy MagHook cable kept them attached. Bars flew straight up the exhaust shaft, and the long, fiery columns issuing from the rocket paws threatened to set Belka and Strelka alight.

* * *

The Galactanauts watched the dog food melt off their screens and gasped in horror. Bars had come to a halt in the bright silver shaft, hovering as Flumpy dangled beneath. He blasted all four of Nicky's rocket engines at maximum burn. Temperature warning gauges lit up on Flumpy's control panel, and it became obvious if they remained in the shaft, the ATV would be cooked. Belka reluctantly pressed "DeMag" on the MagHook. As it disengaged, the craft fell back through the shaft, tumbling and bouncing violently from side to side. Flumpy dropped toward the cold, hard road. Belka quickly reactivated the MagHook, and it clamped on to the exhaust shaft's metal rim. They dangled for a while before Strelka slowly unwound the cable, lowering the ATV to the ground.

The strange six-wheeled machine arrived, pedaled on either side by a damp Lucy and Sam.

twenty-three

Dr. Macheski was parked in the street overlooking the motor-way tunnel exit and saw the dachshund emerge from an exhaust vent and fly off. He sped off in pursuit—then his Datsun stalled. He swore, brushed aside the bits of model rocket that had been flung onto the seat beside him, restarted the engine, and sped off again.

Beth surveyed the deserted backyard. No Amy, no Lucy. Dion's distinctive gold helmet was there, however, abandoned by the shed. He was usually inseparable from it! She hoped Amy wasn't skylarking about with him on that ridiculous lawn-mower scooter thing.

"So if the girls aren't out in the backyard, where are they, Tom?" Beth demanded, storming in and waving the helmet at him.

Tom didn't answer. He was looking at a TV news item about

176

the State Premier being doused by a rainstorm inside some tunnel.

"Where *are* they?" Beth repeated. She reached for the TV to turn it off but then froze in her tracks.

The image on the screen filled her with horror. It was fuzzy, but she immediately recognized the two dogs from the backyard—followed by Lucy! Clinging to an amazingly fast bike!

The smile dropped from Tom's face.

"Where's that? WHERE'S THAT TUNNEL?" Beth shrieked.

"The M12!" Tom yelped, jumping to his feet. "I'll get the car."

Dion watched in utter horror as the taxi's meter crept toward $100. "Can't you drive any faster, buddy?" he shouted over the unbearably loud techno music. The driver shrugged in response.

"Let me make a call on your cell please, Dion," Amy requested.

"Why? Who to?" Dion asked suspiciously.

Amy thought quickly about her reply. There was nothing more uncool than ringing your parents, but that's what she wanted to do—and desperately. There was a side to Dion emerging in this taxi ride she didn't like at all. Usually he was so . . . well, nice wasn't the word, but interested in her. Often it made her blush. But now he was obsessed with getting his dumb scooter back. Obsessed with the taxi meter. Getting so *angry*. She took the phone from him.

"I'm calling a friend about something," Amy lied. "I'll pay for it."

Dion sighed and reached for the taxi's radio. "Would you turn the music down PLEASE?" he bellowed at the driver.

* * *

The phone rang in the empty Buckley household, while in the driveway the Buckleys' battered Toyota Crown reversed inexpertly, dropped off the curb, and roared down the street.

Two minutes later it was outside the Van Steenwyk residence. Beth wound down her window and looked out. There was a poplar in the front yard, a freshly painted mailbox, and an overdressed fourteen-year-old girl standing nearby.

"Miranda!" Tom called.

"What?" Miranda looked around in surprise.

"Is Amy here?"

"No. I mean, I don't know."

"Are you here to see Dion?"

"No—I was just passing," Miranda said, blushing.

"Do you know where Amy is?" Beth called.

"How would I know?"

"Is Amy with Dion?"

Anger surged through Miranda at the very thought. "Who cares?" she snapped.

"Are you able to *contact* Dion?" Beth shouted.

"I'll call his cell . . ."

She was diverted to Dion's voice mail.

"He's not answering . . . ," Miranda said, her mind suddenly awash with appalling visions of Dion and Amy eloping to Las Vegas.

"Come with us in case Dion calls," Beth insisted. Miranda obeyed, and the Toyota Crown charged down the street.

Miranda was flung about in the backseat as she pulled her seat belt tight about her. "You really should get a new car," Miranda said. "In some of the modern, better cars you don't even need a map. The car tells you where to go."

"I'll tell *you* where to go if you open that pretentious yap of yours one more time, Miranda," Beth replied under her breath.

The six-wheeled machine rolled out of the M12 tunnel, and Lucy and Sam stopped pedaling in relief. Since the scooter's engine had exploded, they had cycled their connected bikes many miles, not to mention the many *before* the tunnel. Flumpy leapt out from under Lucy's arm and quickly identified the distant speck in the sky as the dachshund en route to the D.O.G.

"Attention, young Earth people. We will have to pursue Colonel Bars by means of perambulation until we locate another vehicle," Belka ordered over the loudspeaker. "Follow us!"

Lucy looked at Sam. Sam shook his head.

"He means we're going to *run* after them, guys," Strelka spoke up.

Lucy and Sam scrambled off their bikes as the terrier bolted over the nearby embankment and onto a golf course.

Colonel Bars stretched back in his chair and checked the location monitor with a smile. The D.O.G. position was creeping nearer; Belka and Strelka's position was so far behind it was a joke; Flanger was quiet, and the dachshund was flying steadily forward on autopilot. He looked out on the receding suburbs of the city and saw the great dusty sweep of the countryside looming in all directions.

"Hideous planet," said Bars.

Flanger wasn't listening. She had her eyes closed, and her favorite heavy metal could be heard pounding away from her headphones. As Bars walked over to the Meals/Beverages Unit and dialed up a beer, neither of them saw the "Low Fuel" warning blink repeatedly on the forward screens.

On Gersbach the intercom sprang to life on the Chief Controller's desk. His Number Two at the Hole Observatory Center shouted excitedly down the line.

"The wormhole, sir! Right on schedule, just as predicted—it's closing!"

"That is good news . . . ," the Chief said.

"Surely that's better than good news, sir! When the hole shuts, the planet's saved, isn't it?"

"When the hole shuts, we're saved, yes," the Chief said, and switched off the intercom.

He let his Number Two believe the best, but the Chief knew the worst.

If the hole closed right now, we'd be saved, he thought as he poured a very large drink into his last unbroken glass. *But our planet will be destroyed long before the wormhole closes completely.*

His alerter buzzed on the desk. He read the ominous message from the Gersbach Seismology Center displayed upon it: "Core of planet now dangerously unstable. Volcanoes erupting. Molten magma levels undermining core integrity—pressure on planet's crust at crisis point. Irreversible damage to planet structure imminent."

The Disturbance Of Gravity funneling through the wormhole was dramatically increasing in strength, and the Chief wondered what dark evil was responsible for it.

*   *   *

Gavin Buckley posed for photos with the Japanese tourists who had just unearthed the last corner of "Gav's Big Bone." The group laughed heartily as they posed in front of the now fully exposed D.O.G.

Gav scanned its length and realized it looked precisely like a classic cartoon version of a dog bone.

"Jeez, what a big bone!" he gasped. "Must be twenty yards!"

Belka and Strelka ran the terrier onto the ninth hole of the Royal Golf Club. As two elderly golfers teed off nearby, Sam ran up and jumped into their golf cart, standing on the accelerator and brake so that his feet could reach the controls. Lucy sprang into the passenger seat and Flumpy leapt into her lap. Sam released the brake, and the cart shot forward, bumping jauntily down the fairway.

"Look! There it is! My scooter! Pull up, driver!"

In the space of one breath Dion had seen his abandoned scooter on the new motorway, yelled to the driver, and leapt out of the cab. Amy scrambled down the embankment and gingerly stepped onto the road surface. She had hoped Dion would lift her down the last bit—but that was wishful thinking, considering his current state of mind.

Dion was devastated his scooter had been treated so barbarically. The engine was missing; the steering column was attached to two stupid bikes . . . he just couldn't believe this was happening!

"I just don't understand how a dog . . . ," he muttered. He pulled what was left of his scooter from the strangely cobbled-together vehicle. Lucy's elderly bike fell onto the road. Dion couldn't help but give it a spiteful kick as he headed back to the taxi.

"Careful!" Amy said. "That's Lucy's bike."

"Piece of junk," Dion spat nastily, barely breaking his stride.

"Dion . . ." Amy was unable to hide her disappointment. "We can't just leave it here."

Something in Amy's tone made Dion stop. He ran back, ever mindful of the taxi's meter, and, with a scowl, hoisted Lucy's bike on his shoulder.

"We *should* just leave it. What kind of moron is your sister?" he said.

"Well, I'm sure she's got her reasons. We don't know the whole story."

Dion rolled his eyes and marched up the embankment.

Amy wondered where Flanger was. She tried to remember what she had said about surviving a relationship's first fight. Amy just wanted her to come back and wave her magic wand.

Lucy saw the last house of the city drift past, and now they were officially in the country. The golf cart cruised along at an unremarkable speed, but it was much easier than riding their bikes. Sam sat at the wheel, a golf club holding the accelerator pedal to the floor. Up ahead they saw a Datsun 180B parked on the shoulder and an old man scanning the nearby field with binoculars. As they passed, Lucy recognized him.

"That's the Russian rocket man from school," she said. "Dr. Macheski."

And then Lucy and Sam saw what Macheski was looking at. A flying dachshund was veering toward a sheep truck.

"WHY DIDN'T YOU TELL ME THE FUEL WAS LOW?!" shouted Bars.

"I DID!" Flanger shouted back. "Maybe if you hadn't wasted it on flame throwers in tunnels, we'd have some! Are we going to crash?"

"Not with *me* in the seat," Bars replied. He angrily canceled the annoying "Low Fuel—DANGER!" warning blinking on the screens. Wiping the sweat from his brow, he assessed the situation. He knew he had the auxiliary fuel tank at his disposal, but that would barely service the homeward launch back through the wormhole.

There was only one thing for it. Take a leaf out of Belka and Strelka's book and use an Earth vehicle.

twenty-four

Dr. Macheski watched in wonderment as the dachshund's flames cut out and it plummeted—dramatically but accurately—into a semitrailer loaded with sheep. There was a distant "Baa!" as it landed, and the truck proceeded to turn and rumble down a gravel track. Macheski leapt into his car and exited the freeway at the next turn. In front of him was a golf cart with a very eager terrier sitting between two kids.

Belka saw the dachshund kill its engines and land in the sheep truck. He checked the location monitor and saw the source of D.O.G. loom closer. They were on track. He didn't know where the truck was headed but hoped it would take Bars and Flanger way off course.

"Sam," he said over the loudspeaker. "Follow this road to the hill and then turn left. I've got a shortcut in mind."

* * *

"Follow this road to the hill and then turn left," Dion said. The taxi driver did as commanded.

"But that takes us back home," Amy said. "We've got to find Lucy."

"I can't spend any more time *or money* chasing after your idiot sister. I've got appointments this afternoon."

"She's my little sister and she needs help. We can't just leave her," Amy said, surprised at the authority in her voice.

"Look at the meter on this taxi! The chasing of crazy sisters is not tax deductible!"

"Are you saying that your bank account is more important than our relationship?"

Dion sighed heavily and leaned forward.

His jacket rode up. Amy could read some of the words on the back of his T-shirt: BY LIVESTOCK SOMETIMES.

"Lean forward more, Dion," Amy asked sweetly.

"Huh?" Dion replied, then found himself being shoved forward.

A wave of humiliation washed over Amy. The back of Dion's T-shirt read: WE ALL HAVE OUR HEARTS BROKEN BY LIVESTOCK SOMETIMES. It was what Dion had said to her that night after the Winona story was revealed. Amy pushed Dion back into his seat, ripped his jacket clear from his chest, and gasped at what was on the front of the shirt. A fat cow, with the word "Winona" written on it, and MOO! printed below.

A thousand playground incidents replayed in Amy's mind with new understanding.

Dion realized what he was wearing and bit his lip. Amy felt a humiliated heat rise through her body and fought back tears.

"Well, this is business, baby," Dion said. "You understand, don't you? It's been a great seller!"

"How could you do this to me?" Amy wailed.

"If you want to be in business, you've got to *be in business*," Dion said.

Amy's look of fury stopped him from saying more. Dion's cell phone rang and he hastily answered it. It was Miranda Hunter.

"I'm with Amy's parents, Dion, and they are just so *amazingly* rude!" Miranda explained. "They're worried about Amy's sister. Do you know where she is?" Miranda asked under Beth Buckley's glare.

"Kind of . . . ," Dion admitted. "I wish I didn't, but I do."

"Yeah, the whole family is trouble. Hey, what are you doing tonight? Maybe we could—"

Tom reached over from the front seat and snatched the cell from Miranda's hand. "Who am I talking to?" he demanded.

"It's Dion Van Steenwyk, Mr. Buckley."

"Is my daughter with you?"

"Which one?"

"Which one have you got?"

"Amy's here and Lucy's . . . oh, somewhere around."

"Put Amy on!" Tom ordered.

"Pleasure." Dion handed the phone to Amy. He just wanted to be somewhere else.

"Where are you, Amy?" Tom asked.

"With Dion in a taxi," Amy said, relieved to hear her father's voice.

"What's happened? Where are you going? Are you OK?" Tom asked. Beth looked at him in dread.

"I'm fine . . . we just went after Flumpy, who took Dion's scooter."

"Flumpy took Dion's scooter?"

"Yes, Dad, Flumpy took it. After Nicky flew away."

Tom found the image of Nicky hovering outside his bedroom window coming back to haunt him.

"Where's Lucy?" Beth asked, frowning with worry. "Does Amy know where *Lucy* is?"

Tom asked her.

"I don't know, Dad. She went through that new road tunnel. But why would she be out here? Where's she going?"

"She wants to go back to the country," Tom guessed. "Beth—take us to Tubby Flats!"

Sam Chan wasn't an experienced driver and got a little muddled between the brake and the accelerator of the golf cart. It's a shame this confusion took place after they'd left the road, bumped across a wheat field, and found themselves perched on top of a ravine.

In a near-fatal error of judgment, Sam hit the accelerator, and the cart was propelled off the imposing cliff.

"Instigate Emergency Landing Procedures," Flumpy's computer announced. "A full surface impact from this height will destroy the ATV."

Belka and Strelka looked at each other blankly, then through the forward screens saw a rapidly approaching river.

The cart fell from under Lucy and Sam's feet and plummeted toward the water. Flumpy tumbled from Lucy's grasp.

"Instigate Emergency Landing Procedures," the ATV computer repeated. "Or Automatic Safety System will engage."

"Engage Safety System!" shouted Belka.

The cart broke the surface of the river in a great plume of water.

"Instigate Emergency Landing Procedures," the computer continued. "Or Automatic Safety System will engage."

Lucy and Sam splashed into the swirling depths.

"Automatic Safety System engaging," the computer announced calmly.

When the ATV was three feet above the river, Lucy and Sam witnessed an amazing transformation. Flumpy's head retracted into his body. So did his legs, and the torso expanded here while contracting there—turning the ATV into a furry ball. It splashed into the water, bobbed unharmed to the surface, and was swept away by the current. Lucy and Sam immediately began to swim after it, but then Sam grabbed Lucy's shoulder.

"This current—it's too dangerous. We've got to get to shore," he cautioned. Reluctantly they swam to the river's edge and hauled themselves onto the gray stones.

Belka and Strelka had no need to hold on to their seats. The Automatic Safety System featured form-fitting, transparent, rubber-like sheets that emerged from the back of their chairs and held the Galactanauts so securely in place they could barely breathe. An ominous, deep rumbling shook the ship. The powerful torrent kept pushing the craft under, toying with it like some crazed marine monster. Water sloshed about the cockpit floor, raining in from the ceiling before draining out into the lower decks. The forward screens revealed a furious swirl of dark water, a startled school of carp, a foaming wall of bubbles—and suddenly the ATV was flung from the top of a waterfall.

The craft bounced violently from one great stone on the surrounding cliff face to another, rolled across a gravel verge, and plummeted to a sticky finale in a pile of rotting vegetable matter.

"Automatic Safety System Procedure has been completed," the onboard computer announced. "Thank you for your cooperation."

The rubber sheets shot back into their receptacles, and Strelka gulped the air hungrily. Outside, the ATV sprouted legs and extended its head to the proper place; then, with a determined grimace, it powerfully shook itself.

Belka looked up at the fine trail of water dripping in from the ceiling.

"The seal's been breached," Strelka muttered, checking the ship's diagnostics report. "Back at the gnome, when the ATV fell onto the backpack of explosives!" His ears seemed to ring a little in recollection.

"If we're not watertight, we're not *airtight*. . . ." Belka frowned, shaking his head in disbelief. "Even if we could get this thing flying again, we can't use it to get home."

Strelka stared off into space. He was probably panicking, Belka thought, but with Strelka he could never really tell.

Belka switched on the windshield wipers, dislodging a moldy lettuce leaf from Flumpy's eyes. The view revealed was shocking—a windy landscape strewn with plastic bags, piles of rotting vegetables, and rusting machinery of all kinds.

"Extraordinary," said Belka. "Humans are amazing the way they waste their—" His diatribe was cut short when a filthy plastic bag blew onto Flumpy's face, wrapping around his ears. And there it stayed, billowing around them like a large white parachute.

"Firing laser," announced Strelka. As the Galactanauts watched the snout of the ATV, the laser beam shot from the left nostril and made a neat hole in the plastic bag over the craft's nose. A small twirl of smoke appeared, then the superheated plastic caught fire.

"Stay calm!" shouted Belka.

"I am," replied Strelka.

Belka quickly accessed ATV Weapons Command and Missile Launch Control. His fingers moving with precision, he removed the deadly missile in the right nostril and placed it in storage, then fired.

Firing an empty missile chamber may seem a silly thing to do. But Belka realized that water from the river would have pooled inside the missile tube, so as he pressed the launch button, a powerful spray of fish-scented water blasted the growing flames and extinguished them.

Strelka regarded his fellow Commander with the closest look to admiration he could muster. "You're a Gersbach Field Weapons Officer Class 1, right?"

"Of course." Belka smiled.

Strelka emerged from the hatch between the ATV ears. He now understood what Belka had experienced earlier. Earth's gravity was crippling for such a small man! And the stench of this garbage dump made him nauseated. He gathered his faculties and focused on their current problem. One of the handles of the plastic bag had wrapped itself twice around the ATV's left ear, leaving Flumpy's entire face covered in plastic.

"OK, Belka," he wheezed into the intercom strapped to his chest. "Rotate the left radar twice counterclockwise. That should release it."

In the cockpit Belka did as requested. The bag slipped off and blew away with the breeze.

"Yer mother," the translator announced.

Belka looked up at the screens at the same time Strelka gazed forward. There, six feet away, was a pack of large, nasty, and very hungry feral cats.

"Yer mother!" the translator repeated.

"Yer mother yer mother yer mother yer mother yer mother yer mother!" the translator added, desperately interpreting a chorus of feline voices.

A piercing alarm sounded.

"Life-forms approaching," the computer intoned. "Hostile."

"That'll be five dollars," the manager of the Tubby Flats Go-Kart Club said to Sam. Sam reached into his muddy trousers, produced a very damp bill, and scrambled into a battered, lime green go-kart.

"The starting line's over there by the old septic tank," the manager began. "Swing 'round the tractor, don't hit the chickens, go over the—"

Sam suddenly pulled the ripcord and the engine burst to life. Lucy ran around the corner of the nearby shed and leapt in. The noisy vehicle shot forward.

"Hey!" the manager called. "You can't have two drivers!"

* * *

The leader of the garbage-dump feral cats—a wild-eyed orange tomcat with mangy fur and a mangy personality to match—sniffed the air with excitement. Strelka gazed down at the spray of fish-scented water glinting on the ATV's nose. He slowly and casually turned to enter the hatch.

"Move, Strelka!" Belka barked. The tomcat rushed forward and swiped its paw at the ATV's face. Belka didn't dare move the craft for fear of dislodging Strelka. The surveillance monitor revealed a black-and-white image of Strelka moving as fast as gravity would allow him back to the outer hatch. Belka fired the empty missile tube again, and a rather pathetic spurt of water only served to anger the tomcat.

"Fire the missile!" Strelka wheezed over the intercom.

"That's our last resort," Belka said. "It'd probably blow *us* up at this range."

The tomcat gave a long, low growl of disapproval . . . and the battle was on. A vicious black cat with flaming eyes leapt onto the ATV's back. Another bit savagely into the tail, then shrank back as its fangs struck metal instead of flesh.

Strelka was one step from the elevator door when the tomcat saw him, swiped at him, and sent him flying toward the ground. Belka responded intuitively, swinging out the ATV's left paw so that Strelka landed safely in its fur. Belka fired the laser and singed the tomcat. It hissed and bared its fangs.

The black cat clinging to the ATV's back unfurled its paw, and Strelka looked up in horror as its claws descended upon him.

* * *

In the sheep truck the dachshund was shaken off its precarious woolen perch, tumbling down its host's flank into a nightmarish jungle of endless, restless sheep hooves.

Bars succeeded in navigating the dachshund to the calmest corner of the semi and looked at the location monitor.

"Belka and Strelka! Those Space Command scum!" he roared. "They're closer to the D.O.G. than we are!"

twenty-five

Beth Buckley turned the Toyota Crown off the freeway and found she was automatically driving back to their old property. It created more emotion than she cared for, coming back. The fields of wheat and old tumbledown fences looked the same, and she remembered the feeling she and Tom had shared when they first came down this road many years before.

They did have some fun back then. Mucking about like kids, the fun of being newlyweds, the amazing experience of being a mum for the first time. Watching the dazzling wrap of stars emerge from the clean twilight as Tom walked back to the homestead, smiling that lopsided grin of his.

Then the other memories flooded in. Seeing Tom smile less and less. The farm not doing so well anymore. The bottom falling out of the wool business. Gavin turning up and buying the property next to them, and his incessant visits and advice.

Finally, Tom hurting his back from working too late and too tired; then all the loans and bank business.

Their dream had fizzled so quickly.

She looked over at Tom and saw his eyes were equally misty as he looked over the familiar fields of the journey home. And then with a loud BANG, the left rear tire of the old car gave out. Miranda screamed and Beth pulled the Toyota over.

Eric Harvey's old tractor sat a short distance down the road. FOR SALE was written in red paint across its scoop. Tom leapt out of the car. He didn't want to buy the tractor, but he would *borrow* it.

The black cat swung its paw viciously at Strelka. It missed by a fraction of an inch. The sudden displacement of air (mixed with the cat's foul stench) almost sent Strelka tumbling to his doom. He grabbed even tighter to tufts of Flumpy's artificial fur. The cat's flaming eyes loomed above him, and its paw blocked out the sun.

A savage attack by a dirty white feral cat rocked the ATV, distracting the black beast and rupturing a fuel line. The white cat sprang back snarling, a fine spray of fuel from the ATV belly stinging its eyes.

Belka hopped Flumpy about, keeping the left front paw outstretched, where Strelka clung desperately. The determined black cat gripped Flumpy's head with its right front paw and swung at Strelka with its left. Strelka hurled abuse at the creature, but it had no effect. The cat secured its grip on Flumpy's head, its paw covering the ATV's eyes.

In the cockpit Belka was alarmed to see the black cat's paw unfurl across the forward screens. He was driving blind but continued to hop in a circle, singeing the cats with the laser and keeping them at a distance. His heart rate accelerated as the life-form detector screen indicated thirty more feral cats closing in.

"YER MOTHER YER MOTHER YER MOTHER!"

Belka reached for the translator. "Back off!" he commanded the cats. "Stand down!"

"YER MOTHER YER MOTHER YER MOTHER YER MOTHER!" came the angry response. Belka could swear there was a haughty sarcasm in the words too. Cats are *not* creatures to order about.

He summoned up Missile Launch Control. He knew he could easily wipe the cats out, but Strelka would probably go with them. The ship *might* survive. But he couldn't stay here forever if it meant Bars getting to the D.O.G. first. The computer announced there would be a slight delay as the missile was loaded.

"Where could they have gone?" Lucy shouted over the go-kart's wailing engine. Sam clumsily steered the machine across the dusty countryside.

"Well, they turned into a ball . . . ," Sam replied, "so they'd be pushed downstream . . ."

They drove back to the river and followed it until they reached a waterfall. Sam slowed them to a halt. Over the idling engine he could make out two sounds. One was the pleasant SWOOSH of the waterfall, and the other was the terrible howling of angry cats.

Belka's hopping-in-a-circle method had not only made Strelka physically ill all over the left paw, but had also created a moat of fuel around the ship from the ruptured fuel line. The advancing cats had grown wise to the firing laser and were leaping aside. One laser beam just missed a gray, homicidal-looking cat and shot into a pile of broken glass bottles. The laser beam hit a reflective surface, bounced back at an angle, narrowly missed one of Flumpy's legs, and plowed into the moat of fuel.

The fuel detonated.

A circular wall of flame erupted around the ATV to a height of two yards, and an enormous BANG! echoed about the garbage dump. When the smoke cleared, the cats were gone.

Belka smiled, stood the missile down, and observed a warning signal indicating the fuel-line rupture. Fuel wasn't really an issue for them anymore, as they would never fly with only one operational rocket leg, but he didn't like the idea of trailing an explosive liquid behind them. He flipped on the intercom as he raised the left front paw up to the cockpit windows. There was Strelka, still clinging on, though a bit worse for wear.

"While you're out there, do you mind having a look at a fuel-line problem?" Belka suggested.

Strelka was about to make a particularly rude gesture when he was distracted by the squealing engine of an approaching go-kart.

A relieved Lucy held Flumpy on her lap as the go-kart shot across the landscape of scribbly-gum trees. Within the ATV Strelka emerged from the bathroom and sat stiffly in his chair. He burped as Belka entered the cockpit and announced that the fuel line had been resealed.

"Terrific," Strelka said, without enthusiasm.

"How are you feeling?"

"Bit funny," Strelka replied. He hiccuped loudly. His body suddenly convulsed, and he disgorged a matted lump of fur onto the console.

"What's that?" Belka asked with disgust.

"Fur ball," Strelka said wearily. "Feel much better now."

"Bars!" Belka exclaimed, observing the location monitor. "He's right beside us!" He turned Flumpy's head and saw the sheep truck rumbling parallel to them.

"Why *are* they in that truck?" Strelka asked.

"Perhaps their flight system is damaged . . . ," Belka suggested, frowning.

"If they can't fly anymore, *we* can't get home either!"

"We're all marooned on Earth together, in that case," Belka said.

Strelka looked aghast at the thought.

"Well, until the ATV life-support systems give out, anyway," Belka added. "Which wouldn't be long."

Belka noticed Strelka's growing unease at these revelations and decided to shut up. He studied the location monitor, saw the D.O.G. position indicator drift onto the screen, and flipped on the loudspeaker. "Sam, veer left a bit. Only two miles to go!"

"That'd be Uncle Gav's farm!" Lucy exclaimed. "What's on Uncle Gav's farm?"

"The source of danger to their planet!" Sam said, realizing. "Remember how they said they had to get to it? It must be on your Uncle Gav's farm!"

The go-kart emerged from a small thicket of trees and hurtled through the Tubby Flats Dog Show. Groomed hounds and the show judge looked up at the approaching engine sound as

Sam split the group like Moses parting the Red Sea. From the ATV Strelka saw a wall of legs scrambling for cover and instinctively hit the horn in the cockpit. Flumpy barked loudly. The show dogs, excited by the speeding terrier, gave chase, and a great pack of perfectly shampooed and clipped pets ran off after the go-kart.

The dachshund popped its head out the side of the sheep truck. Bars was standing in the cockpit, fists clenched with excitement as he watched the location monitor and the approaching D.O.G. At the rear of the truck he saw a go-kart bounce onto the road and squeal up behind them in pursuit. The smile faded from Bars' face when he saw a familiar terrier stand up in Lucy's lap and woof at him.

"Your friends are back," Flanger observed coolly. "Persistent, aren't they?"

Bars turned a deep, throbbing shade of red.

The go-kart caught up easily with the truck and attempted to overtake it. The truck driver, smiling warmly as he jigged along to a yodeling medley, never looked in his rearview mirrors and trundled down the center of the road as he always did. Sam drew the go-kart alongside the truck and hastily braked, just avoiding the treacherous ditch that ate into the road's edge.

"It's no good!" he yelled over the engine roar. "The road's too narrow! We can't pass!"

"If we stop the truck, I'm pretty sure we'll trap Bars," Belka said over the loudspeaker.

"I'll climb along the truck to the driver," Sam said. "Get him to stop."

"That's too dangerous!" Lucy yelled, feeling a sweat break across her brow.

"What else can we do?" Sam stated. "Take the wheel, Lucy."

"But I'm the better climber!"

"You? You can't even swing on the monkey bars anymore."

Lucy turned crimson. Sam moved aside, easing Lucy's foot into place on the accelerator and putting her hands on the steering wheel.

"Keep it steady," Sam said.

Lucy felt terrified. The go-kart was not actually going *that* fast, but the wind blowing through her hair and the occasional wisp of wool in her face had her senses on edge. Sam slid slowly from the seat. Flumpy sat motionless on Lucy's lap. Sam balanced precariously, his feet on either side of Lucy. He was absolutely terrified but refused to let it show.

"Take us closer to the truck, Lucy!" he shouted over the wind and noise.

Lucy pushed gradually on the accelerator, and the go-kart eased up to the truck's rear.

Sam raised his hands, fingers poised to grab the truck's railings.

"Here I go!" he shouted. Leaping at the truck with all his might, he flew a yard and grabbed a railing—then slipped and fell. Lucy screamed as Sam missed every handhold before his jacket sleeve caught on a rail edge and jerked him to a halt. He dangled from the truck like a broken puppet, secured only by a thin strip of cheap material. Terrified, he reached up with his free hand to secure a hold. His feet barely swung clear of the gravel road racing by underneath.

Lucy was paralyzed with fear. She knew she had the ability to save him—but something was once again holding her back. She heard a chorus of her classmates' voices chanting, "Bush monkey! Bush monkey! BUSH MONKEY!"

"Help me!" Sam shouted.

"I . . . I just can't . . ."

"I can't hold on forever!"

"It's just that I'm . . . I can't do it anymore, I'm . . ."

Sam's foot dragged across the ground, and a shower of stones kicked up at the go-kart. He tried to swing himself up but caught his foot between the railings. Suddenly his jacket ripped, his body twisted, and he was left dangling upside down with his hair running through the gravel.

"LUCY! PLEASE!"

Lucy trembled uncontrollably. She hated this feeling. She despised feeling weak. She hated her body—it felt like someone else controlled it.

"What are you waiting for?" Strelka snapped. "What's eating you?"

"The kids in school!" Lucy blurted out.

"What about them?" Strelka asked.

"They call me *bush monkey*!"

"Big deal. Who cares what they say?"

"I do. Dad says I've got to fit in. But the kids say I'm dumb and I'm just a stupid monkey up a tree." Tears were rolling down Lucy's face. "They tease me and they hate me and I'll never have any friends there."

"But isn't Sam your friend?" Strelka asked.

"He's my only friend!" Lucy cried out.

"Well, help him then!"

Lucy started to move, then stopped.

"Oh, stop feeling sorry for yourself. So what if you're a monkey!" Strelka exclaimed. "We're *all* monkeys! But you're a very *good* monkey. Those kids at school are *lousy* monkeys. I bet they can't climb a tree as well as you. I bet they can't run as fast as you or jump as far. I bet they can't do anything! Look, Lucy—if you're a monkey, then you're a monkey, and you shouldn't try and be anything else! Just be a *great* monkey. Right?"

"Yes . . . ," Lucy replied uncertainly.

"So get your great baboon butt up there and save your friend!"

Lucy felt a little wave of confidence break over her. Strelka was right. Why should she change because she was in the city? Who gave anyone the right to tell Lucy Buckley what to do and what to enjoy? Lucy could jump! And leap! She was good at it, and that's what she was going to do!

"Flumpy—take the wheel!" she ordered.

Belka immediately grabbed the steering wheel with Flumpy's mouth. Strelka extended the hind paw to press down on the accelerator.

Sam stared at Lucy, terrified.

"Don't worry, Sam!" Lucy called out bravely. She stood up. "Take me close, Flumpy!" she commanded. The go-kart pulled in directly behind the truck. A stray piece of gravel whizzed through the air and struck Lucy's cheek. She paid it no attention. This truck wasn't going to get the best of her. It was a tree, that's all it was. A tree like any other she used to leap on and climb up.

In her mind she saw Melissa Blume and Bradley Ditchfield

and all the others teasing her—and bet not one of them would've been half as brave as Sam had been today.

Lucy focused on the truck's middle railing and imagined grabbing it and swinging her feet under the lower rung for support. That's the way it's done. Visualize success.

The truck rumbled and shook.

Sam looked at her with pleading eyes.

The wind roared through Lucy's hair and stung her eyes.

As she concentrated, the sound seemed to die down, and in the calm silence all she could see was that rail. That was where she was going. Nothing could stop her.

Lucy leapt.

Her hands grabbed the intended rail, and her sneakers swung under the lower railing. The sound of the world snapped back into place around her, and Lucy smiled in satisfaction. Her body had a new manager—and that manager's name was Lucy Buckley.

"Way to go, Lucy!" Belka shouted. And Lucy felt the happiest she had in a long, long time.

twenty-six

"Belka and Strelka are right behind us!" Flanger nagged, pointing at the location monitor.

"I don't care!" Bars retorted. "We've got to find a way out of this sheep hell!"

The dachshund waddled under the thick canopy of heaving sheep, looking for an escape route. As it scraped one ovine belly after another, it was kicked about by bad-tempered legs.

Lucy leapt across the fluffy sea of sheep and hammered furiously on the truck cabin's roof. The driver looked out of his window in shock.

"Crikey!" he said, and hit the brakes.

Lucy ran to the rear of the truck, clambered down like a monkey, and eased the upended Sam to the ground.

"Thanks, Lucy," Sam breathed in relief, his face red as a beet. The go-kart skidded to a stop, and Flumpy leapt out.

A loud commotion erupted at the back of the truck when a familiar dachshund popped out from between the startled sheep and pulled up the gate handle. A quick head-butt pushed the gate open, and Nicky prepared to spring to freedom. But he was instantly swamped by a flood of escaping sheep leaping onto the ground.

"Enough!" Bars shouted as he was thrown about inside the cockpit. "Launch!"

The sheep scattered as the dachshund rose on a tower of fire, cleared the truck, and flew at great speed toward Uncle Gav's farm.

Flumpy ran after Nicky. The sheep chased after Flumpy.

Sam and Lucy followed in the go-kart. A rattling Datsun 180B joined in the chase, and a wall of impeccably groomed dogs brought up the rear.

Sergeant Terry O'Loghlin of the Tubby Flats Police Department was never *that* busy as a rule. He was the only police officer for one hundred miles of farms, and the only police incident he could remember was last year's feisty refusal by Tom Buckley to leave his property when the bank foreclosed on him. O'Loghlin had intervened, but it was Tom's brother, Gav, who had talked him into behaving reasonably.

The funny thing was, the *very next day* Sergeant O'Loghlin was paying his rent at the Tubby Flats Real Estate/Burger Bar when he bumped into Gav, who was suddenly the new owner of Tom Buckley's land. O'Loghlin sometimes wondered about that chain of events.

Regardless, the district was abuzz with news of Gav's Big Bone. Literally busloads of tourists were coming in, digging it out, and enjoying a barbecue of Gav's funny-tasting (but top-selling) "gourmet" sausages.

But right now the thing uppermost in Sergeant O'Loghlin's mind was a small white terrier dog running toward him at amazing speed. Behind it was a flock of sheep moving with a conviction O'Loghlin had never seen before, and behind them a go-kart, a Datsun 180B, and an amazing cross section of beautifully coiffed dogs belted along in close formation. O'Loghlin stood in front of the charging group and, not knowing quite what else to do, held up his hand as if stopping traffic. A thin red beam shot out of the terrier's nose and made O'Loghlin's leather boot sizzle. He shoved his burning foot into a cowpat by the side of the road and watched the curious procession scamper by.

"Missile in range," the computer announced.

"What's that?" Belka asked.

"I programmed the computer to let us know when the missile was in striking range of the D.O.G.," Strelka explained. "I figured we could just blow it up—no more problem."

Belka looked at the location monitor. The D.O.G. was now just over the hill. Right next to the D.O.G., however, was a human life-form indicator; and bearing down on both of them was Nicky. Belka sighed in exasperation and sank in his chair.

"A missile strike now would take them *all* out," he declared. "Including that human."

"No more bad guys, no more D.O.G.—one human down, is that such a big deal versus all of Gersbach?" Strelka asked.

Belka thought, his fingers drumming the console in front of him.

"The missile is a last resort," he affirmed, and thrust the throttle forward.

On Gersbach, Space Command's Chief Controller studied the seismology report as the latest earthquake cracked his computer screen in two. In the fragments of screen left operational, he read:

"Planet Gersbach's core is moments from critical chain reaction. If Disturbance Of Gravity not terminated immediately, entire surface of Gersbach will be inundated with molten lava. Damage irreversible. Expect total extinction of life."

The Chief Controller did not, for the first time in his long career, know precisely how to react. Then he did, and the impulse to do so was overwhelming.

He screamed.

twenty-seven

Gavin Buckley had just shooed the last of the Big Bone tourists away. He was reluctant to do so, but his supply of gourmet sausages was running low, and that meant firing up the slaughterhouse again. It seemed best not to have tourists witnessing *that* part of his operation. Shame the Big Bone happened to be in eyeshot of the slaughterhouse. Still, now that the Big Bone was raking in the bucks, he could probably afford to move the slaughterhouse over the hill and keep the blades turning day and night! He headed to the shed to fetch some animals. The supply of them was running low too. . . .

He looked up and thought his dreams had been answered. Running down the hill toward him, leaping through any available gap in the wooden fence, was a beautiful selection of perfectly sized sheep and dogs. Though they were still way off, he could tell from their speed they were young and sprightly—not an ounce of fat or rangy meat on them! He rushed to the corralling gates of his slaughterhouse but lost his smile as he saw the police SUV of Sergeant O'Loghlin pull up on the hill. The policeman leapt out and clambered over the fence. Behind him two kids in a go-kart—one of whom looked just like Lucy—skidded to a stop. A Datsun 180B arrived in a cloud of dust, and behind it a taxi lurched to a halt. Behind *that* a tractor arrived—with the unmistakable form of Gav's brother, Tom Buckley, at the wheel. Beth clung to Tom's waist, while some weedy city girl clung to her.

Gav had a sinking feeling.

The taxi driver finally switched off the deafening music. He turned to Dion and Amy, who picked themselves off the floor after the abrupt halt.

"That'll be $350, mate," he said. "Plus the tolls . . . $430."

As Dion handed over his credit card, Amy thought she saw his hand tremble.

"Do you want me to stay?" the driver asked cheerfully. "Are you going back?"

"Are you kidding? I'd rather walk," Dion said.

Amy didn't know what to say. Where was Flanger?

Belka and Strelka pulled up at Gav's Big Bone. The D.O.G. location monitor beeped triumphantly, and Belka knew they had finally made it. Sheep and show dogs gathered around them, panting and shuffling. Belka reached for the translator, but Strelka pushed his hand away. Belka studied his colleague as Strelka rose solemnly to his feet. There was something unusual about his demeanor. His stance was proud and dignified—not unlike that of Napoleon before addressing his troops.

"Furry animals of Earth!" Strelka commanded. "Cover the big white thing!"

The assembly of dogs and sheep bounded off and surrounded the Big Bone. A regiment of German shepherds plumed dirt across it, their paws working feverishly, excited barks echoing across the paddocks. The flock of sheep nosed whatever they could find over the bone, and Gav's crowning achievement was soon disappearing under a mound of dirt and debris.

"NO!" bellowed Gav. "Get away, you mongrels! GO ON! SHOO!"

He tried to move the animals from their task, but they growled ferociously, holding their ground.

Bars and Flanger, meanwhile, were running across Gav's Big Bone, trying to find a loose enough piece of D.O.G. to place in the cargo hold. It was no easy task, as the great white bone was very solid, and by standing directly on it they ran the risk of being buried under a mound of dirt. Occasionally they saw Belka and Strelka's ATV sniffing them out, its little head and bright eyes popping up over the backs of animals, trying to find them.

"Over there!" Bars snapped at Flanger, pointing to the far side of the Big Bone.

There lay his prize.

A crumbling edge of D.O.G. made easy pickings, and Nicky tore free a foot-long chunk. Handlike clamps descended from the belly, grasped the Big Bone piece, and began winching it into the cargo hold. As Flanger completed the stowage process, Bars switched to the auxiliary fuel tank and fired up the ATV for one last flight—the flight back home. As the rocket paws belched smoke, the cloud of exhaust began to frighten away nearby animals. Belka realized immediately what was happening.

"Get us over there, Strelka!" Belka commanded. "They're taking off with that piece of D.O.G.!"

Strelka ran Flumpy over to the dachshund and stood nose to nose with it. Through the screens they saw Bars laughing at them, waving goodbye. The cargo doors in the dachshund's belly began to close, and the spacecraft began to ascend.

"Fire me as a missile," Belka commanded, "into the cargo hold of that ship."

"That's, ah, risky . . . you probably won't—" Strelka began, but Belka cut him off.

"Just do it!" he ordered, rifling through the Weapons Store. He grabbed a canister of Personal Anti-Flea Spray, pushed it down his boot, and ran off to Flumpy's nose. Strelka switched the panel in front of him to Missile Launch Control.

The dachshund rose slowly into the sky. Flanger joined Bars in the cockpit.

"The D.O.G. is almost in place," she informed him. "Can we get off this boring planet and go home now?"

"Home . . . ," Bars said, almost whimsically. "When I get home, I'm going to sit on the beach, breathe in the ocean air, and watch the sunset with a bottle of vintage champagne. Then I'm going to have everyone in Space Command thrown into a vat of boiling acid. And I think I'll put all left-handed people in chains . . ."

"But, evil overlord—if we take the D.O.G. to Gersbach, won't it destroy *us* too?"

"Oh, we won't land with it! We'll put this craft into orbit around Gersbach. The wormhole will close behind us, but the earthquakes will continue. *We'll* be perfectly safe up here in the cockpit." Bars smiled. "The government will yield to our ransom demands within minutes. They'll have to."

Flanger looked at her nails.

"Anyway, then I've got a score to settle with my old football coach. What about you? What will you do?"

For some reason a vision of Flanger's parents flashed into her mind, and for some even stranger reason she didn't want to laugh at them and tell them how old and stupid they were like she usually did. In fact, she almost felt like she wanted to give them a hug. Flanger took a deep breath, and the silly feeling soon passed.

Inside the missile tube Belka folded his arms across his chest and braced himself for launch. When Strelka saw his fellow Galactanaut on the Missile Status Screen, he aimed the red gun sight at the dachshund's rapidly closing cargo doors.

"Locked on," the computer confirmed.

"Fire!" said Strelka, hitting the launch button.

Belka flew between the front paws of the flying dachshund and collided with a folding cargo door, but a remnant lump of putrid dog food cushioned his impact. As he hauled himself clear of the mess, he rolled dangerously close to the door's edge. He just missed being cut in two as the cargo doors clanged shut, locking him in.

The enormous piece of Gav's Big Bone swung heavily above him as the engines roared deafeningly. The smell of rotting dog food was overwhelming. Belka ran to the Manual Cargo Door

Control at the rear of the ship, narrowly avoiding slipping in a puddle of marrowbone jelly.

"One of them's onboard!" Bars bellowed, stabbing his greasy fingers at the little figure on the surveillance monitor. "He's in the cargo hold!"

He turned to Flanger like a patronizing parent. "Now, I'm going to ask you to do something . . ."

"Yeah?"

"I want you to go down to the hold, find the man who's come onboard, and kill him. Do you think you can do that, or do you want *me* to go while you stay here?"

"All right! I can go!" Flanger shouted, not appreciating his condescending tone. She snapped her fingers and strode from the cockpit. Her gang of fleas bounced after her.

Strelka watched the dachshund turn slowly as it rose higher and higher in the sky. Dangerous amounts of time were passing. Belka had probably failed, he thought reluctantly. Now he had to make a difficult decision. He activated Missile Launch Control once again and locked in the coordinates of the ascending craft.

"Locked on," the computer confirmed without emotion.

Strelka hit a series of buttons and watched the monitor as the missile was rolled into the launch tube and secured.

"Missile ready for launch," the computer said. Strelka reluctantly reached for the bright red "Fire" button.

Belka found the manual controls for the cargo doors, pulled the "Open" lever, and watched the heavy doors swing open. Noise and wind enveloped him, bashing every crevice of the ship. He realized the piece of D.O.G. was held at either end by large black metal clamps that resembled two robotic hands. He triumphantly pressed the "Release" button on the Manual Clamp Control, and the clamp closest to him sprang open—but the one by the dachshund's front paws did not. The heavy piece of D.O.G. swung down and forward as the front clamp stubbornly held on. The dachshund's head was dragged earthward by the sudden shift of weight. Belka tumbled through the open cargo doors and out into the blinding sunlight. A hand reached out to grab him and pulled him effortlessly back into the hold.

"Commander Belka," Flanger said. "So nice to finally meet you."

twenty-eight

Strelka saw the piece of D.O.G. dangling from the dachshund and smiled in relief. The craft couldn't fly into space like that. In fact, it had lost altitude.

"Missile stand-down," Strelka commanded.

"Confirmed," the computer said.

With a roar from the front-paw rockets, the dachshund's grimy metal deck leveled beneath Flanger's feet. "Commander Sparkleman: *hero*," she said, circling Belka and sizing him up. "Is that on your job description?"

"Flanger Damka, I am an officer of Gersbach Space Command and I am placing you under arrest."

"You haven't read me my rights."

"What rights?" Belka asked, thrown by her question.

"Do I have the right to remain silent?"

"Yes."

"Do I have the right to kick you in the bum?"

"Certainly not."

Flanger leapt behind him in a heartbeat and, despite knowing full well she had absolutely no right, swung her boot into Belka's rear end.

"Do I have the right to punch you in the stomach?"

"NO," Belka fumed, turning to her.

She immediately doubled him over with two rapid blows to his midsection.

"I suppose pinning you to the floor with my boot isn't on either?"

Belka had no time to answer before his legs were kicked out from under him and he felt Flanger's heel pressing against his chest.

"I don't understand, Commander, there seems to be something *wrong* with your *rights*."

Belka realized words were obviously going to have no effect on Flanger. In a flash he whipped the canister of Anti-Flea Spray out of his boot. But Flanger's reaction was even faster. She snatched the canister from his hand and threw it up into the hold. It clattered to a halt on the central walkway one floor up.

"*Never* threaten me," Flanger said, driving her boot harder into Belka's chest.

"Ms. Damka, can I ask you something?" Belka managed to say, despite difficulty breathing.

"Oh, I'm sorry, Commander, but I can't go out with you," Flanger said with false sincerity. "I mean, I'm flattered, but I don't think of you like that." She applied more pressure with her boot. "It's just not there. We're like brother and sister. It'd ruin our friendship. I'm not looking at the moment. There's somebody else. I'm too busy with my career. I'm thinking of going overseas soon, so I don't want to start anything right now. I don't go out with guys I work with. But most of all . . . you're just too UGLY!" With this, Flanger pushed down as hard as she could. She pushed so hard, in fact, that it was easy for Belka to yank her other leg from under her and scramble free. Flanger fell to the floor. Belka leapt on her chest and pinned her down.

"Are you stalking me?" Flanger asked, keeping up her act.

"I'm placing you under—" Belka began, but before he could finish, a dozen fleas jumped him and splayed him across the floor.

"Why are you doing this, Ms. Damka?" Belka asked. He decided to try and reason with her. "Why are you working for a madman like Colonel Bars?"

Flanger saw red. "I'm not working for HIM!" she screamed, towering above Belka. "I work for ME!"

"You're not very grateful," Belka said, sensing her weakness. "After all he's done for you."

"He's done *nothing* for me! I busted *him* out of jail!"

"So you're partners? Gersbach can look forward to being reigned over by King Bars and Queen Flanger for the next hundred years, can it?"

Flanger had never thought about that. She certainly didn't want to stay with Bars forever. The very idea made her feel ill.

"Of course, if you're not here under your own free will, that would be different," Belka continued. "If you were brainwashed by him, then you're just as much a victim of Bars' evil as the rest of us. We're after *Bars*. We don't want you," Belka said, offering her a way out. "Well, Strelka wants you, I suppose," he added as an afterthought.

"Strelka?"

"My partner is a fan of yours," Belka said, rolling his eyes.

"Just what I need. Another straight-laced official type telling me how to run my life!"

This description of Strelka would have made Belka laugh out loud had he not been in a situation of extreme danger. Or if he had a sense of humor.

"Of course, if you'd prefer to spend the rest of your life with Colonel Bars . . . ," Belka said.

Flanger stared back at Belka as the image of Bars and herself sitting on matching thrones flashed into her mind.

"Nice try, Commander," Flanger said. "But your amateur psychology won't work on me."

Nevertheless, whether it was Belka's doing or not, Flanger couldn't rid herself of the terrible thought of being with the repulsive Bars for the rest of her life.

Bars hauled the straining dachshund craft a few feet higher and looked at the cargo-hold monitor screen. Flanger was circling a spread-eagled Belka, toying with him.

"Will you stop playing around down there and kill him!" he bawled over the intercom. "Get the D.O.G. back in the hold and get up here!"

The dachshund craft again pitched forward, dragged earthward when a gusty breeze caught the piece of D.O.G. Cursing, Bars compensated by putting full power to the front-paw rockets, and the craft leveled again.

*　*　*

Time was slipping away. Belka raised his watch and checked the wormhole countdown. Only ninety minutes left until it closed. He had to reassess his strategy.

He stopped trying to bring Flanger into his confidence and tried to put her into a headlock instead.

She sprang easily from his grasp. Two of Flanger's flea friends rammed Belka from behind, and he teetered dangerously over the edge of the open cargo doors. He jumped to safety and Flanger leapt upon him. She wrestled him facedown to the floor, twisting his arms painfully behind his back.

Belka sprang onto his back in a wrestling move, pressing Flanger to the floor. She squirmed and shouted beneath him, and her fleas bounced in for a vicious attack. Their bites were painful—but the overexcited fleas were also biting into Flanger's flailing limbs, and she screamed at them to back off. They jumped into the hold to watch the Gersbacians fight it out.

With a yell Flanger hurled Belka into the air. He was astonished at her strength—he almost hit the ceiling. He grabbed for a rocket engine coolant pipe, missed, and began falling to certain death through the open cargo doors, but just managed to grab the guardrails of the central walkway one floor up. As he dangled precariously over the yawning chasm, Flanger leapt up onto the walkway in one effortless bound and strolled casually in his direction. Belka hauled himself over the rail and collapsed. Flanger ran at him, her face contorted in fury. A rush of turbulence dipped the craft momentarily, and a small metal cylinder rolled down the walkway to Belka. It was the canister of Personal Anti-Flea Spray. He threw himself at the can and pointed it at Flanger, uncertain how effective the spray would be on a half-flea person.

Flanger saw the spray can and stopped dead.

"There's a certain flea component to you that doesn't like this stuff, isn't there, Flanger?" Belka said, getting to his feet and backing her slowly down the walkway. A flea sprang at him from behind, and Belka quickly spun around and sprayed it, instantly knocking it out. Flanger leapt toward the distracted Belka and raised her fist to strike him. Belka swung back and calmly delivered a precise dose of spray in her direction. She crumpled to the ground, clasping her chest. Belka stepped across her and slid down the ladder to the cargo hold's lower level.

The fleas gathered angrily, furious at this man for treating their mistress so contemptibly.

"You don't belong here, you know," Belka told them.

He was playing a dangerous card. No one but Colonel Bars really knew the IQ of the super fleas, but Belka was about to find out.

"Your kind originally came from Earth," Belka explained. One of the fleas cocked its head to one side, as a dog does when trying to understand something.

"Your kind is *meant to live on Earth,* on the furry creatures," Belka continued. "Ask yourselves, have you ever really felt completely at home on Gersbach? How would you like living here on Earth . . . on the dog animals? Sucking the *delicious* blood through the *succulent* skins!"

One of the fleas scurried over to the open cargo doors. It looked over the edge and saw the pack of dogs burying the Big Bone below. The rest of the fleas joined their friend and saw one dog in particular standing out—a fat, shaggy, juicy sheepdog.

"So what do you say?" Belka asked smoothly. "More life as slaves and pets, or . . . ?"

The fleas seemed to think for a moment before one leapt over the edge. It floated down and landed on the sheepdog. The other fleas quickly followed, jumping out like a squad of paratroopers.

As his new residents touched down, their canine home had a quick scratch, then resumed burying the Big Bone.

Belka swung to the Manual Cargo Door Control and punched the "Shut" button. The doors whirred into place.

"NO!!" bellowed Flanger.

As the doors boomed shut, the front clamp's cable was severed. The piece of D.O.G. plummeted to the ground and shattered, then was promptly covered in dirt by a dozen dog muzzles.

In the dachshund cockpit, Bars was flung to the rear of the cabin. His head hit the bulkhead, which knocked him out. The drop of the D.O.G. had removed the weight for which the front-paw rockets had been so powerfully compensating. Now that the D.O.G. was gone, the rockets shot the craft into an almost vertical position.

Strelka saw his chance. Flumpy couldn't fly, but he could *jump*. Strelka leapt the ATV into the air on a direct collision course with the dachshund's butt.

But he didn't collide. He docked.

A loud CLANG reverberated throughout both ships, and the connected craft sank two yards in the air. They started a slow spin—the dachshund's rocket paws keeping them airborne at a tremendous cost to fuel.

* * *

A revived Flanger had sprung toward Belka at the same time the dachshund was upended. With a startled cry she fell through the hold to the A.N.O.S., then through an exit she'd never seen before. It was the brilliantly lit docking tunnel from ATV to ATV, and Flanger ramped down Flumpy's tongue and landed heavily on the Throat-Level Elevator doors. The air was punched from her body, and she felt like she was going to pass out.

Bruised and fighting for consciousness, she tried to sit upright but instead toppled toward Flumpy's cargo hold. As the ship was now vertical, this was not unlike falling down an empty, pitch-black, ten-story grain silo toward a certain death. She was bracing herself for the long drop when the elevator doors hissed open and an arm reached out and grabbed her wrist. The arm strained with her weight but managed to pull her to safety. Flanger's eyes flickered open and settled upon the flushed face of her savior, Commander Strelka Frunkmaster. She instinctively kicked back from her sworn enemy and began to topple into the cargo hold again. But again Strelka caught her, drawing her close. She gazed up at his concerned eyes, bewildered by his gallant rescue but grateful nonetheless. With a slight smile she fell unconscious in his arms.

Strelka gazed at the woman he had pursued for so long. She was even more beautiful than in any of her photos—and he had dozens of them. In fact, she was without a doubt the most beautiful woman he'd ever seen.

It was true that she was a dangerous criminal, and it was true she probably wanted to kill him, but he'd had much worse starts to relationships.

twenty-nine

Belka had been mentally prepared for the upending of the dachshund. In fact, he had been counting on it to dispose of Flanger. He sprang to the central walkway, which, now vertical, served as an excellent ladder up to the cockpit.

He patted himself on the back for successfully disposing of the D.O.G., but now he needed to secure the dachshund for the flight home.

He gazed at his watch. The wormhole was due to close in eighty minutes! Only eighty minutes to take over this ship and get Strelka and himself back home. It was possible . . . in fact, only one thing stood in Belka's way: Colonel Bars.

Bars regained consciousness in the upturned dachshund cabin and wiped the bleeding gash on his head. Woozy, he scrambled up the handrails to the cockpit controls and lay back in his seat. A quick scan of the ship's diagnostic report revealed he'd lost his cargo. The precious piece of D.O.G. *was gone*! He convulsed in rage and beat the console until he managed to settle down enough to study the rest of the report.

He made an amazing discovery. The other ATV was attached to the dachshund's rear! And more interesting—if he was reading the data correctly—he seemed to be able to communicate with the other ship's computer! He logged into it and activated the camera in the rival ATV's cockpit. Flanger seemed to have Strelka tied to his chair! Excellent! He studied the other ship's status and found, amidst a long list of systems operating below par, that it had breached the seal on its outer hatch. He smiled as he realized the enemy ship was no longer spaceworthy. He checked out Flumpy's rocket legs and found all but the left rear were disabled.

A thought struck him. Could he *command* this other ship? He connected the two ATV computers and realized he could. He powered up a program and assumed control of the two spacecraft.

"Very good idea, Colonel Bars," Belka's voice whispered in his ear. Bars spun to face him but was immediately handcuffed. Belka then reached over and fired Flumpy's rear rocket leg. The craft powered upward, and the docked ATVs shot into a level position. Bars huffed in fury as Belka wrestled him expertly to the floor and secured his feet with electrical tape from the Weapons Store.

* * *

Strelka was a little concerned. He thought back to his training. Had he been taught about securing hostile combatants in battle conditions? If he had, was it okay to let them have a nice hot bath?

Flanger emerged from Flumpy's bathroom. She looked, and felt, *beautiful*. The dog food was out of her hair and her nails, her teeth were clean, and she was wearing a nice, fresh bathrobe. The scent of perfume drifted pleasantly behind her.

"Boy! Does that feel good!" she said. "You've no idea what it was like on that prototype ship—those *primitive* facilities!"

Strelka eyed her uneasily from his chair. Flanger's bright red scarf bound him to it.

"I thought fleas didn't like water," he said.

"I'm still a woman, Commander Strelka," Flanger purred. "Now, what shall I do with you?"

Belka took the dachshund's controls and began piloting the docked ships back to the ground. They dropped slowly, inch by inch. Belka was acutely aware he could not afford to damage the craft in any way. It was their one way home.

Suddenly he felt, more than heard, a curious sound. It was a kind of whistling, almost beyond his upper limit of hearing. He turned to Bars and saw him sitting up awkwardly and pursing his lips.

"What are you . . . ," Belka began, then followed Bars' gaze to the ceiling. Scuttling from a duct were six large, glistening black fleas. They surveyed the scene below and sprang to the floor. Belka felt a pit in his stomach. These weren't ordinary fleas. They came up to Belka's knees in height, moved in formation, and gleamed an almost impossibly shiny black.

"Not only are they ten times the size, Belka," Bars laughed. "They're ten times as smart, and will defend me to the death. Meet my Elite Guard!"

In a creepy display of superior intelligence, one flea ripped the electrical tape effortlessly from Bars' ankles while another chomped through his handcuffs. Belka was shocked to see bright, sharp teeth make easy work of the sturdy metal chain. Bars stood up menacingly. The fleas gathered on either side of him, in full battle readiness.

"Kill him! Now!" Bars ordered. "And try and make it hurt a lot too."

The fleas sprang forward. Belka dove under the pack, pulling out his canister of flea spray. As the fleas quickly turned after him, he hit the closest beast with a full blast. It coughed momentarily, then resumed its attack.

"I improved the species with this batch," Bars explained, leisurely taking a seat to watch the battle. "You'll be impressed . . ."

The first flea leapt at Belka's head. The Galactanaut ducked, and the creature sailed through the open door of the latrine. Belka dove after it and slammed the door shut behind them. Great dents rippled along the door surface as the flea's fellow soldiers tried to gain entrance. The captured flea sprang onto Belka's face. It took all of Belka's strength to keep its rows of deadly teeth at a safe distance. The flea's six legs encircled his throat and began to squeeze the life out of him. Twin hooks at the end of each leg began to pierce his flesh. He rammed the beast against the cistern, desperately trying to dislodge it. The flea's proboscis—a slashing, blood-sucking tube powerful enough to puncture animal hide—extended toward Belka's face. It loomed grotesquely, quivered in bloodlust, and aimed for Belka's throat.

"If you want it, you can have it!" Belka yelled. He bent the end of the proboscis, and the flea sprang back in pain. Belka shoved the creature into the toilet bowl and held it there, flushing the latrine repeatedly until the beast grew still.

Belka burst back into the cockpit and slammed the door shut behind him. Bars laughed at the strain on Belka's face.

"Be careful about angering the fleas, Belka! They might damage the ship!"

Bars snapped his fingers, pointed at the location monitor, and an elite flea dove into it, smashing it to pieces in an explosion of glass and sparks. Bars snapped his fingers again, and another flea destroyed the right guidance column. Bars pointed ahead, and yet another of his hardcore guard rammed a forward screen and splintered it. Belka knew another hit would cause irreparable damage.

Belka swiped the discarded flea spray canister from the floor and threw it into the heated remains of the monitor. It exploded and set fire to the nearest pilot seat. Black strips of vinyl curled back and melted, sending a plume of dark smoke up to the Cockpit Environment Monitor. The antifire system reacted. A large surge of gas descended, and Belka and Bars coughed and spluttered. The fire was extinguished, and the fleas were momentarily confused.

"Ah! Good try, Belka! Fleas hate water, but the antifire systems are gas based nowadays!" Bars called out through the haze.

Belka knew this but hoped the gas would have some effect on the fleas. Though the comment about water had given him an idea. He ran to the fire cabinet at the rear of the cockpit. A determined flea cartwheeled through the air toward him like a huge ninja star. Belka sank to his knees, grabbed its proboscis, and flung the creature into the fire cabinet. The glass panel shattered, and Belka grabbed the ax within.

"Oh, come on, Belka! What are you going to do with that?" Bars sneered.

Two fleas attacked. Belka wielded his ax left and right through the air and sliced both fleas in two. Part of a beast's body splattered against Bars, and the Colonel's cocky attitude began to desert him.

"Attack him!" Bars ordered his three remaining warriors. "Tear him to shreds!"

The first flea sprang on Belka's back. Belka slammed it against the bulkhead as he dueled the creature in front of him. He swung the ax repeatedly, but the flea dodged at every turn. The flea on his back attacked his neck while the third Elite Guard went for his legs. The first flea scrambled onto his chest, and Belka fell to the ground.

Belka had never felt pain quite like being bitten all over before, and he knew the creatures were only toying with him before they sank their tubes into him and drained his entire blood supply. He had one option and took it. He sprang headfirst into the Meals/Beverages Unit, and a fountain of Gersbacian Premium Beer sloshed across them. The fleas sprang back.

Belka nursed his wounds and turned on Bars. "So—they're still afraid of water, huh?"

Bars tried to stare him down but failed. The fleas shook off the beer and prepared to fight once more.

"You can't win, Commander Belka," Bars said. "There's not enough water in here to hurt them."

The nimblest flea sprang forward for the kill. Belka summoned his nerve, aimed, and flung his ax through the air. It tomahawked across the cockpit, split the flea in two, and thudded to a halt in the rocket coolant line that ran along the bare cockpit walls. An explosion of water drenched the cabin, and the remaining two fleas ran for cover. Belka watched them scuttle out of the cockpit and down into the hold.

Bars hauled the ax from the pipe, kicked the wounded Belka to the ground, and loomed above him, the water coursing down his face.

"Good play, Belka, but I'm afraid it's Game Over," Bars sneered, raising the ax for a vicious blow.

Flanger burst into the room, wearing Strelka's spare uniform. Belka's heart sank at the sight.

"What have you done to Strelka?"

"I wouldn't worry about that," Flanger said, grinning. "Concern yourself with what I'm going to do to . . . Colonel Bars."

Flanger hurled Bars across the cabin into the smoldering pilot seat. The ax clattered to the floor, and Flanger snapped it over her knee. Bars looked up at her in utter bewilderment.

"You traitor!" Bars shouted. "I created you!"

"Yes, well—you *bore* me," Flanger stated. She leapt onto her former leader and pinned him to the floor. "And if you think I'm going to spend the rest of my life at your beck and call . . . I mean, come on, seriously."

Strelka entered the room. Any other Space Commander would have run in, or perhaps even bounded in. Strelka sort of ambled in.

"What's going on?" Belka asked. Strelka went over to the control panel and stopped the coolant leak.

"I told you all Flanger needed was a little understanding," Strelka explained. "And a shower. Oh, and a guaranteed pardon back on Gersbach," he added quietly.

Belka frowned as Strelka took the dachshund's controls. There were red welts all over Strelka's neck, and it seemed most unlikely they came from combat. Belka had no further time to consider this as warning lights began to flash across the panel.

"We're out of fuel!" Strelka shouted.

The rumbling of engines abruptly ceased. Flanger looked at Strelka in horror and braced herself on Bars for impact. The connected ATVs dropped like a stone.

"Engage Automatic Safety System!" Belka ordered, staggering to his feet.

"This ATV features no such system," the computer replied.

"Retract legs for impact!" Strelka commanded.

"No such function available," the computer said. "Attached ATV is instigating its Automatic Safety System in ten seconds."

"Of course! Everyone—quickly! Evacuate to the other ship!" Belka ordered. "And keep your eyes on Bars!"

The group sprinted down the dachshund's cargo hold toward the docking tunnel. Strelka was helping Flanger through when the two remaining Elite Guard fleas came out of nowhere. They cartwheeled expertly through the air and attacked Belka and Strelka, forcing them back into the dachshund's hold. Bars seized his chance. He laughed as he pushed Flanger through the docking tunnel into the Flumpy ATV and slid after her.

Belka avoided his flea assailant's stabbing proboscis and heaved the creature off the walkway. It bounced back from the depths in a second and charged Belka from the rear. It was on course to plunge its blood-sucking tube straight through Belka's head when Strelka hurled the other flea into its path. The beasts collided with a sticky thud.

Flumpy disconnected from the dachshund with a loud CRACK, and sunlight flooded the dark hold. Dazed by the bright light, Belka and Strelka made easy targets as the fleas recovered and raced in to attack. The last thing Belka felt was six glistening black legs wrapping about his body; and the last thing he saw was Flumpy converting into the furry safety ball. Then the dachshund impacted, hard, on the ground.

Belka stirred a few moments later, feeling like steel rods had been inserted down the length of his body. Both Galactanauts had taken the full impact of the crash, bouncing on solid steel flooring. It was testament to Belka's regular exercise regime, he thought, that he was fit enough to sustain such a battering and still get to his feet. Then he realized he had been cushioned by the two fleas, which were now dead and squashed on the floor. Out of the A.N.O.S. he saw a distant Flumpy return to normal proportions, having bounced harmlessly as a ball across the dirt to the slaughterhouse door.

Uncle Gav appeared, looking fearfully toward the hill at the rumble of approaching people. He hooked his boot under Flumpy and heaved him into the slaughterhouse's gloomy interior.

"Come on, Strelka!" Belka ordered, pulling his severely bruised colleague to his feet. "It's not over yet."

"Flanger . . . ," Strelka managed. "Where's Flanger?"

"Bars has taken her into our ship."

Without hesitation Strelka ran to the cockpit.

Sergeant O'Loghlin had seen most of it but still couldn't figure it out. *Were they kids' toys? Flying dogs, connected in the air, turning into bouncing balls? They didn't have toys like that when he was a kid. Gavin didn't have kids, did he?*

As Gav withdrew into the slaughterhouse, a dachshund ran inside behind him. There was the sound of a metal door clanging shut and a large bolt being rammed into place. O'Loghlin ran to the door and, sure enough, Gav had locked himself in.

Gav's wife, Judy, walked over the opposite rise from the homestead. She raised her eyebrows at the sight of so many people gathering and shouting.

When the slaughterhouse door slammed shut, Belka could barely make out a thing in the gloom. "Switch on the headlights," he ordered.

Strelka swept the dachshund's powerful beams around the converted barn. It was a creepy place. Great hooks hung from greater chains secured to the rickety timbers of the roof. Corralling gates lined the floor. Huge quantities of dog and cat collars were piled about the perimeter. But when the headlights happened upon the center of the room, Belka and Strelka realized the full horror of Gav's operation. There was a huge hole in the floor, giving way to a wide concrete bowl that sloped toward a two-foot-wide opening in the bottom. Within the opening a complex series of blades—like a giant's kitchen food processor descending into hell—stood silent and waiting. Fluorescent lights across the ceiling suddenly burst to life and glowed a sickly green. Flumpy skidded into view, tethered to a very angry Uncle Gav. He tied the terrier to a nearby post.

"You bloody dogs! Covering up my Big Bone!" Gav roared, scooping up the dachshund and marching to a dusty corner. He punched a large green industrial button and a grating sound began. From deep below, a motor wailed louder and louder. The blades in the pit began to rotate, slowly at first, then faster and faster. Gav held the little dog high above the greasy, swirling blades that viciously chopped the air. Belka and Strelka looked through the terrible mouth of the machine—its blades spinning so fast they were almost invisible—into the foul chute below.

"So let's see how good a sausage dog you actually are!" Gav laughed.

"Can I ask you something?" Strelka inquired over the loudspeaker. Gav stumbled backward in shock and looked curiously into the dachshund's face. Strelka continued, "When you gather up your animals, do you spotlight them?"

"What?" Gav mumbled.

Strelka blasted high-beam headlights directly into Gav's eyes. Gav shrieked in alarm and dropped the dachshund, rubbing his dazzled eyeballs and sinking to his knees in fear.

Belka and Strelka landed directly on the lip of the concrete bowl. For a moment they had control of their craft, then the sausage dog's little paws began to slide down the greasy surface. Slowly, inexorably, they were slipping into the whirling blades of death.

thirty

In Flumpy's cockpit Flanger punched Bars as hard as she could. He winced and sneered at her.

"You'll have to do much better than that, my girl. If you're going to change sides, don't play with the guy who knows all your weaknesses." Effortlessly he pushed her to the floor at the rear of the cabin and took a seat. He reached into his jacket and produced a slim can of flea spray. It was different from cans Flanger had seen before: larger, and painted red. "A little insurance policy if you turned on me. Just one puff and it's curtains for you, sister!" Bars laughed. "Now, let's watch our friends get minced."

Flanger kept her distance from Bars as they looked out the forward screens. Gav was recovering, and the little head of the dachshund was slipping slowly out of view, sliding down the greasy concrete to the waiting blades. Its shoulders heaved up and down as it ran on the spot.

"The human will take *us* out next," Flanger said, pointing to Gav. "We're tied up and we can't run away."

"In that case I'd better look at what weapons we have at our disposal, now we're in the *better* ship," Bars said, his fingers speeding across the console. "Mmm . . . yes, yes . . . ah!" He smiled. "A missile."

He pressed a series of buttons on the control panel with relish. The missile was loaded into the launch tube.

"Don't you think Belka and Strelka would have used that *on us* by now if they could have?" Flanger asked.

"Don't be stupid. They're too moral to *kill* us," Bars sniggered.

"Or maybe the missile is so powerful you can't use it at close range," Flanger suggested. "Let me ask the computer. Computer—*instigate Automatic Safety System!*"

It was a deft move. The Safety System's rubber restraints shot out of Bars' seat and trapped him. The flea spray clattered to the deck. Flumpy converted into a ball, popped out of the collar and leash attaching him to the post, and rolled toward Nicky. Flanger braced herself against Bars' chair, grabbed the spray can bouncing about the cabin, and held it to Bars' face.

"One move when I release you, buddy, and I empty this whole can onto you. It may be flea spray, but I bet a blast wouldn't do a Gersbacian Colonel a world of good."

If Bars could have nodded, he would have, but the rubber held him securely in place.

"Computer—disengage Safety System," Flanger ordered.

The rubber sheet unwrapped from Bars and he gasped for air. "I hate that system!" he snapped, regarding Flanger and the spray can warily. The ATV rolled to a halt and resumed normal proportions.

"Computer—list your weapons and utilities on the forward screen," Flanger commanded. She saw immediately what she needed.

Belka and Strelka held the dachshund's one functioning guidance column so firmly forward it threatened to break. Nicky only succeeded in running on the spot, and indeed was steadily losing ground as he slid down the greasy slope toward the pit of blades.

"Is there no fuel for flight at all? Not even in the auxiliary tanks?" Belka shouted in panic.

"Nothing! Bars used the lot!" Strelka yelled back. "But it doesn't matter—the crash landing shattered the rocket engines! This'll never fly again!"

Belka looked at Strelka in alarm. "Well, we really are trapped on this planet, then; there's no way off now . . ."

A loud clunk shook the cabin. The Galactanauts looked at the forward screens. Flumpy stood at the edge of the pit, the MagHook cable secured between his nose and the dachshund's forehead. Flumpy slowly wound them in, stepping back from the edge as he did so. With a great smile Strelka walked the dachshund over the pit's edge and away from the danger while the MagHook wound them up to Flumpy's nose. In the cockpit they saw Flanger smiling back at them, with Bars—looking disgusted—by her side. Flanger held a red can to his face. Flanger and Strelka stood waving at each other.

"What is it with you two?" Belka finally asked.

"Animal magnetism," Strelka said. With a clunk the MagHook disengaged and rolled back into Flumpy's nostril.

"You stupid dogs!" Gav cried out. He stumbled onto his feet and lunged toward them. "Right! Into the mincer!"

But in his frenzy he slipped. His headlight-dazzled vision had led him *into* the blade pit rather than around it. Teetering on the edge of the ramp, he began to skid toward the blades. "Help me!" he cried. "HELP ME!"

Tom Buckley's hand shot out; he seized his brother and hauled him to safety. Gav looked at him with relief and surprise.

"You don't mind us letting ourselves in, do you?" Tom said.

Judy Buckley stood nearby, holding the slaughterhouse keys.

"Gav! This place is disgusting!" Tom said, shaking his head.

Lucy ran in and scooped up Flumpy, cradling him to her, happy he was safe. Amy grabbed Nicky, clearly relieved. Sergeant O'Loghlin strode in with the rest of the city folk close behind him and switched off the mincer. As the blades churned to a halt, the converted barn sunk into silence.

"Now, what the hell is going on?" Tom demanded. A moment passed, and then Lucy, Sam, Amy, Dion, Miranda, and Gav all began to give their version of events, each talking louder over the other, squabbling between themselves. Only Dr. Macheski held his tongue.

"One at a time!" Tom shouted over them, motioning them quiet. He turned to Lucy. "Just tell us what's been happening, love."

"Well, basically, Flumpy here has the good aliens and Nicky has the bad aliens . . . ," Lucy began to explain.

Inside Nicky's cockpit Strelka paced up and down.

"Stay calm!" Belka ordered.

"How can I? Flanger is in there with that maniac! He could turn on her at any second. . . ."

"She could turn *on us* at any second, more likely," Belka reasoned. "She's always got a flea in her ear about something. They found the MagHook—what happens when they find the missile?"

Bars grabbed the spray can from Flanger as she gazed into the other cockpit. "Ain't love grand?" he chuckled. "Gets you all distracted."

He activated Missile Launch Control and dialed in the coordinates of the dachshund. Flanger reached over to stop him, but Bars waved her away with a tiny puff of flea spray. It burned deep in Flanger's lungs, and for the first time she felt real fear in the presence of the mad Bars.

He reached for the bright red launch button.

"Target confirmed," the computer announced.

Bars hit the button. The missile shot out of Flumpy's right nostril and punched a foot-wide hole in the rickety slaughterhouse wall.

Warning alarms began to shriek inside the dachshund cabin.

"The missile!" Belka shouted. "Bars has fired the missile AT US!"

"But it's heading away . . . ," Strelka said.

"It'll loop back. It's been given our coordinates—it'll track us!"

"Missile locked on," the dachshund's computer announced calmly. "Time until impact—three minutes, fifteen seconds. Take evasive measures."

"We must get clear of the humans, or the missile will destroy us all," Belka announced. "But we have to lock down Bars first."

He thought for a moment. "Bars took remote control of our ship from here before . . . ," he recalled.

"We still are in control!" Strelka said, studying the console. "This ship learned Flumpy's control frequency!"

"Shut Flumpy down," Belka ordered. "Let's trap them!"

Strelka entered a code and flicked a switch.

Flumpy grew limp in Lucy's hands. She looked down at the terrier in alarm. "What's wrong?" she yelled. "Flumpy? I mean, Belka? Strelka? Are you sick?"

Belka, of course, was actually at the controls of Nicky. He wrenched the dachshund from Amy's grasp and ran it out of the slaughterhouse. Lucy ran after it, thrusting the floppy Flumpy at Sam as she went.

"Bars is not getting away again!" she announced dramatically. "I'm going after him!"

Inside Flumpy, Bars chuckled at her confusion.

"Missile impact—two minutes, fifty-five seconds and counting. Take evasive measures," the dachshund's computer declared. As Strelka ran the ATV away from the humans, Belka worked frantically at thwarting the pursuing missile. His fingers punched a code into the console.

"Sending self-destruct order to missile!" Belka shouted in triumph.

"Missile impact—two minutes, fifty seconds and counting. Take evasive measures," the computer said.

"Report on self-destruct order!" Belka snapped.

"Self-destruct order received by missile," the computer said. Belka and Strelka breathed a sigh of relief. The computer whirred to life again. "Self-destruct order not accepted."

"Why not?" Belka shouted.

"A bar has been placed on self-destruct instructions by launch initiator," the computer announced. "Missile impact—two minutes, forty seconds and counting. Take evasive measures."

In Flumpy's lifeless cockpit Flanger tried desperately to operate the loudspeaker. "Sam! Lucy!" she shouted. "BARS IS IN HERE! Belka and Strelka are in Nicky, and the missile is *aimed at them*!" She punched the dead controls of the ship in frustration. Not a single light shone on the panel in front of her.

"Such a pity you can't warn your new friends," Bars sneered. "And such a shame your Space Command boyfriend is about to be battered and fried. Oh well!"

Flanger raised her fist to strike Bars, but he warded her off with a puff from his spray can.

"Temper, temper," he laughed.

"Missile impact—two minutes, thirty seconds and counting. Take evasive measures," the dachshund computer announced.

"Redirect it! Send it somewhere else!" Strelka yelled at Belka, running the dachshund across the dusty ground.

Belka set to work at the console with renewed vigor.

Dr. Macheski noticed the little missile far up in the brilliant blue sky. He watched it make a leisurely hairpin turn and thread a fine vapor trail behind it. It took a new trajectory and began a murderously fast descent, and Dr. Macheski understood immediately where it was headed. "Stay back!" he commanded the group of humans. "The missile is aimed at the dachshund."

Lucy ran on ahead, oblivious to the danger.

"Lucy!" Tom shouted after his daughter. But she hadn't heard. Without hesitation Tom ran after her, easily breaking the Tubby Flats Sports Day 100-yard record he had set eighteen years earlier.

"Missile impact—two minutes, fifteen seconds and counting. Take evasive measures," the computer said. Lucy loomed in the dachshund's rearview display.

"Lucy!" Strelka ordered over the loudspeaker. "Don't follow us! Stay back!"

Lucy continued running. The wind was whistling in her ears, and she didn't hear the warning.

"Missile impact—two minutes, ten seconds and counting."

Belka entered a redirection code and punched the transmission button.

"Missile redirection order not accepted," the computer announced.

"WHY?" Strelka roared in disbelief.

"There is a bar on redirection orders," the computer said.

"A bar by Bars, I suspect," said Belka, fuming. "He's had his grubby little fingers in Flumpy's computer and anticipated our every move."

"Missile impact—two minutes and counting. Take evasive measures."

"Dr. Macheski!" Sam yelled, tugging at the Russian's hand. "Can't you do something? Launch your rocket at that missile and bring it down?"

"I . . . well, we could use that new mini-engine I was testing . . ."

"Do you have it here?"

"Of course. In my car . . ."

Dr. Macheski barely had the words out before Sam was pushing him up the hill and back to his old Datsun.

"You won't get away again, Bars!" Lucy shouted. Despite her recent ordeal she felt great. She was running again. She was in the country. She felt alive and happy, and she wasn't going to let her new friends down. She became aware of someone shouting behind her and a high-pitched squealing above.

"Lucy!" Tom yelled as his old shoes pounded through the dust. "Get back! The missile is going to strike!"

Lucy looked up and saw a tiny streak of silver bearing down on the dachshund, dipping and weaving through the sky, matching the dog-craft's every move.

"Missile impact—one minute, forty seconds and counting," the computer said.

"DO SOMETHING!" Strelka screamed.

"What can I do? We can't self-destruct it and we can't redirect it," Belka said.

Strelka looked at his partner in disbelief. "How can you *not* know what to do? You *always* know what to do! You tell *me* what to do, you tell *everyone* what to do, but for the first time it's really *important* . . . the one time you could *not* get away with *not* knowing what to do, you DON'T KNOW WHAT TO DO!"

"Stay calm, Strelka."

"Yeah, right. And just when I'd finally met the perfect woman."

There was an uneasy silence.

"Missile impact—one minute, twenty seconds and counting."

Strelka is right, Belka thought. He didn't know what to do. The mission had failed, their annihilation was imminent, and even if they did escape, there was no way home. Worse still, Gersbach remained under dire threat from the D.O.G.

He turned to face his fellow Galactanaut. "I know what to do with the missile. We're going to aim it at the D.O.G."

"But I thought you couldn't redirect the missile."

"We can't. But we could *lead* it somewhere."

Strelka felt his mouth go dry.

"Covering the bone is no real solution," Belka continued. "Like the gnome, it has to be destroyed. It's what we came to Earth to do."

"But for the bone to be destroyed, it means that we'll be . . ."

"Yes," said Belka, and drove the dachshund toward the bone.

thirty-one

Dr. Macheski's mini-rocket shot into the sky. Standing atop the hill, Dr. Macheski and Sam had a perfect view of the drama unfolding below. The plucky dachshund was running at full speed toward the gleaming white bone, scattering the sheep and show dogs from their burying duties. Tom Buckley was sprinting after his daughter. The little silver missile, glinting in the sunshine, was bearing down on Nicky, with Lucy right behind the sausage dog. Correcting course as often as it did, the missile seemed to possess a malicious mind—ruthless, and determined to kill.

Dr. Macheski knew he wouldn't have many chances to knock the missile off course. His hands were sweating as he gripped his mini-rocket's remote control.

He steeled himself and went into action.

The mini-rocket made a speedy arc through the air and caught up with the missile. The crowd below gasped in astonishment as the new rocket made an appearance. When they realized Dr. Macheski was controlling it, they began to shout encouragement.

The mini-rocket dwarfed the missile in size but not, unfortunately, in grace and accuracy.

It lunged at the missile. It missed. The crowd held its breath.

"Try again, Dr. Macheski!" Sam shouted. "TAKE IT OUT!"

Tom Buckley loped up behind Lucy, scooped her into his arms, and sprinted as far from the dachshund as he could. The air screamed through his lungs, and excruciating pain shot down his back as he held his daughter aloft. The sausage dog, meanwhile, scaled the large mound of dirt that almost completely covered Gav's Big Bone and skidded to a halt.

The missile hurtled earthward, its eerie squeal growing louder as it pushed the air angrily out of the way. Amy screamed as it powered toward the dachshund sitting atop the bone. As the deadly missile accelerated, fire and thick black smoke spewed from its tail.

"Missile impact—fifty seconds and counting," the dachshund computer announced.

Belka and Strelka regarded each other in the quiet cabin. It felt very wrong, after battling through so many dangerous situations, to just sit there as a willing target. But it was what they had to do.

It was difficult to know what to say to each other. The only recorded fatality in the history of Gersbach Space Command was that of Lieutenant Nash, and he perished not so much from a mission gone wrong but rather from sleeping in, missing his mission launch, and being sucked into his Living Unit's cleaning system—which had assumed the house to be empty at the time.

There had certainly never been any *martyrs* for Gersbach. Belka wondered if they would name a building after him. They would probably name the Space Command Tavern after Strelka.

Strelka, meanwhile, studied his fingernails with an unnatural interest, unable to look his colleague in the eye.

Belka broke the emotion-charged silence. "Commander Strelka, I know we've had our differences, but overall it has been an honor and a privilege to serve with—"

"Hey, there's another rocket out there," Strelka interrupted, looking out the forward screens. "We've got two after us now."

Dr. Macheski flew his mini-rocket at the missile. The trajectory was looking good—the mini-rocket would surely collide with its target. The watching crowd held its breath.

There was a small, anticlimactic sound of metal against metal, and the crowd burst into wild cheering. The mini-rocket had knocked the missile aside and sent it spinning in the opposite direction.

"Missile impact—twenty-five seconds and . . . correction. Stand by, new data . . . ," the dachshund computer announced.

Belka and Strelka's hearts seemed to stop as they waited.

"Missile countdown resumed. Missile impact—*thirty* seconds and counting."

* * *

Though flung substantially off course, the silver missile quickly recovered and resumed its run at the dachshund. The sausage dog sat on Gav's Big Bone, almost noble in its stance, its little body absolutely still and resolute.

"They mean to sacrifice themselves," Dr. Macheski said. "They are going to die to destroy that bone!"

"Why would Bars do that?" Sam asked. "He's a criminal. He'd never do anything *good* like that . . ." A terrible thought struck him. He held up the limp Flumpy and looked into the eyes carefully. He strained and strained, focusing as closely as possible, tilting the cockpit this way and that to get some light onto the people within.

"NO!" Sam yelled. He could see into the cockpit all right. It was Bars in there, making rude gestures at him and laughing. "Belka and Strelka are in the sausage dog!" Sam shouted. "They're going to kill themselves to save their planet!" He grabbed the remote control from Dr. Macheski's hands. The mini-rocket veered crazily through the sky before chasing the missile one more time.

"Missile impact—eighteen seconds and counting."

Strelka looked at Belka. "I'm sorry I called you Golden Boy. I know it annoyed you."

"Thank you, Strelka."

"Missile impact—twelve seconds and counting."

The mini-rocket raced past the missile and missed it by the barest fraction. Rough hands grabbed the remote control from Sam.

"Give that to me, boy," Gav said. "That bloody dog

deserves everything it gets! It ruined everything!" He fumbled with the remote control. "Die, you mongrel!"

Gav meant to deliver the dachshund the deathblow, but since he knew so very little about technology, he managed to send the mini-rocket screaming back toward the watching group. They flattened themselves on the dirt as Sam and Dr. Macheski tried to wrestle the remote from Gav.

"Missile impact—five seconds and counting."

Belka and Strelka could see the missile plainly now. Its silver body glinted in the sun as fire and gritty black smoke filled the sky behind it.

Sergeant O'Loghlin hauled Gav aside. The mini-rocket remote control dropped from his hands. It tumbled down the hill, its joystick bashed from side to side before coming to rest. The mini-rocket spun through the air and then shot at full throttle toward Gav's Big Bone.

"Missile impact—three, two . . ."

The explosion was devastating.

Gav's Big Bone and the mound of dirt were incinerated in an enormous firestorm. The ground collapsed for yards around.

"Nicky! Flanger!" Amy cried out, and burst into tears.

A massive shock wave hit the group of humans soon after, and they fell in an undignified heap. Only Dion remained upright, with Miranda clinging to his legs. He didn't think to help her up.

The group was silent. As the people scrambled to their feet, everyone's eyes turned to the far side of the field, peering keenly through the smoke and dust for any sign of Tom and Lucy.

There was the ominous sound of creaking wood and metal, and suddenly Gav's slaughterhouse collapsed, its elderly structure shattered by the shock wave.

Gav realized his Big Bone had been vaporized and his slaughterhouse completely destroyed. His two biggest money earners gone in an instant. For the first time he was speechless.

A rain of dirt fell as if from nowhere, and then all was silent. The birds had been scared away. Only a gentle wind could be heard, slowly dispersing the great curtain of dust.

A sheep trotted out of the clearing haze. A pair of bouncing cattle dogs ran out, playfully nipping at each other. And then, off in the distance, Beth saw Tom cradling Lucy in his arms. He was walking toward them with an enormous lopsided grin on his face and just avoided stepping into the gaping hole that was once Gav's Big Bone.

"Oh, thank God you're alive!" Gav shouted, mainly for the group's benefit. "Are you OK?"

"To be honest," Tom called back, placing Lucy on the ground, where she walked unsteadily, "that was a bit of a hoot!"

Beth broke into a nervous laugh and ran to hug them. Amy impulsively wrapped her arms about her family, and Gav sprinted across to do the same.

"Ah, fantastic! It all worked out fine then, eh?" Gav said. But no one was listening to him. They were watching, fascinated, as a shower of money began to flutter down upon them—blown from its secret, tax-free hiding place in Gav's slaughterhouse roof. Tom gazed at his brother steadily.

"Gee, Gav," Tom said, peeling a hundred-dollar bill from his face. "I thought you had cash-flow problems. I thought you couldn't help us out with our mortgage."

"Fair go, mate, I couldn't," Gav began awkwardly. A thick wad of hundred-dollar bills fell hard on his head. "I'm doing it tough like everyone else."

"But you could still afford to buy our farm," Beth ventured.

Tom was actually shocked. "*Gav* bought it?"

"Sergeant O'Loghlin told me," Beth announced. "Got it for a song."

"Now, mate!" Gav nervously explained to Tom, aware of the many eyes upon him. "I'd never do *anything* bad to you or the kids!"

"RUBBISH!" shouted Judy Buckley. "You set your brother up, Gavin! You plotted the whole thing with your real-estate and bank mates!"

Tom and Beth were amazed. They were amazed at this revelation, but they were even more amazed at Judy's sudden stream of words. They could barely recall a time when Judy had said *anything,* let alone criticize her husband.

"You let Tom and Beth go under," Judy continued yelling at Gav, "so you could expand your hideous pet-killing business!"

"Pet killing?" Sergeant O'Loghlin asked. "Am I to understand, Gav, your 'boutique' sausages are—sorry, *were*—actually comprised of people's pets?"

"It was quality stuff, mate. Prime cuts," Gav said. "The odd stray dog, maybe. People don't look after their pets . . . ," he trailed feebly.

"Lucy," Sam said as she approached. "I've got bad news . . ."

"Bad news? After what just happened? Are you crazy?" Lucy

smiled as she took the limp Flumpy from Sam and held him in her arms. "Good news, Belka and Strelka! The bad people are gone now, and so is the threat to your planet. The Big Bone's blown up."

Flumpy burst into life. The shock wave had broken the electronic lock on its system and rebooted the ATV. Flanger took advantage of the distraction and slapped the flea spray from Bars' fist. She lassoed the startled Colonel with her belt and pinned him to the floor.

"Belka and Strelka aren't here, Lucy!" Flanger shouted over the loudspeaker, above Bars' shouts of protest. "They were in the dachshund! They were running away to save us from the missile!"

"But the dachshund and Big Bone were blown up," Lucy said.

"I know. I'm so sorry."

"But that means . . . ," Lucy began. "Belka and Strelka . . . are dead?"

"Flanger? Is that you in there?" Amy asked urgently.

"Yes, Amy."

"You're alive!"

"Yes . . ."

Amy let rip with a barrage of questions. "Why did you run away? Why are you in Flumpy now? Is there a man in there with you? What should I do about Dion?"

"Calm down, Amy," Flanger explained. "I've got Colonel Bars tied up now, that's the important thing."

"So . . . Belka and Strelka aren't in there with you?" Lucy asked.

"No, I'm sorry. They were in the dachshund," Flanger said quietly.

Lucy began to cry.

Amy put her arm about her sister. "If this is another trick, Flanger, I'll be very, VERY angry!" she shouted.

"It's no trick. They really were in the dachshund," Flanger assured her.

Sam walked over and comforted Lucy as she sobbed big, salty tears. Beth and Tom gathered about her and, distressed, felt tears rise up also.

"I hate you, Flanger," Lucy managed between sobs. "They were *my friends*!"

A door fell off the shed behind the slaughterhouse ruins. The explosion had rocked the rickety structure to its foundations, and the broken door had finally teetered forward into the dust. A cowering group of kangaroos and emus emerged into the sunlight, confused and frightened.

"Now, there should be a law against putting the Aussie Coat of Arms through a mincer," Sergeant O'Loghlin said.

"Oh, mate, emus are perfect for slaughterhouses!" Gav replied, digging his grave that little bit deeper. "They can't walk backward in the feeder lanes!"

"You're under arrest, Gavin Buckley," Sergeant O'Loghlin said.

"And a good thing too," Judy muttered.

A cow ambled out after the emus and kangaroos. It looked at the gathered crowd and gave a gentle "moo."

"Look!" Tom said. "It's Winona!"

Amy looked up in horror. Miranda Hunter laughed out loud and looked around, fully expecting to see everyone else in hysterics. Strangely, no one was.

                              * * *

Lucy wiped away her tears, and then couldn't believe what she
saw. A dachshund stumbled forward from Winona's shed and
trotted up to her.

"Hello, Lucy!" Belka announced cheerily.

Lucy burst into a fresh round of tears. But they were happy
tears this time, and she hugged the dachshund joyfully. "How
did you escape the missile?" she asked.

"Well, a rocket collided with our A.N.O.S.," Belka explained.
Strelka's eyes widened at the memory.

"My mini-rocket!" Dr. Macheski gasped. "It saved you?"

"It thrust us clear of the missile and propelled us through
the slaughterhouse, and then we ran into the shed," Belka continued. "The missile hit the bone instead."

The humans stopped to regard the animals. They had yet to
fully accept talking dogs, and their minds were spinning trying
to explain it.

"These dogs really *do* talk . . . ," Sergeant O'Loghlin said,
scratching his head.

"They're not dogs, they're spaceships," Lucy explained.
"They've got people in them. Flumpy here," she said, holding
up the little terrier, "usually has Commander Belka and
Commander Strelka running him. They came to Earth to stop
Colonel Bars and Flanger getting a piece of the D.O.G.—you
know, the Big Bone—in the dachshund. But Belka and Strelka
are in the dachshund at the moment."

"Why did you come here in dogs?" Dr. Macheski asked, his
eyes marveling at the supreme engineering of the alien ATVs.

"Because you sent one into space," Belka explained. "We
thought they were the ones in charge down here."

"Laika!" Dr. Macheski said, smiling. "You found Laika! I was there when we *launched* her! I used to feed her biscuits!"

Belka's mind reeled. If ever there was a good story to relate in the *Space Academy Gazette,* it would be Dr. Macheski's story. There were so many questions Belka wanted to ask him, and so many explanations he wanted to give of what had happened to Laika, and how important Laika had been to Gersbach.

But now Belka suddenly felt defeated. He looked at his watch and saw the wormhole countdown click into its final minutes. He lay the dachshund down in the dirt and resigned himself to the fact that a conversation with Dr. Macheski would probably be the last thing he did . . . ever.

"What's the matter, my little friend?" Dr. Macheski asked.

"We're trapped on your planet with no way home," Belka explained. "We've accomplished our mission, but without a booster capable of escaping Earth's gravity, I'm afraid we'll never see Gersbach again."

"That's quite a problem. You'd have to be a rocket scientist to solve it," Dr. Macheski said. "Fortunately, I happen to be a rocket scientist."

thirty-two

Once again Macheski One stood proud and ready. Dr. Macheski had fetched the components of his powerful rocket from the Datsun and quickly reassembled it for flight. He removed the nose cone to make way for a little dachshund-sized cargo hold. Dr. Macheski cautiously refueled the rocket before turning his attention to the remote control sitting nearby.

The dachshund lay on the ground—a fuel-less, flightless spacecraft; but it did serve as an airtight capsule for the Galactanauts' homeward journey.

"If I put the engines at full burn, and give you maximum thrust, I'm certain you'll achieve escape velocity," Dr. Macheski explained proudly. "I can put you into orbit around the Earth—but I don't understand, what good would that do you?"

"We'll use your planet's gravitational pull to slingshot us into the wormhole," Strelka replied over the loudspeaker.

"That's how you got here? Through a w-w-wormhole?"

Dr. Macheski stammered in excitement, looking vainly into the bright blue sky for a glimpse of it.

"Please, Dr. Macheski, we're running out of time!"

"Of course, forgive me!" Dr. Macheski exclaimed, and turned to Flumpy. "Let's get *you* aboard!"

Beth and Tom Buckley watched in amazement as Lucy held out her hand to Flumpy's mouth. The jaws opened and steps rose from the pink tongue.

Bars came first, prodded forward by Flanger. A belt securely bound the villain's arms to his sides as he staggered onto Lucy's hand.

"You're a very bad man," Lucy said. "You're lucky they don't leave you here. I wouldn't treat you nicely at all."

Without the translator Bars didn't understand Lucy, but he understood her tone well enough. He lapsed into a sulk. Flanger pushed him forward and smiled up at Lucy.

Lucy didn't know whether to forgive Flanger or not, but Belka and Strelka said she was OK now. Lucy carefully lifted Bars and Flanger over to the dachshund and eased them through the A.N.O.S., where Strelka was waiting. He and Flanger hugged each other, and Lucy smiled.

Amy sidled over and whispered into Nicky's ear. "Flanger, why do you have to leave now? Miranda's horrible to me, and Dion and I had a fight. I need your magic," she said, trying not to let anyone else hear.

Flanger flicked on the speaker, and her voice burst forth loud and clear. "Amy, I don't know any magic. I'm an *alien,* not a fairy."

The gathered group couldn't help but listen in.

256

"*You* made Dion like me," Amy said. Miranda craned her head forward.

"No, I didn't," Flanger explained. "*You* made Dion like you. It's not magic. It's confidence. It's believing in yourself."

"But he's being a creep. He did something really rotten," Amy pleaded. "Can't you change him back to how he was before?"

"I can't change him back because he never changed *in the first place*," Flanger said. "He's *never* been different. You've just got to decide whether he's worth it or not. It's up to you."

Amy looked across to Dion, who smiled back at her sweetly. She wanted him to run to her, kiss her, and swing her about in his arms—but he didn't move. This was because he was standing on several of Gav's hundred-dollar bills.

"It's up to me, is it?" Amy said uncertainly. "What do I do about Miranda?"

"Just rise above her!" Flanger replied. "You can fight her, sure, but you'd be dragged down to her level to do it. It'd be so easy to tell her she's got no fashion sense, she puts on makeup with a trowel, that she throws herself at any good-looking boy . . ."

Miranda went pale. She was mortified at being publicly ridiculed. Especially by a sausage dog.

"That's how things are on Planet Miranda," Flanger continued. "But it's a lot harder to rise above people like her, Amy. To be yourself. To set your own standards."

The eyes of the group focused keenly on Miranda.

"You are all *so* stupid, I'm going home!" Miranda shouted defiantly, and stormed off. After a few steps she was confused to find herself walking only in her socks. She looked back and saw that her brand-new shoes were stuck fast in a fresh cowpat.

"Moo," Winona said.

"But what about Dion?" Amy implored.

"Don't obsess about guys too much just now," Flanger said. "Just focus on the people who *you know* really love you."

"Who do you mean?"

"Like your dad and your mum," Flanger said. "And your sister too."

Amy looked at Lucy, who nodded.

"Yeah . . . ," Lucy agreed. "Sometimes."

"You've always got your family, Amy," Flanger continued. "Look—times are tough for you. You all get on each other's nerves and you're adjusting to the city, but you look out for each other. With a family like that you can do anything. You really can."

She's right, Amy thought. *My family is pretty good.*

It's just a pity they're not as cute as Dion.

Dr. Macheski ushered the group a safe distance from Macheski One. He took the dachshund gently from Lucy's arms.

"I'm afraid it's time, Lucy," he said.

He carried the dog to the launch site. He gently lowered the sausage dog's long body into the top of the rocket, and soon all that remained visible was its little head, dwarfed by six feet of shiny metal rocket below it. He secured the nose cone and bolted it into place.

Tom held Lucy to him, and she hugged her dad back. Beth looked down and realized Amy was holding her hand for the first time in years.

Judy looked about to see no one was looking and gave Gav a swift kick. Gav looked down mournfully at the handcuffs Sergeant O'Loghlin had placed on him.

"Goodbye, Lucy. Goodbye, everybody," Belka announced from the deck of the dachshund. "And thanks."

Macheski One gave a short puff of steam.

"Ready, Dr. Macheski," Strelka announced. "On my mark: five, four, three, two . . ."

"ONE!" shouted Lucy.

Dr. Macheski hit the button on the remote control, and the engines burst into life. Atop a huge ball of fire the rocket and its dachshund payload soared heavenward.

There was another surge of blue-and-red flame, and the rocket accelerated.

"Look after Flumpy!" came Belka's distant voice as he sailed faster and faster into the sky. "He looked after us!" In a moment the dachshund rocket was a small black dot in the afternoon sky, and a moment later it couldn't be seen at all.

The humans turned to Flumpy, who stood eerily motionless.

"Now there's a pet that's easy to look after," Tom laughed.

Surprisingly, Belka and Strelka had no further mission difficulties. They looped the Earth and shot back through the wormhole as it closed behind them for another year.

Safely back on Gersbach, Belka and Strelka were feted as heroes. They were given ticker-tape parades, keys to the city, and even had a cameo appearance in a feature film about their adventure called *Hole of Death*.

They were accosted daily by wide-eyed youths seeking stories about life on Earth. They didn't get much response from

Strelka. He always had some reason why he couldn't spare time for his fans, although he did sign autographs for women in a certain age bracket. Belka, however, gave generously of his time. He related stories of giant Earthlings, feral cats, flying creatures, exploding gnomes—and the genuine fun of chasing tennis balls. The crowds would grow about him. It was all most gratifying.

For all his newfound acquaintances, though, Belka would often look up at the nighttime sky from his Living Unit and wonder what had happened to Lucy and his other human friends.

He didn't know that Gav had gone to prison for fraud and innumerable charges under the Animal and Livestock Act, and was named the Humane Society's "Creep of the Year." He didn't know that Gav had put all his property under Judy's name for tax purposes, and that Judy then sold some of it to set up an animal refuge, which stood proudly on the old slaughterhouse site. He also didn't know that Judy had helped Tom and Beth, who moved into a bigger house with full-length mirrors and a genuinely attractive gnome.

Belka didn't know that Lucy now had a real dog she'd named Laika, who scampered with the best of them and loved to chase a ball. Lucy and Sam played with her in the nature reserve that adjoined the Buckleys' backyard.

Belka didn't know Lucy was now a star athlete for her school, excelling at state-level long jump and gymnastics. And Belka also didn't know that Tom and Beth had a shop doing so well they were opening another like it very soon. It was called The Peppermint Place and sold every type of peppermint imaginable—except peppermint balls.